Fear the Moonlight

Hal McFarland

authorHOUSE®

AuthorHouse™
1663 Liberty Drive
Bloomington, IN 47403
www.authorhouse.com
Phone: 1 (800) 839-8640

Published by AuthorHouse 02/25/2015

ISBN: 978-1-4969-7025-1 (sc)
ISBN: 978-1-4969-7024-4 (e)

Print information available on the last page.

Print information available on the last page.

THANKS TO BARBARA, MY WIFE, WHO VERY PATIENTLY ALLOWED ME TO BOUNCE IDEAS OFF HER, ESPECIALLY AS RELATED TO CHARACTER DEVELOPMENT, AND WHO PUT UP WITH MY WRITING ALL NIGHT AND SLEEPING ALL DAY!

TO JACKLYN OLINGER, OUR NEXT DOOR NEIGHBOR AND FRIEND, WHO UNDERTOOK THE JOB OF EDITING THIS 80,000 WORD NOVEL AND SUGGESTING ITS COVER PICTURE,

AND TO WILLIAM HENRY GROTH, THE MAN WITH THE ARTISTIC EYE:

THE DREAM TEAM!

BOOK ONE

COMING OF AGE

CHAPTER 1

In the beginning there were three. They had arrived, surrounded by fire and thunder; but they existed, now, in the sterile silence of a laboratory, their history unknown, their awareness unverified; and from this beginning, an industry sprang up, growing by the decades, gaining secrecy and importance by the centuries.

They came as three, outliving their interrogators one after the other, but they aged, too, only more slowly; yet, by half a millennium, but one remained: and as the guardians hovered over him, traveling through him, monitoring every living molecule, it was apparent that death was not far off.

Billions of dollars had been spent on trying to unravel the secrets, which they brought with them--the technology of their existence, of their present, and their past. And they had names--names given to them by the scientists who extracted them one by one from their cocoon: male 1, the oldest, female 1, and male 2, the last survivor and their final hope for unraveling the secrets of the universe.

Until now, the research was focused, not on the future, but on the past and the present: the 3W's, who, where, and why: who were they, where were they from, and why were they here? And overriding all of this was the determination to learn the how.

But with male 2's last breath, the researchers' quest would also end—unless--and it had not been considered before; it had not, because, as long as at least one of the three remained alive, there was the certainty that on some tomorrow, the breakthrough would occur, and the mysteries which had arrived so suddenly would give way to answers. The questions the scientists had were legion and filled many of the lab's repositories. They began with such obvious ones as, how had their bodies healed themselves so quickly, so completely, after the grievous injuries of the crash? How had they survived for centuries? How had they continued to exist with no brainwave activity and no nourishment? Were they in some type of suspended animation?

The other two were declared dead with the cessation of the one beat per minute of their hearts, their bodies placed in a frigid morgue, with no absolute certainty that they, in fact, *were* really dead, because life and death as understood by the interrogators may or may not apply to these two.

The one that remained, clung tenaciously to what the researchers had defined as life; and as the heartbeats continued to slow, the decision was made to extract the male's living sperm and impregnate a young female researcher who had volunteered. This offspring, if the experiment were successful, would provide the secret city with a reason for its continued existence: it would be quite like the take over of the lives of the Dionne quintuplets by the Canadian government some centuries ago: the children would be under the microscope twenty-four-seven for their entire lives.

Once the sperm was extracted, the researchers realized that they would be able to impregnate more than one volunteer; therefore, three others were chosen to be the recipients of this desperate undertaking; and so, for the next year, they became the observed rather than the observers.

The nine-month timeline came and went: it was obvious that each of the four volunteers carried a living being inside her, but they had willingly crossed the threshold of the known and were now in uncharted territory.

During the fourth week of the twelfth month, shortly after midnight on the extreme night of the full Moon, Uno felt something moving on her inner thigh near her vagina. Reaching her hand down to feel herself, she was startled when her fingers were grabbed forcefully and tugged on with an impatience, which was unnerving. Her reaction was to pull against this force; and as she did, she realized that she was giving birth. The baby was pulling itself from her womb.

That same night, researchers Dos and Tres gave birth in the same manner--but the observers acted swiftly, removing the babies from the mothers' arms even before each was able to see her child's face; and when they had recovered from the rigors of childbearing, the mothers were transferred to another location, the logic being that they could no longer be objective in their duties within this secretive lab. The children, too, three boys, were separated from one another, never to be made aware of their sameness, their uniqueness, their kinship.

The fourth mother had disappeared during her eleventh month. No trace of her or of her child was ever found.

The years passed, and as the observers waited anxiously for the emergence of characteristics or actions which would separate these three from the billions of babies born around the world, they grew old and the children remained children--unremarkable children--that is, from the point of view of those who observed, who measured, who probed and pricked; but the three youngsters, at about the fifth earth-year after their birth, became aware of each other and shared with one another their thoughts and their feelings and their plans--plans that no one their ages would even consider.

Alpha, the eldest (but only by a mere few minutes), transmitted the image of an Indian pointing into the distance—an Indian on a gigantic horse; and he shared his feelings of the tranquility, peace, and safety that existed under this Indian's outstretched arm--so the three met there at the age of five--met there without leaving the confines of their prison, and they renewed their strength in this sacred land under the protection of the icon called Crazy Horse. This was their refuge, and they would spirit themselves away from the laboratory whenever the pressures and the expectations became too great.

As they grew, the powers came to them in surprising ways: Alpha was being asked if he could make a spoon on the table move by simply concentrating on it and contemplating its new location. As he concentrated, he suddenly realized he was intercepting the thoughts and feelings of the interrogator. He zeroed in on this activity, as opposed to that of the spoon; and as he did, he felt that the interrogator was at peace with himself, was not an evil circus master--and as Alpha's skills grew, he understood that the group who studied him were all good people, intending him no harm. He shared that with the other two and they, in turn, revealed more of their strengths--Beta, in particular, indicated that he was able to influence the actions of his main overseer by mentally broadcasting suggestions of activities which should be followed.

As the three sat under the gigantic, outstretched arm of their Indian guardian, at various times over the ensuing years, they eventually came to realize that they could learn no more within the confines of the laboratory, and that it was time to bring their bodies with them and join the world that they had only read about.

Their teachers had made sure that they were fluent in multiple languages and that they had more than a layman's understanding of science and math. However, several areas which they would need to survive outside their bubble of safety were neglected--but neglected because it never occurred to the three, that their education would require information on how to live in the real world, how to be taxpaying citizens, how to find and succeed at a job, and how to deal with income. The concept of food, clothing, housing, and money were never integrated into their lesson plans; and as they later readily admitted, they did not grasp the real-world need for such knowledge. Food had always been there three times a day, lodging was, for their entire lives, a given--their every need, as well as most of their wants, was provided for. The one essential ingredient, which was beginning to demand their attention, as they matured, however, was that of freedom: the same compulsion, which brought the Pilgrims to America, the Jews to Israel, and, more recently, caused aspiring Colonists to gaze toward the Moon, seeing it as a world away from the craziness which now surrounded them.

But they instinctively knew that if they simply disappeared, they would be hounded for the rest of their lives. Each understood, at a basic level, their importance to the men and women who served them, who guarded them, who taught them, whose lives were committed to them. Although the three had no way of knowing why they were such an intriguing part of all the activities which enveloped them, it was obvious that they were essential to the needs of those people who hovered over them, from the food servers, to the doctors, to the psychologists who were omnipresent in their lives.

They understood the finality of death, too, and realized that if they could just convince everyone that they had died, that they would be free: there would be no search and rescue, no dragnet, no frantic, determined effort to locate them and return them to the laboratory. Death would bring freedom!

So in their 15th year, as they sat with Crazy Horse, the three plotted the perfect accidents: how to die convincingly, leaving no trace, no way which would allow the searchers to say, "They may still be alive--we must not stop searching."

They continued to sit in the shadow of the sacred structure in this area so peaceful, so serene, so spiritual, and so undemanding, planning, at great length, their eventual deaths--an oxymoron if there ever was one.

Alpha, after a long pause in their brainstorming, said, "I think, for me, I want to die at sea."

The other two thought a moment about that: Alpha was the one who loved his swimming lessons—he would stay in the Olympic-sized pool long after his coach had left. He'd always say that he did his best thinking while doing the laps. Another positive to the swimming was that his shoulders were broadening, making his waist seem much slimmer, a characteristic the other two brothers envied.

"They won't let you walk the plank!" Beta replied, laughing at the idea. He turned over on his stomach, beginning to do pushups, willing to try anything to improve his physique. (The three were becoming more competitive all the time.)

"No. Now wait. Hear me out. I convince my handlers to take me on a sea voyage--help me expand my experiences--make them think that this will, somehow, benefit their research on me--you know, dangle the carrot."

"Then what?" Gamma asked. He did not do pushups, hated to do laps, was the couch potato of the three.

"Then I'll find a way to fall overboard; and as soon as I'm in the water, I'll transport myself here to our special retreat."

"You know what would happen, then?" Gamma asked. He was the irritatingly logical one: A precedes B; 2 comes after 1....

"They wouldn't be able to find me--would believe I was dead. No way they'd locate my body at sea--they would understand that."

"Yeah, you're right." Alpha agreed, "but you can be sure that the two of us left would never get a chance to see the real world again. We'd be locked up securely in the lab for the rest of our lives!" He thought about the "Time Outs" when they were younger and would be isolated for doing something their teacher felt was bad or dumb (there was a separate room with padded walls that they would be placed in, maybe for 15 minutes—sometimes for an hour. Alpha hated that!

"You have a better idea?"

"Yes and no. We have to die at the same time--I don't know how--but we can't give them the opportunity to make plans to lock up whoever was left."

Shading his eyes from the afternoon sun, Alpha thought out loud: "If we all three want to do something unusual, like go to the ocean, and want to do it at the same time, our handlers will know that, somehow, we're communicating. They aren't stupid! But ... what if we string this out over a few months, ask to see some of the places we've read about, you know, the Statue of Liberty, the Declaration of Independence, Mount Rushmore—things like that. Let them get used to our asking to go out into the world. And what if, after a few trips, we start moving that damned spoon across the table. That will make them think that one thing is causing the other thing, and they may, in fact, begin suggesting, on their own, trips that we should be taking."

"Yeah," Beta replied, "Make them think that the more we see and do in the real world, the more weird spoon-like stuff we're able to do!"

Alpha stood, stretching. He was the tallest of the three, brown hair, blue eyes and already with the muscular and fit body of an adult. Though the three were brothers, there wasn't a connectivity that would easily brand them as such. Gamma was thinner, more scholarly looking, and less inclined to show his emotions. Beta was ruddy, sandy-haired-- the bon vivant of the three.

Alpha thought a minute: "All that's good, but how are we going to die at the same time? How do we manipulate our handlers to let us go where we have to go and do what we have to do to make our deaths not only coincidental but sudden, irrevocable, and very believable?"

Alpha looked at his WristLink and turned toward his two brothers, "We'd better be getting back. Siesta time on the ranch is about over!"

Beta broke in, "Wait, we haven't solved our problem." But he was speaking to the empty air--Alpha had already transported.

He and Gamma looked around. They hated to leave the sanctuary.

"There was one other thing I wanted to bring up," Beta insisted. "I don't like not having a real name: Alpha, Gamma, Beta--that's like we're not real people--we need names."

"Agreed!" Gamma said, enthusiastically. "We'll share that idea with Alpha--and the next time we meet here, we'll unveil our new choices!"

And with that, they wheeled, calibrated, and disappeared.

Alpha rejoined his sleeping body--but his mind was whirling as he transitioned back here to his home at the Greenbrier, an epiphany in motion: what if the three of us were able to escape this compound? We could meet up somewhere, get on a ship, and, at the right time, with cameras rolling, jump to our deaths. That way our handlers would not have to be manipulated. The three of us would be in the real world, finally, at the same time; and our lives would change forever.

In the ensuing days, he started looking at his total environment in a different light: where were the chinks in their security? What was the weakest link? What could the three brothers use to exploit their surroundings and achieve their freedom?

As he began to look closely at all aspects of his everyday existence, he realized, for the first time, that there would be parts of this life that he would miss: the daily routines, although occasionally frustrating, gave structure to his life. His handler was a kind man, a brilliant scientist, yet a philosopher at heart. Alpha, in a passing thought, asked himself-- Can I make it without Samuel? And he realized that this man was and would always be a father figure for him. A moment of angst overcame him as he anticipated freedom: escape to a world without rules, routine, or structure. What would that do to my life? He mused; and here, for the first time, came a question: What would *I* really like to do?

As far back as he could recall, in his entire life, all activities were determined by others--he planned for nothing, could anticipate nothing on his own, could expect every day to be filled with interesting and challenging ideas and activities; but all of this was beyond his control: he was not privy to anything that would happen to him one hour, one day, or one year from right now. But what if he were able to shake the shackles of the laboratory? What if he were the one who would decide his future? That was a scary thought: to be able to plan one's own day, one's own week, one's whole life—choose activities with purposes that he understood and that he agreed with: challenging!

At the same time that all of these ideas were bouncing around inside his consciousness, he was making notes of every security camera, every monitor, every Xirate light barrier, as well as every heat detector. All of these devices were subtly placed, but this had been his whole world for the last 15 years, and he understood every nook and cranny of his prison.

One of the more interesting features of Alpha's quarters was that no exit door had a knob or a handle on the inside--only on the outside. Somehow, his handler and others were able to leave the compound simply by approaching the door: a chip or other device on their bodies seemed to be the activator.

His living quarters consisted of an open kitchen–living room and a bedroom, as well as a small bathroom: most of the appliances and devices were voice-activated. One wall across from the couch was the Learning Center, an important part of his daily routine.

Samuel, his instructor, mentor, and friend used it to highlight aspects on any particular topic that was chosen for the day, and it provided visual stimulation during his unstructured times. Of the various helpers who came and went in his life, Samuel was the constant--the even-tempered, all-knowing companion who grew old as Alpha moved from childhood to his teenage years.

Time revealed the disconnect between his own slow maturity and Samuel's metamorphosis from youthful vigor and enthusiasm to the equanimity of the long-suffering Sage: Alpha asked him why it was taking so long for him to reach adulthood. Samuel's laugh took the edge off of his answer as he replied that one should not wish for adulthood--that the longer we lived, the faster time would consume us all.

Most of his daily lessons were crisp and precise, containing no sphinxlike riddles--but sometimes.... Sometimes, and it became more noticeable as Alpha matured and asked more pointed questions about life in the world outside his cubicle: at those moments, Samuel resorted to obfuscation rather than answers. For example, Samuel had often explained to Alpha that the reasons for the daily lessons, tests, and experiments was that he was preparing him for the future--for life as an adult; and when Alpha would ask if there were other young people like him who were, likewise, being trained, the answer was always the same: "You are the only one that matters to me."

Alpha, of course, knew about Beta and Gamma, but he could never get Samuel to comment on anyone else. Maybe it was, for some reason, a secret he had to keep–- but another possibility was that Samuel was just as insulated and isolated from the greater world as were the three brothers.

After the last meeting at the Crazy Horse Monument, Alpha begin thinking more and more about escape: it became apparent to him that escape was more realistic than trying to manipulate the handlers into a situation, which would allow the brothers to die convincingly at the same time, yet providing no corpses to verify their deaths.

But escape brought to the fore puzzling questions, which, up until now, none of the three had considered: What would life be like for them outside this petri dish? Who would provide for them--find them clothing, shelter, and food? Where would they get the wherewithal necessary to survive outside the bubble, and what exactly did wherewithal mean?

Many more questions had to be answered before they were ready to leave the laboratory; and as they continued to meet at the Monument and contemplate the realities to come, they made a prioritized list of to-do's:

A. Determine an escape plan.
B. Find out specifically what was required to live independently.
1. What skills do we need?
2. What would be necessary in order for us to assimilate?
3. How would we convince someone to take care of us--provide food, clothing, and shelter?
4. What would our long-term goals be?

And they realized, too, that they all could not be asking the same series of questions, could not suddenly become curious about the same things. They diversified:

Alpha worked on the skills needed in the outside world; Beta dealt with assimilation; and Gamma zeroed in on the basics of food clothing and shelter. And, they were determined that when they did leave the compound, they would do so with names which they, themselves, had chosen:

Alpha decided to take his mentor's name--Samuel, abbreviating it to Sam; Beta's handler was fond of saying to him, almost like a mantra, "Well done! Well done!" So Beta chose "well done," then shortened it to Weld as his first name; and Gamma's favorite writer from long ago was Mark Twain, so he chose to become Mark.

Each began working on his specific assignment, but at the same time, there was an overriding goal--the escape itself!

Early on, they understood that they simply could not transport out of the compound and be on their own--they would be free, but they would be creating a greater problem. With all the cameras and other devices, it would be obvious what they had done; and the search for them would begin immediately.

Unknown to the brothers was the Consortium and its one trillion dollar investment—an investment they expected the three to transform into world domination. For many lifetimes, those who passed through the sheltered world of the three—the many investors, known and unknown, lived and died with the hope and expectation of eventual other worldly revelations; and their vote had always been to continue funding this gamble. Their faith had not faltered even though the three had been so careful not to reveal any of their unusual and expanding talents—not to share their growing number of secrets with their mentors, their handlers—they continued to provide everyone with the visual living proof that they were simply talentless teenagers.

And an Ah Ha moment came on their tenth meeting at the Monument: Beta postulated, "What if we don't escape. What if instead we are kidnapped?"

"Kidnapped?" The other two shouted in unison.

"Yes!"

"Sounds stupid, but run with it," Alpha said.

"In the middle of the night, once I have snuggled down under my blanket--I would have brought several extra pillows with me under that blanket, so I'll arrange them like a body, and then I'll transport to the outside area near one of your doors. I'll have a blanket over my body and a see-through sock over my head. I'll grab you and cover both of us with a blanket and transport. And then to make it convincing, I'll go to my own quarters, grab the pillows, which represent me and, again, transport."

There was silence.

"What then?" Alpha asked, his mind beginning to acquire these simple, yet strange plans.

"Then we hide out, send a ransom note, and wait for the troops to arrive."

"Where would we hide?"

"Well, I think we've decided that the best place to die is in the ocean: our bodies could never be found--so I've been doing some research--the luxury liner, King William, makes the Atlantic crossing every week. We can transport to it in mid- ocean and make our handlers aware of where we are."

"Then what?" Gamma asked, with some impatience.

"Simple," Beta said, grinning, "When we're sure that they have identified us, surrounded us, and are ready for the capture, I push the two of you over the rail!"

"Okay, we're dead, in the middle of the Atlantic—so far so good, but what about you?" Gamma asked.

"Well, then I jump over and join you in Davy Jones' locker."

The two listeners shook their heads in unison.

"It won't work." Alpha said, "Frankly, that's an embarrassing plan! You have to do better than that!" He hoped his brother was just joking— the plan was that bad! Sometimes Beta was in a weird world of his own, marooned somewhere between a dilatant and a ding a ling! Alpha smiles at his choice of words—a perfect description, he felt.

"What's wrong with it?"

"Think. Who and where are the kidnappers? There have to be kidnappers-- kidnappers with unique abilities—special powers that the camera will have recorded when everyone disappears. Where are they? What about the ransom? It all seems a little too contrived."

After a few more moments of fruitless thinking, Beta provided a ray of hope, "Well, at least we've decided on one thing."

"What's that?"

"Our names! I'm really happy, finally, to be finished with these lab-rat names: now Alpha is Sam; Gamma is Weld; and I am Mark! Let's never mention those old monikers again!"

"Agreed!" The other two brothers rejoined, giving each other the fist twist.

Sam was the eldest and, true to his birth order, was the natural leader: "Wait, now, if we want these to be the names we keep after we leave this place, we don't want anyone knowing them--ever—we can't use them until we're out of here: we're still Alpha, Beta, and Gamma. Sorry."

Seeing the disappointment on his brothers' faces, he quickly switched topics:

"My mentor says that we can't leave our training program until we exhibit characteristics which qualify us to be part of the general population--that all young people our age have to go through this orientation; but he also says that I'm lagging behind."

"It's that darn spoon again, isn't it?" Weld growled, with some frustration. "Why don't we go ahead and move it around just enough to satisfy everybody? You know, if we don't, we may be in here for the rest of our lives."

"Or dead!" Sam interrupted. "I'm telling you, it doesn't make financial sense for them to keep training us, if there's no indication that we'll ever be ready to leave."

Mark, usually the up-beat, optimistic one, reflected, "There's something wrong with the whole set up--you can't tell me that it takes so long to prepare every young person for the real world--at least not the way we've been schooled. Think of all the people who've come and grown old in the time that we've been here. We don't change quickly, don't have health problems, colds, aches, and pains--the only thing that's ever been human about us is that you, Weld (We can use our real names when we're alone, can't we?)—you've had to wear dark glasses. We're not like any of the people who've been assigned to us—we're somehow different."

"Different doesn't explain why we've had such a prolonged and lavish education--everything provided for us," Weld volunteered.

"I've been thinking the same thing," Sam agreed. "There's something about the three of us, in the minds of those who train us or maybe their leaders, that makes no expense too extreme for our well-being and our education. Somehow, they have great expectations for us." He paused. "But, what the heck could it be? Sure, sure, we *could* move that spoon--nothing great about that. Do you suppose that we're the *only* ones able to do that? Surely that can't be the reason we're important to them. There's no indication, that I can think of anywhere in my life--and you tell me if I'm wrong—nothing that any of us can recall, to suggest that we've revealed any unusual talents or characteristics. We've shown them nothing! Why, then, do they expect so much?" He continued. "Weld, have you or Mark, picked up any thought transfers that would make you believe that there might be others like us in or outside this compound?"

They both shook their heads.

"We *are* special, then. Each of us should make an effort to find out exactly who we are, where we really came from, and how we're of benefit to them?"

Weld adjusted his glasses: "We've all read the thoughts and feelings of those who're working with us, and we agree that they truly are interested in our improvement and that they all have very positive feelings toward us. But if what we're saying is accurate, then we're pawns in someone's or something's long range plans. I don't know about you, but I don't want to be anybody's puppet—even if it is for a good and worthwhile cause! And for all we knew, it's not!"

"Yeah, Sam replied softly—we have to learn how to extend our thought probes and be able to search well beyond these dormitories—we need answers--let's work on that."

CHAPTER 2

While the three brothers were struggling with their problems, on the top floor of the Greenbrier Resort in Sulfur Springs, West Virginia, two women sat at a conference table, looked out past the bucolic lawn and gazed, in the distance, at one of the five golf courses. They, too, were troubled:

"I think it's time," the gray-haired one in the black pantsuit stated.

There was silence, each drinking slowly from her tall, ice-cold afternoon Refresher.

The younger one shook her head, her auburn hair reflecting red and gold in the afternoon sun.

"If we *do* advise the Consortium to pull the plug, we're admitting to a one trillion dollar mistake."

"The mistake may be to continue and to squander another trillion over the next century. Let's go with Professor Raucous' idea--he's the genetic genius. His plan is to turn the three loose---supervise them only at a distance. Let them experience the real world---succeed or fail as we all do---let them fall in love and marry. The professor seems to think that the talents that we're looking for, the solutions to the world beyond our telescopes, will come in their children---that the special DNA of the Original One has skipped a generation. He feels that the Consortium should follow the lives of the offspring of Alpha, Beta, and Gamma. We've learned nothing from these three brothers. Unfortunately, they are just like us—not that that's so bad, but when one spends a trillion dollars expecting a quantum leap in science and physics, one cannot settle for just ordinary."

"Of course, you're right—but our sponsors, those in the Consortium, although they have deep pockets, may simply want to put this whole program, including our three, on the garbage heap of past failures, light a torch and make it all disappear. Are we deciding, here, today, that we *have* failed? Do we suggest that they end this experiment? If so, we need to send them, along with our recommendation and the professor's suggestions, our letters of resignation.

The room was silent for a long time.

* * *

The Greenbrier has held many secrets in its lifetime: It began humbly in the mid-1800s as a trading post; and because of a mineral spring located nearby, a sulfur spring, a few houses were built to accommodate those who came for its medicinally rejuvenating properties. Over the years, more and more people learned of the springs and began making the difficult sojourn there. Eventually, a railroad laid tracks to this West Virginia spa, and from that time forward, it grew by leaps and bounds. It is, today, the playground of the rich and famous, having 10,000 private acres, the unsurpassed mineral spring, as well as a plethora of sporting and social activities, especially a series of championship golf courses called, today, the Justice courses, named after a local entrepreneur, Jim Justice, who, in about 2010, purchased the entire resort, guaranteeing all past debts and thus removing it from an imminent bankruptcy suit. The Justice golf courses have seen most of the major golfers in the world take their turn on these challenging links.

Yet the national attention of this secluded West Virginia playground came only in the mid-20th century with the building of an underground series of bunkers designed to be the go-to housing for the entire United States Congress, in case the Soviet Union's bombers targeted Washington, D.C. with a nuclear attack.

This vast undertaking was disguised as simply an enlargement of the resort, as well as a remodeling project, code-named *Project Greek island*. During the height of what was called the Cold War--a period of extreme hostility between the United States and the Soviet Union, a time when there was no declaration of war, and yet both sides seemed to be on a wartime footing.

The endeavor began in 1958 and was ready for occupancy by 1961. Individuals and companies who were working on the project had to sign a lifetime commitment to total secrecy--a secret so sacrosanct that there was an unwritten understanding that if any leak were to take place and be traced back to a person or a company, that individual or that entity would simply disappear--would cease to exist.

Also, the government's lease agreement signed by both the resort owners and a clandestine wing of the Defense Department was that if the secrets of the bunkers were ever exposed, the government would cease to fund the original project and everything would be reassigned to the Resort, itself.

For 30 years, the illusion of the nature of the Greenbrier remained intact. This city within a resort was self-sufficient. It had its own power plant, purification and decontamination equipment, its own water and air systems, and it contained dormitories enough to house over 1100 people.

Finally, in May 1992, the Washington Post exposed the project, and it, therefore, according to the original agreement made between the Greenbrier and the government, had to be returned to the Greenbrier management. It was then opened as a tourist attraction.

The Post was, at first, cast as the bad guy--the un-American newspaper that exposed one of The United States' most precious secrets--but there was more to the unveiling than met the eye.

The Greenbrier was several hours from Washington, D.C. by train, but back when the USSR depended upon its bombers to deliver a nuclear payload, two hours was adequate to get Congress to the bunkers. However, with the perfection of the long-range nuclear-tipped rockets, the escape to West Virginia became unfeasible, time wise. Since the annual upkeep of this secret out-of-date war-ready facility was costing the American taxpayers millions of dollars, the practical reason for the leak (by our own government) to the Washington Post was simply to break the lease agreement with the Greenbrier and, thereby, return the control of and the expenses of the bunkers to the Resort.

Again, about 200 years later, during the Great Famine and the virulent Pestilence, the bunkers were used as a pristine storage facility for seeds from every imaginable crop, worldwide, as well as for stockpiling the strategic food, water, and other necessities for the directors of the fight for the world's survival. These leaders lived here, as well, and controlled all aspects of this struggle, which eventually resulted in the resurgence of mankind; but they led the fight from the comfort and safety of West Virginia's plush Greenbrier bunkers—not an unusual or unexpected decision, given the perilous nature of this last-ditch undertaking.

CHAPTER 3

The Consortium was a recent creation, occurring just after the Pestilence—a time when the Government was scraping the bottom of the barrel just to survive; and its purpose was to bring together teams from across the nation to resist mother nature's latest onslaught. There were still a few very wealthy families in America, the same families who had always been the major contributors to its politicians, influencing their rise or their fall—so it was these six families who banded together to save the centuries-old attempt to learn from those beings who came here—who remained Earth's ultimate puzzle–the eternal promise of greatness, of power, and wealth—it was at this fateful point in time that the newly founded Consortium accepted from the nearly destitute Government the responsibility and the expense of continuing this ancient experiment. They were an independent entity, no longer directly affiliated with the Federal Government and connected to the Greenbrier only peripherally, through their decision to continue renting space from them.

Now, just as the Government had done 200 years ago, the Consortium leaders of SpaceQuest again met to decide the fate of three children, the offspring of the last Alien to come here a millennium ago, and they met with the same concerns and the same constraints.

The decision on the table today, the one they had been struggling with for some time, was whether their efforts and the efforts of all those who had gone before were of value and were worth continuing or whether it was time to accept the futility of expending another trillion dollars over the next century on this project.

Jonathan Zobek had the floor and was expounding on his favorite theme, "Kill the project and reassign the monies to the continued attempt to repopulate the Moon, and to use it as a jumping off place toward a Mars' transplantation and then look toward the stars." He was an excellent speaker, his ideas always well thought out, his gesticulations perfectly timed, and his eye contact riveting. He was dressed today, as usual, in black, with a white handkerchief slightly visible in his left breast pocket, his cravat matching perfectly.

Of the five who were listening, three were leaning forward, elbows anchored to the conference table, obviously in complete agreement.

He continued, "We've had failures, of course, in trying to make the Moon's North Pole Colony a success, but we shouldn't be distracted or deterred by a few missteps."

Jack O'Rourke interrupted: "Few missteps! Hell, JZ, we've lost the entire Colony twice! It's been no more successful then our project, StarQuest."

A small, shriveled, shadow of a man sitting in the end chair cleared his throat. The talking stopped.

"We're changing the direction of our oldest experiment, but we aren't ending it."

He was obviously a man who commanded the respect of the other five.

"But this change will free up most of our funds for other considerations-- considerations which we don't have to decide on right now. Before we leave here today, we need to figure out what to do with our three boys."

Jonathan filled in the void from the pause in Chairman Blount's pronouncement:

"Carlton, these three boys, as you call them, have had more years on this Earth then my grandfather, my father, and me combined! They're simply a liability to us. Why plan for their future? We need to plan for their demise. They've given us absolutely no reason for spending another dollar on them!"

The Chairman glanced over his bushy eyebrows, proffering his inscrutable but curious look-- "We've always been able to find consensus--where do you see the middle ground being on this?"

Jonathan pursed his lips--thankful for the Chairman's giving him a foot in the door: "Why do we need all three? I say, choose just one, and we'll cut our expenses by two thirds."

"Go on," the Chairman encouraged.

Jonathan never was sure whether Chairman Blount was in agreement on any topic or was just giving him enough rope to hang himself.

He trod carefully: "From all the test results and psychological assessments, it seems that Alpha is the brightest--holds the most promise--but, I'll have to admit, there's not that much difference in the three. I don't think it matters. Let's just choose one, turn him loose in our real world, and see what he does."

Jamaal Kurdish had not joined in the conversation, as yet, but he was following the logic closely: he interrupted. "According to Dr. Raucous, there's no longer any hope for these boys. All of us were convinced that the onset of puberty in the three would unleash the secrets, which the Original Ones brought with them. Unfortunately, that has not happened; so it's their offspring that we must look to for the answers we've been seeking for so long. I say, once they produce children, end their useless lives and focus on the offspring!"

Chairman Blount looked around the room, assessing the effects of the discussion so far, and he saw the tide beginning to turn from his original pronouncement.

"I suggest we accept Jamaal's plan--put it in play on the boys' 16th birthday. In the meantime, let's see what being part of our chosen families--part of today's world-- has on Alpha, Beta, and Gamma. For all we know, that exposure with real-life might, in itself, prove to be eventful!"

"I second the Chairman's plan," Jonathan immediately offered, never losing a chance to come down on the side of the current leadership.

CHAPTER 4

Weeks went by, tortured weeks of trying to find a weakness in the underground bunkers' security system. The prisoners of Chillon felt no more hatred for their incarceration then did the three Newall brothers--but the brothers' odium was recent and, unknown to them, was to be short-lived. The only positive since their last meeting at the Monument was a decision on their last name: Their choice was simply a play on words: all three had concerns about stepping out from the well-organized, well-planned activities of their confinement to the freedom of the outside world where all would be new to them. They took the *all new*, reversed it and had a last name that they were excited about.

There was a disappointment, however, which overshadowed their name choice: they found no weakness in the security system which surrounded their compound and, equally disappointing, was the fact that, even by joining their minds for a linkup with others beyond their compound, success alluded them.

But then, one day--not an important or eventful day--ordinary as any other day in their lives, everything in their past became but a memory: everything in their future suddenly reflected hope, excitement--freedom.

Samuel came to Alpha's room during their lunch break--he looked 10 years older than he did an hour earlier: his high forehead was deeply creased, the muscles in his jaw twitched, and his eyes were lifeless--he was, by now, of course, an old man; but he had always carried himself with pride and purpose. Samuel was suddenly a shell of himself.

"Sit down, Alpha," he said, in a funereal tone. "I have some unexpected information for you." Suddenly this calm man of learning began crying. After a minute or so, and with some effort, he regained his composure.

Sam was touched by all that he was seeing and hearing. He had no idea where Samuel was leading him, but he understood that it was only with great effort and self-control that this was being done.

He waited, patiently.

Samuel continued: "Very soon you will be placed with a family outside our compound. You will be leaving me—leaving all of us here who have loved you and worked for you and for your best interests. You are ready to join the rest of the world."

He bowed his head, holding onto a stair railing to steady himself. The teacher in him paused, waiting for Alpha to process this new knowledge.

"Do you understand what I'm saying?"

Sam did not reply immediately for, in truth, he did not understand. There had never been any hint that this moment was on the horizon. It must be one of Samuel's teaching tactics: a test of the intellect or of the emotions.

The silence was prolonged.

Finally, realizing that Samuel had passed the ball to him; and unsure of what the game was, Sam went right to the heart of the situation:

"When do I leave?"

"When would you like to leave?"

"Now!"

"Are you sure I have prepared you?" With this question, Samuel set on the steps, shaking his head. "Alpha, I must tell you, this wasn't my idea--there is so much more you need to know--so much more I need to share...."

So this was no test on Samuel's part--the grief he was projecting was real--the message he came to deliver contained no subterfuge--the three brothers were free. The search for a way out of this compound, the secret meetings at the Monument, the endless lessons and tests, the unspoken need on the part of his team for him to perform some unexplained action--all that was in the past.

Sam walked over to his teacher: "Samuel, you will be with me wherever I go, for the rest of my life--your spirit and mine will be linked forever--you can rest now. I *am* ready."

Samuel smiled. His shoulders straightened. "Thanks, Alpha. God speed, wherever fate send you."

And not looking back, Samuel left the room. Sam never saw him again.

* * *

It was the middle of the week, and for the first time in his memory at this time in the afternoon, all was quiet. The place seemed deserted--no sounds, no smells, no thought activity within range. Hour after hour passed. Dinnertime came and went. It was all very disconcerting. Sam checked his WristLink. Food was always brought to him, to his kitchen, by one of the many forgettable faces--those who smiled and served, and left him to enjoy his meal. This afternoon, just a few hours following Samuel's emotional message that he was free, Sam was still here--but this time, and it was a new sensation to him, he was feeling the hunger pains he had only read about during his anatomy classes.

Finally his outer door was opened and two men in suits and a young lady in a lab coat entered.

"Are you Alpha?"

"Yes, what's going on? Where's my dinner?" Sam was in no mood for pleasantries. He did not like feeling that sensation in his stomach.

"We're here to give you your Biometric Wallet and the other necessities you'll need on the top side."

"Topside?"

"Yes. They're required before you leave us here at the Compound."

Another orderly-type person came to the door, pulling a wheeled apparatus, which hummed impatiently and emitted, every few seconds, a series of multicolored flashes.

The smaller of the two men, the one who had first mentioned a wallet, noticed that Sam was eyeing the machine:

"Your Fuji Scanner Facilitator."

"My what?" All this was very confusing: it was not presented in a coherent way--not like Samuel would have arranged it. Sam did not like these people--they had no business here in his private quarters, and he was disoriented by their cacophonous chatter.

"Your hand, please," Lab Coat said, in a bored voice.

Sam was resistant. "Why? What do you need my hand for? Why are you here? Where are the food servers?"

"Your hand," she said again, looking him in the eye as though she has some authority to make him obey.

Sam did not move--did not offer his hand--did not even return her look.

"Alpha," the technician said firmly, pausing in his key-pushing activities--do we need to call security? It would be in your best interests to cooperate. If you continue to resist, you will be strapped to your bed while we complete our assignment."

The effrontery on the part of these petty people was inexcusable. Sam had never been spoken to in such a manner--had never been threatened. He had always felt that he was the central player in some, as yet, unidentified, role.

The woman said for the third time, "Alpha, give me your hand."

Sam's mind reached out to her.

Boredom echoed back. No evil intent, just boredom, as though she was doing this same activity for the thousandth time.

He extended his hand, seeing no other choice. She gently covered it with a dry, yet liquid solution and waited a few seconds for it to evaporate. Then she placed his hand in a slot in the FujiReader—a plaque on the machine's side suggesting its name.

"What does the FujiReader do?" Sam asked, trying to diffuse this near confrontation.

"Never had one before, have you?" She grinned for the first time. "It analyzes the veins in your hand and imprints them in a form that all Readers can identify."

Sam was sorry he had asked. Doesn't make sense, he thought. Why would anybody be interested in a picture of the veins in my hand?

As he considered this, there was a sudden pain in his left arm just above his elbow.

"Damn!" He exploded. "What the hell are you doing to me?"

"Your Biometric Wallet," the technician replied. "You act like you've never had one before."

"Damn right, I haven't! Call security. What you're doing to me can't be approved. Who are you, anyway?"

The lab-coated lady turned to her cohorts: "Are we finished? What a prima donna we have here."

"Not yet. Gotta get an iris scan--then we'll be through."

Another 15 minutes and they were gone. Sam's body was shaking, he was so upset. He reached out to Weld and Mark. It was Mark who responded. "Yeah, they're here now--what's it all about?"

Sam was in the midst of explaining the recent encounter with these people, when his exterior door opened again, and Dr. Alex walked through.

"How're you doing, Alpha? I just passed the ID team, so I guess you're about ready to exit our secret city?"

Sam's arm was still aching. "Doc, what's happening? What's an ID team?"

"Oh, I've forgotten that this is your first time. The Identification Team's very necessary to your transition. They've given you all you'll need in order to become a functioning member of your new family."

Sam looked puzzled.

Dr. Alex responded to that look. "You've had your exit interview, haven't you?"

"All I've had is verbal and physical abuse! I've no idea what this is all about."

"Shit." The doctor muttered, and he walked out.

An hour later, another intruder walked in and, by now, Sam was ready to throw a few punches, except....

"Alpha, I'm so sorry. It must have been awful--not knowing what was going on. I'll explain everything. I was to be the first one to see you. The day's been so hectic--so many leaving us. It's as though they're releasing everybody at the same time. Anyway, I'm here to orient you and to help you plan the transition to your new family." He was a short, roly-poly looking worrier, with sweaty hands and an unpleasant body odor. He kept adjusting himself, as he talked, and would move his notes from one hand to the other as he performed this obviously gratifying activity.

Sam just listened. Maybe things would finally make sense.

"It's hard to know where to start. Before you can become part of the new order, you need identification, you need a bank account, and you need the various protocols required for your new life." He kept approaching Alpha, as he explained, and Alpha, kept backing up, trying to maintain a comfortable conversational distance.

"The shot in your arm--I see you rubbing it--that shot inserted a life chip which contains all of your basic information and serves, as well, as a banking mechanism. Occasionally, it will have to be reloaded as you become low on funds. Just find a FujiReader outlet and let it scan your hand. It'll read and identify your one-of-a-kind vein structure. It's such a foolproof system, anymore, plus there's no need to carry a physical wallet. How cumbersome that must have been.

"And I remember the stories they used to tell about the old fingerprint system--I'm sure you've read about that antique--the one long before the FujiReaders? A person needing cash would go to an ATM machine, place a finger in a slot and be identified, and then would be able to withdraw physical money. The problem was, the ID thieves thought nothing of chopping off someone's finger, taking it to an ATM machine, and using it to withdraw the cash--how barbarous!"

Sam had a sudden image of someone cutting off his hand and taking it to a FujiReader.

"What makes this new system any more foolproof?" He asked, rubbing his wrist.

The Orientation man laughed. "Oh, the Fuji machine reads the blood as well as the veins. In the beginning, the ID thieves tried the same horrible method to thwart the machines, but that would never work--so you see, your hand is in no danger!"

"You said I'd be assigned a family. What's that all about?"

"Every young person who leaves our Greenbrier program is matched with a family best suited for the personality of that person. You will stay there until you're 18 years old and then, off you go for your specialty training at one of our universities."

Sam was tired of having his life planned for him--was hoping and expecting that when he left the lab, he would be making his own decisions. And now, more schooling! He'd been in school all his life--was tired of the regimen--was ready to be his own man.

"What if I don't want more schooling?" He bristled.

"Oh, there *are* some who make that decision. It's up to you--but once you've committed, there's no changing your mind." Orientation Man's tone of voice was such that Sam could tell he was totally against turning down the university opportunity; but, of course, he hadn't been in school his entire life, Sam was sure. How much education does one need to survive, he wondered, having already made the decision that he wanted no more of it!

"If I choose not to go to the University, what then?"

"Most likely, you'll work in one of our Agro businesses."

"Outdoors?"

"Probably."

"I think I'd like that," Sam reflected. "I've been in the same building all my life--It would be great to breathe fresh air, feel rain on my face--even get sunburned, if I want to!"

Orientation man began packing up his equipment. "Think about what you need to take with you—I doubt that you'll ever be back. Your ride will be here for you about eight o'clock this evening."

CHAPTER 5

Mark awoke with a start. Groggy and disoriented, he spun his legs over the side of the bed, expecting to encounter the heated floor of his bedroom. Instead, he felt cold, textured tile. As he looked around, it all began coming back: the secretive exit from the Greenbrier compound, the all-night drive out of West Virginia, the arrival at a hotel in Indianapolis, Indiana, the interminable wait, as his new handlers reconnoitered the area, and finally--a room, a bed, and sleep!

But a sleep interspersed with contacts from Sam and Weld, who also were on the move: through the darkness and rain, Sam was headed south, leaving Kentucky and Tennessee, still traveling, as Mark awoke to his new life. Weld was, as was Mark, ensconced in a hotel, having been allowed no outside contact, nothing but furtive activity from the Greenbrier, to the van, to a hotel room.

The Chairman's plan was to place each of the offspring of the Alien in a different and unique situation: Mark to a rural farm family in Wisconsin; Sam to a major southern city, Atlanta; and Weld to a family in Alameda, California.

When Mark awoke again, it was in the Wisconsin farmhouse of Allie and Bert Schmidt, an elderly couple whose children had long since fled to the city, numbed by the life of cows and rice. Bert was, to say the least, as Mark assessed him, rough around the edges: a 6'5" giant of a man, who smelled of cow dung and sour milk. Allie, however, was all sweetness and light, seemingly overjoyed to have a teenager in her house once again.

They both were going to take some getting used to, Mark realized. Allie, the night before, after Mark arrived, served him a monstrous farm dinner: ham, mashed potatoes, carrots, peas, cranberry sauce and milk, followed by a generous slice of chocolate cake; and all the while, as she hovered over him, continuing to refill his plate and his glass, she would ask if he needed anything else.

Bert, in contrast, ate quickly and was out of the house, headed for the barn to tend to the milking chores.

The next morning, sometime before sun up, Bert came over to Mark's bed, shaking him gently: "Boy, time to rise and shine. Allie's got a big breakfast ready for us--then you're gonna become a farmer!"

Once again, Allie was the perfect hostess, aware of Mark's every need—yet the breakfast, although prodigious, took less than 30 minutes.

"Come on, Boy," Bert encouraged, pausing for a final gulp of black coffee, "let's get at it."

Hesitating at the side door only long enough to hand Mark a pair of galoshes and, quickly pulling on his own, Bert was eagerly out and into the still dark predawn. The rugged farm clothes Allie had laid out for Mark fit perfectly, and the boots, too, were just right. Wonder how long they had to prepare for me? Mark considered. Wonder what part they had in the decision for my coming here or for choosing me instead of Sam or Weld?

"Let's go, Boy, the cows don't like waitin--they're happier and produce more milk if we get them settled in before 6 o'clock---besides, we gotta be on the tractors by eight--got two more fields of rice to plant! You ever driven a tractor?"

In truth, Mark had never even seen a real field, felt the sting of the early morning air, or, for that matter, ever encountered the smells of 100 Holstein cows!

From what he could see, Bert ran a pretty tight ship: the cows knew where their stanchions were and seemed eager to have the milking machines hooked up to them. Just behind each animal was an 8-inch deep concrete ditch, water constantly flowing through it, to remove the cow dung and urine, which accumulated from the hour or so that they were there for the milking and feeding process.

Bert started Mark off with a no-brainer job: washing down the udders of each cow, before attaching the milking suction cups to the four teats. Dodging the occasional gushes of urine and feces and trying not to inhale the powerful barn smells kept Mark so preoccupied that he did not hear Bert the first time he called from the other end of the barn.

It wasn't until Bert was directly over him and grabbed him by the collar that he was aware of his situation:

"Dammit, boy! You deaf or somethin? You're wastin my time. Let's get this herd to pasture: we gotta get outside—there's a lota no-till plantin to do this mornin!"

As they approached the smaller of the two farm tractors, an International 12 M, Bert began Mark's training: "Now look, it's exactly like programmin a car--what you're wantin to do is just go in straight lines, across the field, 10 feet apart. Watch me. Here's how you program this tractor's computer."

And Mark did watch. And he understood. Computers he could deal with--cows … he wasn't so sure.

The morning went by quickly, and in spite of the occasional rumblings in his stomach, for the first time in his life, he felt really alive. The tractor that he was in charge of had an open cockpit, so he was able to take in the many smells of the Earth in the spring, as well as the multiplicity of sounds: above the muffled steady refrain of the tractor, he could hear birds and the occasional yelps of the distant coyotes--Mark had no way to connect these sounds to specific birds or animals, but he appreciated the fact that he was now part of something that was real, that was palpable--and he dared to embrace it.

Allie had lunch set up at a picnic table behind the old clapboard, two-story house, beneath an ancient tulip poplar tree, which was just beginning to bloom. There was a gentle breeze blowing, and Mark lifted his arms, reveling in these new sensations-- feelings the air cool down his sweating and dust-covered body.

The iced tea was like an elixir--and he drank glass after glass.

"Boy, go easy on that tea--don't want you to get all bloated on me. We aren't halfway through our day yet!"

Allie corrected her husband: "His name's Mark, honey. Mark, not Boy."

"Yeah, yeah, I know. Well, the Boy did okay today, so I guess we'll keep him," Bert laughed, deep and sincere.

"Course we will, even if he wouldn't of been able to drive that tractor you love so much--he's ours, now." Allie beamed.

It was at this point that Bert began his lecture on the background of the Herford breed of cow; and after about 30 minutes, Mark began thinking TMI, TMI--too much information!

But this was Bert's passion: through constant attempts at selective breeding, he planned to continue producing superior Holsteins and increase milk and meat production, as well; and Mark, as the lecture continued, felt like a captive audience. Allie, on the other hand, busied herself clearing the table of the main courses and preparing to serve dessert. She was obviously not particularly following this discussion, having heard and participated in it a thousand times or more in the past. Bert was very proud of the fact that he had cows, which produced, individually, over 23,000 pounds of milk per year. Mark had no trouble believing those statistics. After all, these were huge animals, over 5 feet tall and weighing in the neighborhood of 1500 pounds!

Bert explained that the Holstein originated in the Netherlands over 2000 years ago, and through selective breeding had become an animal, which would produce high quantities of milk and would be able to subsist on grassland, with little additional expense required.

America's dairymen were so satisfied with the Holstein that 90% of the milk cows in the United States were of that breed.

Bert favored the polled variety: those cows who naturally did not have horns, maybe because of his traumatic experience of years ago: he had borrowed the Holstein bull of a neighbor in an attempt to improve the genetic makeup of his own herd. This bull was a mean-tempered animal with huge hooked horns. And Bert, being accustomed to working with cows and heifers of the poll variety, took his eye off this giant beast for a few seconds too long and was gored in the stomach. Of course, the good news that came from this horrible incident was that it allowed him to meet his wonderful Allie who happened to be on duty as a surgical nurse when he was brought to the hospital.

The following month went by quickly: cows in the morning, planting all day, and cows in the evening. At the end of the third week, Mark could feel that his body was changing, adjusting, evolving: his hands were becoming calloused, his face and arms darkening beneath the Wisconsin sun, and he was acclimating to a life without his teachers and without his daily lessons. A new routine was insinuating itself: rising before sun up, 10 to 12 hours of outdoor physical work, three squares a day, interspersed by Bert's insistence that he learn every practical thing a farmer needed to know: Practicality trumping Academics!

And practicality included the history of their most lucrative crop, rice. Since the Great Pestilence of a few centuries ago, the production of rice in Wisconsin and other northern states has expanded exponentially. Early efforts, spearheaded by firms such as *Uncle Ben,* continued to breed out rice characteristics which reduced the volume of production or exposed the crop to unnecessary risks, such as early frost or disease. Lake-seeded crops of rice were greatly expanded because of the introduction of air boats equipped with collection troughs. With the coming of the Pestilence, many crops in the United States were decimated, including potatoes and corn; but rice, because of its genetically engineered past, withstood the challenge, providing a starving nation with a sustainable food until the genetic manipulation of other native plants became successful. The simple but catastrophic fungi plague, called Super Brown Spot, was finally stopped; and more recently, the maturity time of the rice crop was reduced from 110 days to just a little more than half of that. Efforts to increase the resistance to the early northern frost may, in the near future, allow for two crops to be harvested each year.

Bert was no teacher, but he was a realist, and Mark found himself thinking less and less about the Greenbrier and its, as he looked back, stifling pedagogue. Now, learning was not for the joy of learning: it was in order to survive and prosper, and rice was a big part of Bert's success.

One of the strangest and most rewarding sensations he had ever felt came at the end of a long day in the fifth week of his new placement, as he and Bert were walking from the barn to the house.

"You're doin just fine, Boy!" Bert said, with some admiration; and he put his strong rough hand on Mark's shoulder. "I'm proud of you."

No one at the Greenbrier--no teacher, no handler--no one had ever touched him in such a gentle and accepting way. It was difficult for Mark to understand the feelings that washed over him. To be complemented—accepted--to feel the success of being a contributor to an important and real-life activity!

That evening, after retiring, he connected with his brothers, sharing this new sensation.

CHAPTER 6

As the days piled up, one on top of another, they became months; and gradually Mark found himself looking beyond his immediate chores and the surroundings which were slowly becoming so comfortable; and he decided to ask Bert about the high-rise buildings he could see in the far distance. He tried to picture the state of Wisconsin and determine where he was, geographically: could what he was seeing be the city of Milwaukee?

During the next day's lunch break, he quizzed Bert about exactly where they lived, and if what he saw on the horizon was, in fact, Milwaukee.

Bert's face flushed, "Don't want to talk about it," he said, shaking his head vigorously and leaving the table.

Allie, who was sitting next to Mark, put her hand over his: "You don't want to bring that up, Mark. That subject is off-limits with Bert--he gets so upset." She was comfortable running interference for her husband and was always on the lookout for situations, in which she could intervene and shield him from any kind of anguish or worry.

Mark was surprised by this and curious, so he decided to share his interest with her and to ask if she would explain those buildings to him.

"I'll tell you, Mark, but don't talk to Bert about any of this." She poured another glass of milk and sliced the second piece of apple pie for him. Before beginning, she walked to the door, checking to be sure that Bert was not in range of this conversation.

"Bert's family owned all of this land going back over a 100 years--and they kept adding to it, generation after generation. Now, only Mr. Lukazewski's land separates us from those towers you see."

"What are they?" Mark asked. "Is that Milwaukee?"

"No, no," Allie laughed, "We're nowhere near any big city. Those towers are the way most fruits and vegetables are grown today--the towers are vertical farms--18 to 20 story structures, and each huge building can provide enough food for a small city of maybe 50,000 people. You know, after the Great Pestilence and that global war, a lot of the good land couldn't be used for crops anymore, so those powerful Agro-Businesses came out here, bought up big sections of farmland, and began building their hydroponic and aeroponic towers. There's an outfit called VeryFresh Farms that's been trying to get our neighbor, Mr. Lukazewski, to sell to them. As I said, he's the one that owns the land between us and the towers."

Mark wanted to understand the logic of all of this, but he had no real experience to draw from. He could pull up, in his mind, a map of the United States and could visually see where Wisconsin was, but that was no help. The only reality he had was the long drive here from West Virginia--it seemed to take forever and to cover thousands upon thousands of acres. What made this particular section of ground so important?

"Why don't they just build somewhere else? What does Mr. Lukazewski have that's so important?"

"Oh, the River! Allie gushed. The White River, plus our deep wells! Those towers need lots of water year-round and, in the cold months, lots of electricity. That's why they want our land."

"Your land? You mean they want your and Bert's farm, too?" Mark tried to clarify.

"That's what upsets Bert," Allie said, softly, dabbing her apron to her eyes--there've been different groups coming to offer him money or to help him convert to vertical farming, but he's so stubborn, so set in his ways--wants to use the same old methods that his family has for all the years in the past.

"His family was lucky, 'cause this section of the county wasn't hurt much--which meant Bert's family, at least, didn't *have* to choose the new kind of farming--lots of people and companies in other places had to go the tower-method or starve."

"Yeah," Mark agreed. "But I've read that, after the Die Off, people's lives improved—nations began to prosper again. But, I guess, then the cycle started all over--more money, more children, more need for food and other necessities: the only solution became vertical farming!"

"Well, Bert doesn't pay much attention to the rest of the world--his world is right here, and he's determined to protect it!" Allie made that perfectly clear.

Before Mark left to return to work, Allie cautioned him a second time not to mention any of this conversation to Bert.

* * *

The winter came and went uneventfully--that is if one discounts the horrible storms and eight-foot drifts of snow that Mark experienced. The three brothers were surviving their first year in the real world and, in fact, were finding it exhilarating!

They were hoping to meet in two months, May 29, at the Crazy Horse Monument: their 16th birthday.

Unknown to them, the Consortium had been observing at a distance and was getting reports from their adoptive families as to how the three were progressing. No report, thus far, had indicated any unusual activities, which the Consortium could construe to be promising--so as the month of May approached, they set in motion what they called, "The Breeding Regimen." A bevy of young female laboratory technicians who had been following the progress (or lack thereof) of the brothers, volunteered to bear their children--to become part of this experiment to bring the secrets of the stars home to Earth.

Sam was the first to report on his discovery of girls and sex, and as he relayed his continuing escapades, Mark and Weld were at a loss to understand what was happening to their very controlled and proper brother--but then it happened to each of them. Suddenly there were ladies who were introduced to them by friends and family, and these ladies seemed to be interested in only one thing--getting the two of them alone and making passionate love.

Mark, unlike, the other two, had always been up for anything, willing to experiment, to spurn no adventure; and when the adventure happened to be a beautiful woman, all the better: his first dalliance was with Mr. Lukazewski's daughter, Vita, but then she introduced him to a few of her friends who, as it seemed, had no objections to sharing.

After a few weeks of these unbridled orgies (how else can one describe such activities), the brothers began re-evaluating recent events, trying to determine what was happening and why it was suddenly happening to each one of them.

Sam was the first to push away from the frenzy of coupling and to ask the other two to meet him at their usual spot.

"There's something not right about all this," was his opening remarks.

The other two looked at each another, not yet ready to step back and consider how irrational their activities had been.

"Seems pretty right to me," Mark interjected, grinning widely.

Weld removed his dark glasses, trying to understand where Sam was coming from: "This must be what all teenage boys do as they turn 16."

"I don't think so," Sam declared. "I don't think the average 16-year-old boy has older women jumping in bed with him--not the way it's been happening to us!"

"Then why us?" Weld asked.

"That's what we've been asking ourselves for years: why us?"

There was silence.

Sam continued, "I don't think we're free, yet. We're still being watched and manipulated. There's something that someone wants from us. All of what we've been through since our release from the Greenbrier is being directed. They haven't found what they need yet, and they're looking for it 24-7. Don't you want to know what that is?"

Weld turned this question over in his mind. Everything that had been done since his release had been interesting and rewarding: the family he was living with was refreshing, after the years of schooling and those unemotional contacts of the lab. He was becoming especially close to the eldest son, a senior at Wautoma High School, as well as a tennis and track star. Jim was easy to talk with and very inclusive in his activities, asking Weld, occasionally, to run with him as he trained for a mini marathon. Weld had been placed at a local Bio-Kenetic station for his job and was deeply involved in mastering the skills to become a Transformationalist. He could not understand why some entity would have any particular interest in him, would be pulling the puppet strings, or directing, or trying to influence his future. What would be the purpose of that? As far as any other human being on Earth knew, he was disappointingly normal--no smarter, no dumber--outstanding in no particular area that could be of interest to anyone—unless, and that unless came up now for the first time: unless there was someone or something who could intercept his thoughts--who had discovered his talents--the talents of all the brothers. What if whoever was financing their lives knew everything?

He shared these worries there on their mystical mountain.

Sam was the first to respond. He was suddenly convinced that, once again, they needed to revisit those old childish escape plans. One would think their disappearance would now be so much easier to accomplish: they were at their Monument, presumably free to do as they pleased—as far as they could discern, had no cameras, eyeballs, or electronic devices focused on their every move, every thought.

It was a very warm morning, and the sun was not above the outstretched arm of Crazy Horse yet, so there was no shadow across the three. They reacted to the warmth and to the struggle with their dilemmas by finally removing their shirts and letting the sun beat down upon their fair skins.

Sam looked at Mark, the pale, redheaded brother, thinking that he, too, now had the body of a full-grown man--but a man whose skin could not compete with the sun's rays.

"Better put that shirt back on, Mark--you'll end up red as a lobster!"

As Mark reached for his shirt, Sam zeroed in on his left arm and the Biometric Wallet! He observed, and he understood: they *were* being tracked. He was now sure that the biometric device was their problem: it was inserted into the arm of each of them on the pretense of preparing them for the real world--making them able to secure electronic money, allowing them to more easily identify themselves. "Damn," he whispered--and he thought to himself--we have so much to learn--how can we possibly compete with these people--whoever we're up against. Ours is far from a level playing field. Can they see us? Hear us? Tell what we're thinking? Do they know our plans? Are they aware of all our efforts? Maybe we're no more then lemmings, being marched over some precipice. And after a long pause, he thought: how can I convey this new information to my brothers without making these Observers aware that we know?

Mark was listening to Sam's thoughts, and his mind suddenly flashed back to the earlier months with Allie and Bert--to what was an evening ritual before supper: they would all hold hands, and Bert would close his eyes, as would Allie, and after a moment, he would begin talking. Mark simply observed this one-way conversation. It was sort of like when he was very young, his handler would tell him, as he was put to bed, "Now, if you get scared or if you need anything, just ask for it—we're always here to protect you." For years he accepted this as the truth, and he felt safer knowing that he was being watched over; but as he approached his teenage years, the comforting term, *Watched Over,* came to mean the sinister, *Spied On,* in his own mind. Yet, no matter how he came to view the practice, they were not lying to him. Whenever he needed or even wanted something, all he had to do was vocalize his desire.

He remembered one of Bert's talks with this unknown Observer: Bert was saying, "Lord, we need rain. The crops are so dry, hear this plea and help us if it's your will-- and thank you for the boy. He's workin out real fine--a blessin to our family."

That's when Mark realized that nothing had changed from the Greenbrier: they spied on them there--and he now knew, they were spying on him here. Funny thing is, it did rain the next week after Bert asked for it! Whoever he was talking to was able do all kinds of things.

As he was recalling this earlier scene, he remembered how he and his brothers had, just for the fun of it, developed their own secret language. For some reason, they discovered that each had a fascination with antiquity and they, for the challenge and for research, mastered Sumerian, the ancient language of Mesopotamia.

Mark projected to Sam, *Think in our secret tongue*--and as they continued sitting beneath Crazy Horse, the shadow of his arm gradually provided relief from the sun. For over an hour, there seemed to be complete silence on the mountain; yet from the facial expressions of the three, it was obvious that something was happening in their thoughts.

In Sumerian, Mark was broadcasting to Sam and Weld what he'd found out about his family--about Allie, in particular.

At some point in their many conversations on the farm, he had asked her how she and Bert had gotten together; and she, with some excitement, even after all these years of marriage, explained that she was a trained surgical nurse and that, one day, while she was on duty, Bert was brought in, gored by one of his bulls. She assisted in the surgery and, for some reason, felt the need to visit him every evening after she finished her shift--love and marriage soon followed.

Sam interrupted the thought with one of his own: *Why are you telling us about this?*

Mark grinned at his brother's impatience: *Once we have a plan of escape that's foolproof, we need to get rid of these biometric wallets--Allie can do that for us, using her surgical nurse experience.*

Will she? Weld queried.

I don't know, Mark replied. *When the time is right, I'll find out.*

You have a plan B, I hope, Sam wanted to know.

Sure, we operate on each other.

"Gross!" Weld said aloud, unable to contain his revulsion at the thought of such impending butchery.

"Got to get back for milking time," Mark suddenly interrupted.

And with that, they all vanished.

* * *

A week before his birthday, Mark was having lunch out under the tulip tree, when a Velosocraft landed in the nearby field and a dozen men dismounted and formed up at attention. Their leader and another, walked toward the house. Bert immediately told Allie and Mark to go to the house's cellar. They did, but Mark stayed in Bert's mind, seeing what he saw and hearing what he heard.

The determined old farmer clasp a Thermoshot in each hand and walked out to meet the two who continued to come toward him. They did not appear to be aggressive and carried no visible weapon.

Bert yelled out, "That's close enough! What do you want?"

The man continued advancing. The woman, however, stopped and, turning toward the assembled group by the Velosocraft, signaled to them.

Bert pushed a button on the Thermoshot. It began blinking as he held it over his head. "I said, don't come any closer!"

"Mr. Schmidt, I'm here with our final offer. If you reject it--as you have all of our other generous and peaceful attempts to purchase your land, I can't be responsible for your family's safety!"

"Captain, my wife is now in touch with the police--if I drop my hand, she'll request immediate help."

"That's not going to happen, Mr. Schmidt. All your outgoing messages are being blocked by the Velosocraft's on-board Oslo waves. This is your last chance. I'm leaving our contract here at my feet and returning to my ship. You have five minutes to signal your agreement to its terms."

And with that, Captain Hanover did an about-face and headed towards his platoon. Mark contacted Sam and Weld: *I need you here now!* Seconds later, they appeared in the cellar with Allie and him.

"Shit," Sam exploded. "You didn't tell me you had company!"

"Guys this is Allie--I've told you about her. Bert is outside being confronted by a group of men—they're demanding that he sign over his farm to them."

"What are you going to do?" Weld asked.

"We three need to go out there with Bert. Together, we can force them to leave."

Allie was frightened. She backed herself into the corner of the fruit cellar's shelving.

Mark walked over to her: "These are my brothers—they're here to help Bert. Just stay here, Allie. This shouldn't take too long."

As the three walked out the side door of the old house, Sam said, "How bad you want this to get?"

Mark replied, "They need to get back into that Velosocraft and take off, headed home. When they're away from Bert's farm, they need to crash."

"They're going to see us."

"Yeah, but they won't live long enough to tell about it."

"Okay."

As the three approached Bert, who still had both hands in the air, still gripping the Thermoshots, Mark called to him, "Don't turn around, Bert. And don't lower your arms."

The brothers joined minds and projected their thoughts toward the group, now beginning to unload weapons, including a laser cannon. Suddenly all activity stopped. Frozen motion reigned for a few seconds, then, calmly, the group began returning all weapons to their ship. They boarded it and took off toward the distant towers.

"Now!" Sam commanded. The three minds forced the ship higher and higher in the sky until it was but a speck on the horizon.

"Down!" The three shouted in unison, and the speck grew in size and speed until it was consumed by a ball of flames on the horizon.

"Done!" The three whispered, sweating profusely.

"God Almighty!" Bert burst out, and as he spoke, he turned to face the three.

"My brothers," Mark said, proudly, nodding toward them.

"Where'd you come from?" Bert asked, as though he had witnessed a miracle.

"We were nearby," Sam explained.

"Nobody's nearby out here," Bert laughed. "Now, what's really goin on? Did you have somethin to do with all that out there--that crash and everythin?"

"Ship happens," Mark punned.

Suddenly, Bert looked toward the house, "Is Allie okay?" He strode toward his home.

"Mark, you've got us in something that's going to be hard to explain. Now that these folks have seen this—they may guess at what we're able to do." Sam was concerned that their cover was blown.

"Maybe so, but Bert and Allie are good people. I couldn't stand by and watch those guys push them into giving away everything that had meaning for them."

CHAPTER 7

B y the time they all returned to the kitchen, Bert had brought Allie
from the cellar and was making them a cup of tea. Her eyes darted
from one boy to the other, and she grabbed Bert's hand, looking for
reassurance.

"Bert says these two are your brothers. But I don't understand where
they came from. I never heard them upstairs, and they just suddenly
showed up in our cellar."

"Let's all settle down and talk about this," Sam said. "You're right,
you're right, Allie, we've some explaining to do. Mark knew that those
men who landed on your farm were up to no good. You guys were going
to need help--he was sure of that. Since we were on our way to visit him,
it worked out just right."

"But what did you do?" Bert broke in.

"Ever hear the old saying, 'The enemy of your enemy is your friend'"?

Sam continued, making it up as he went along: "Well, we're being
hunted by the same people who were going to try to take over your farm.
If they find out Mark's our brother, he'll be hunted too."

Allie looked at Mark, reached out for his hand, "That would be
terrible! How can we help you?"

Bert repeated Allie's question: "Somehow you got the Captain and
his men to leave. We owe you. Allie's right—what can we do?"

Sam was creating a road which would lead toward Mark's earlier plan A--that of having Allie remove the biometric devices from their arms.

"Any ideas, Mark?" Sam passed the baton.

"Well, we know our movements are being traced through the sensor implanted in each of our arms. Allie, you used to be a nurse. Could you remove those things for us?"

Allie suddenly became animated: "I've done that procedure many times." She paused for a few seconds: "but I've just about always done it on dead people."

"I hope you can make an exception for us," Sam quipped.

"Well, you see, when someone around here dies, especially a young person, 'cause they've all been implanted—anyway, when they die, they're brought to the hospital. We remove the sensor and then the hospital deactivates it."

Bert intervened: "If you're hidin out from those damned VeryFresh people, you can't just remove the chip. It'd stop reportin your vital signs. That'd make all of them damned curious. They'd come after you, wantin to find out if you're dead or alive."

"So we shouldn't have Allie take them out?" Mark asked.

Bert walked over to Allie's cookie jar—"Tea tastes so much better with one of these peanut butter treats!" He smiled in his wife's direction. It was also giving him time to think of a practical and believable way to solve this problem. He loved dilemmas--always had, whether it was with a recalcitrant tractor or a bull-headed animal. But the word *bullheaded* caused his hand, automatically, to reach for the scar across his abdomen.

He continued his evolving plan, thinking out loud: "If those things are tracin your whereabouts, somebody knows that all of you are here; but I'm guessin you're probably less of a threat here in the middle of nowhere! You think you're in any immediate danger if you just stayed here?"

Sam began shaking his head immediately, "Bert, we can't stay. There are too many things we should be doing."

"I know. I know. All you young folks have agendas. But answer my question, 'Would you be safe here for a while?'"

The three looked at one another. "Maybe," Sam replied. "But I'll bet when those guys in the towers learn about the crash of their ship, they're going to regroup--they'll pay you another visit."

"Well, that's not your problem," Bert countered.

"Let's deal with these things one at a time," Mark jumped in. "Where were you headed with your thinking about the sensors?"

Bert grinned, "Now don't be offended by what I'm gonna suggest: what if Allie took your sensors out and immediately replanted them in three of our pigs?"

The boys laughed. Mark rejoined, "That's the most impractical thing I've ever heard you say, Bert. Where in the heck did that idea come from?"

"I know people, and I know my animals!" Bert began. "And a pig has about the same blood pressure and heart rate that a human does-- plus, if you don't butcher the pigs, they'll live about 25 years or so! Not that you'd want to stay here that long..."

Sam began running this new idea through his head. It was true that they *were* probably being tracked, and now the Greenbrier bunch knew that the three brothers had reunited. But what would they do with that information? Maybe they would see it as a positive move--easier to trace their movements, to pounce on them any time they wanted--plus the three would be isolated from the rest of civilization. He considered for a moment how that would play out: the only downside to the plan would be if their watchdogs were able to make a connection between the crash of the Velosocraft and the presence of the brothers here in farm country.

Sam took a sheet of paper off Allie's kitchen counter and wrote on it as he spoke:

I don't know if they can hear us or not, but just in case, play along:

And he continued talking, explaining that the pig idea was a little too weird but that they would like to stay for a few days and try to figure out just what they should do.

Bert got it: "Sure, but if you're gonna hang around, I'll have to put you to work. We'll be sendin one of our herds off to the stock market next week--also goin will be about 100 head of hogs. You'd be a big help with that."

Allie was following all of this and was quite happy to have two more teenagers on the farm.

"I'll bet the two of you are kinda hungry by now. What if I fix you some lunch? And Bert, Mark, and me—we'll have some of my brownies!"

CHAPTER 8

O n the top floor of the Greenbrier, the six members of the Consortium met once again. Joining them, this time, were the two ladies who originally had been charged with the oversight of the program called StarQuest. So much had changed since their letter recommending that the program be abandoned and that previously allocated monies be set aside and directed toward the resettlement of the Moon. Their letter of resignation, which accompanied the recommendations, at least, in their minds, ended their involvement with this program; and they were quite surprised to be summoned here, especially on such short notice.

In all prior meetings over the years, they had always arrived with an agenda and with a plethora of ideas for the Consortium to consider--various ways to open the portals to the secrets, which these Alien offspring possessed.

Today was different: they were now out of the loop--and increasingly happy because of that fact! They would admit, however, that to be summoned back to the program held some fascination and some excitement; but it also was a commitment, which, in the past, had worn them down and had brought premature wrinkles and sleepless nights.

Chairman Blount wrapped on the table with his martini glass: we are now in session. Mr. Zobek, would you bring us up to date on the StarQuest program?"

Jonathan Zobek scooted his leather chair quietly back and rose ceremoniously to address the seven: "As you are all aware, Alpha, Beta, and Gamma were fitted with new tracking devices and released, last year, to their assigned families. The Breeding Program has now begun and, although it is too early to tell if we have been successful, the boys, I am happy to report, have participated fully."

There were a few head shakes and a chuckle here and there from several members.

Jonathan continued: "We have placed our boys with three families, one in Roswell, Georgia; one in Alameda, California; and one in Wautoma, Wisconsin. They have settled in nicely but, according to reports from the families and from our field observers, none is exhibiting any hoped-for characteristics. Chairman Blount, at an earlier meeting, upon the recommendation of Jammal Kardesha, suggested that if the Breeding Program were successful and if the boys proved to be nothing but normal teenagers, then their involvement in StarQuest would be terminated--that they, in fact, would, themselves, be terminated. We had planned to proceed with this phase on about 29 May--the 29th being the three boys' 16th birthday. Also, at a later sidebar, I recommended that, if the lives of these three were ended, we should make one last effort to find the fourth brother who, as you are aware, was being carried by Asima Sumayyah, one of our lab workers. She disappeared in the 11th month of her pregnancy, and every attempt, so far, to locate her or her son has failed." Jonathan paused here, obviously disturbed by his own revelation: "To leave loose ends like this is very unsettling.

"Another item of interest: Beta, who is in Wisconsin, has had two visitors recently-- Alpha and Gamma. We don't know how they found out about each other or what their plans are. They have now been together at the Schmidt farm for a week. Interestingly enough, during that week, VeryFresh Interprizes lost a Velosocraft and a contingent of freelance soldiers not far from the Schmidt farm.... Coincidence? We don't know. We've been trying to find out why the craft was in the area, and all we've gotten so far from them is 'no comment.'"

Jonathan returned to his seat, taking a long drink from his coffee mug, satisfied with his performance.

Chairman Blount smiled, thinking about his furtive involvement in VeryFresh's long-range game plan. He thanked Johnathan Zobek and, turning to the two ladies: "Miss Kershner and Dr. Farley, thank you for coming. Your services over the years have been of a tremendous help as we've tried to unravel the mysteries of the men and their machine, which came to Earth so many eons ago. We here would like to ask you to perform one last task for us: find Asima Sumayyah and locate her boy--our boy, Delta--or at least be able to tell us the fate of each. Mr. Zobek will give you all the information that we have on the mother." Jonathan rose and motioned for them to follow him out of the room. They looked at one another as they left their chairs, each knowing the answer she would give regarding this request.

CHAPTER 9

They sat on the east side of a stack of circular hay bales, shaded from the afternoon sun. It was their 16th birthday--the coming of age for youth everywhere--but the three brothers seemed to be going nowhere: their past, in its entirety, had been planned and executed by an invisible hand--their future, as they saw it, a perilous journey into the unknown.

Many years ago, they realized that their chronological age was not in sync with the people who serve them. Their handlers, servers, and others aged rapidly, in their opinions, and eventually disappeared from the compound, no explanation ever given. Their 16th birthday, therefore, meant that they had already exceeded the length of live of an ordinary human. Even before they had been aware of this extreme disparity, it was disconcerting to watch the people around them, especially those who were an integral part of their everyday lives, age, become less effective, and eventually vanish.

But now they realized that the lab was forever in the past and that all the experiences, observations, and conclusions associated with that unhappy period had to be put behind them: the freedom which they had longed for was now here and required that they become self-directive. It was an abrupt and jarring adjustment, yet a milestone of gigantic proportions for the three.

Mark rolled over on his side and winced: "Your arms still sore?" he asked Sam and Weld.

"Heck yeah!" They replied, one echoing the other.

Sam was specific, "Allie may have been a surgical nurse at one time, but she really butchered us up good!"

"That's for sure!" Weld laughed, "I think she did a much better job on the pigs!"

"Hey, you got to give her credit for trying--and after all, she *is* old--must be somewhere in her 50s, maybe even older!" Weld continued, "And now, for all that our spy in the sky knows, we're very content running about on the Schmidt farm. If it's just a tracking device that our pigs are carrying, we've bought ourselves some time; but if it's also an audio or visual, it won't take them long to figure out that we're not two feet tall, eating out of a slop trough!"

"Exactly! We need to disappear--need to lose ourselves somewhere in this huge country. You know, the three of us have been schooled for years and years--can tell anyone a million different relevant facts about the United States: size, length, width, population, gross national product--on and on, but..." Mark paused.

"But..." Sam picked up on his thoughts, "But, that's all it is, a lesson! Frankly, I don't have a clue about how to hide, where to go, how even to get our next meal if we were to leave!"

"That's easy," Weld explained, chuckling. "We walk into a fine restaurant, order a fabulous meal, have our first glass of wine ever, and then we just transport out of their... We just vanish."

He was, of course, making a joke. They all knew that--but it could work: anything they needed or wanted would be that easy to obtain. Same way with a hotel room-- enjoy it for a few days--then simply disappear. No tracking devices to give them away.

"Wonder if we'd need that Biometric Wallet in order to be served at a restaurant or to check *into* a hotel?" Mark asked.

"Maybe we should just stay here. The Schmidt's would love that, I think—there's certainly more work here then those old people need to be doing," Weld contemplated.

They saw Bert come out of the barn, headed in their direction. He was walking with purpose, but slowly, seeming to be thinking with every step. It was Sunday, so they weren't afraid of being busted for loafing. He stood over them, his shadow pointing eastward.

"It's May 29th," he said, as though that should have some significance.

"Yeah! Our birthdays!" Mark shouted.

"All three of you?" Bert was very surprised. "What are you, triplets?"

"Sort of," Sam answered, looking at his two dissimilar brothers.

Bert returned to the reason for his walk out here to the haystacks: "Well, anyway, at the end of every month, I have to fill out a report on you, Mark... Kind of an evaluation of your progress." Bert hesitated here, trying to decide how best to ask a question that had been bothering him since the visit of the VeryFresh people.

Easing his huge frame down to a squat position, he eyed the three: "Should I include that part, you know, about those mercenaries, how they just suddenly left and then how their ship crashed? If I don't, they might get suspicious; if I do, same outcome." He pulled a stem from the hay bale and began picking his teeth. "Either way, it could be trouble," he admitted, looking at Mark.

"Do you have a copy of your last report on Mark?" Sam asked.

"Sure. Allie's got it up at the house. Would that help?"

Sam nodded.

"I think she's also got strawberry shortcake ready. Let's go see."

They needed no encouragement!

Sitting around the kitchen table after downing the shortcake, Sam thumbed through the report: "Looks like they're mainly interested in Mark and his activities--nothing about anything outside the farm. I'd say, don't mention it." Turning to Mark, "What do you think?"

"Sounds right," Mark replied, simply.

Allie walked over from the refrigerator: "Let me see your arms--I'm afraid I've done a pretty bad job on all of you--you're going to have scars. I really hate that, and I'm sorry."

"You set us free, Allie," Mark explained, trying to allay her concerns. "Now, we can go wherever we want without big brother checking on us!"

She walked behind Bert--put her hands on his shoulders; "We've been talking. We'd like all of you to stay with us. It's a big place--you need to be somewhere safe, and, Lord knows, we need some young blood around here. Our own kids ran out on us-- don't seem to care about all the extra work it caused--don't seem to worry about what happens here on the farm."

Bert simply nodded his head in agreement.

The boys didn't have a chance to answer. There was a knock on the front door.

Bert jumped up from the kitchen chair, grabbed his Imp from a nearby drawer and said to Allie, "Go answer it--but take your time! I'm goin out the side door and around to the front, just in case."

The boys continued sitting, not sure of what to do.

Allie opened the door to two strangers in suits. On their lapels were EPA insignias; and after their introduction, she led them back to the kitchen. By this time, Bert had come back in the side door and was quickly hiding the Imp in its usual resting place. Following the initial explanation for their visit, the two handed Bert several sheets of paper; as he read them, his face grew redder and more contorted with each second that ticked by.

"This is a damned lie!" He finally shouted. "Sure, my rice fields are planted with modified seeds--but Billy Joe, down at the Co-Op said all of that had been approved—that the new seeds would help me--the new rice would just require less water to get it to maturity! You damned government people need to stay out of the farmers' lives--you get paid the same whether we succeed or fail--whether we live or die!"

"Mr. Schmidt, please read the second document too. I'm really sorry--it isn't personal, I want you to know that. It's just our jobs. We always have in mind the best interests of every farmer in this entire area. Decisions like this are made far above our heads."

Bert suddenly pulled the Imp from the kitchen drawer, "Get out of here! Get off my land--you damn bloodsuckers!"

"Now, Mr. Schmidt, I have to tell you this--the dusters will be finished with your back thousand acres of rice by sundown. Then, starting tomorrow morning at sunup, they'll be getting closer to your house. The dust will make you very sick. You *will* need to be out of here by the end of tonight--and by the way, any animals that you have, should be moved also."

Bert gradually became less bellicose, but he was seething inside. All he had been doing was simply trying to following good farm practices by choosing a new and approved genetically altered form of rice--one that would grow better, faster, and use less water. It was a no-brainer, he thought. Now saying that it was not approved for human consumption was ridiculous!

"Look, maybe we can give you an extra day to relocate, since you do have such a large herd of beef and, evidently, quite a few hogs, also."

Bert did not raise his voice when he said, "Get out," but there was a venom so obvious in his tone that the two government men, without another word, turned, and left the way they had come.

While all this was occurring, there in the Schmidt's kitchen, Mark, whose skills had matured much faster than his brothers, tapped into the minds of the two men; and to his surprise, he realized that they were just actors, not EPA officials--they were hired to convince everyone of the truth of what they were saying.

The Schmidts and the three brothers followed the two men out and watched them drive off. As Bert raised his gaze to the horizon, he pointed: "Looks like they've already started to dust my fields—they're killing my new rice crop. And turning to Allie, he confessed, in a defeated tone, "I don't know what to do now. I just don't know…"

Sam stepped forward: he and Mark had been exchanging thoughts, so he was aware of the subterfuge of the two men.

"Bert, that hovercraft in the shed--does it work?"

"Haven't needed it for quite a while, but, sure, it's a fine machine."

"How much weight will it carry?"

"Oh, I guess fifteen hundred pounds or so--maybe more. Why?"

"If you can trust Mark and the two of us, I think we can make this problem go away."

"Hell, yes, I do! Tell me what you need."

They all ran toward the large shed. Mark opened the doors, and they were soon in the air, headed toward the cloud of poisonous dust.

"Faster, Bert! The sooner we get there, the fewer of your acres will be contaminated!" Mark leaned forward, trying to make contact with the dozen or so planes that were, in a military fashion, going back and forth across the distant acres; and he had no trouble interrupting the pilots' thoughts: they, too, were but hired help--men paid to do a job--men with families, with hopes, and plans. Killing them would be pointless, he knew, but the planes had to be stopped.

As their hovercraft arrived and floated above the precision aerobatics, Mark entered the panic section of each pilot's mind: "Abort!" He broadcast.

Every pilot turned the dusting mechanism off. Mark counted to 10, wanting them to be out of the dust cloud; then he Broadcast, also in the Panic Mode, "Eject!"

For years, thereafter, the men who were now floating gently to Earth would wonder exactly what happened on that cloudless morning in May--would be forever grateful that they had memories to cherish, plans to fulfill, and dreams to ponder. They would never understand the reason for their unpremeditated ejection from their doomed planes; but one way or another, such are the vagaries of life.

Sam reprogrammed the GPS system of each of the planes; and they climbed, turned, and headed back toward Tower 10; and with another slight tweak in the GPS, each plane slammed into a different level of its 20-store structure. Plumes of smoke billowed hundreds of feet into the air, and flames could be seen for miles across the flat terrain as the exploding gas tanks turned the area into a war zone.

As they returned to the farm, Bert said nothing, caught up in his own thoughts-- questioning whether he could find a logical answer to what he had seen: he was a practical man and a problem solver, but he was at a loss to bring his logic to the unfolding drama. It had to be the boys--or maybe the work of God, or …

The brothers, also, were silent, amazed by their own abilities, but troubled as to how they would explain them to Bert.

Weld spoke first, "Bert, can you just forget everything you've seen today?"

"No." The old farmer said, rubbing his knuckles across his eyes. He was such an honest man that he could not dodge this question--he was not able to lie about what was burned in his memory.

"No, I saw what I saw. I don't understand it. I do know that you three are *not* teenage boys, but I sure don't intend to ask just who you are. I don't want to know. And Allie doesn't need to know, either. But..." He paused, trying to regain his composure, "but whatever I can do to help you, just say the word." He looked pointedly at each one to make his words more emphatic.

That was the end of their conversation until they landed, and Bert had taxied the hovercraft into the shed. As he walked out to catch up with the three, they turned and waited: this huge man of interminable patience, logic, and reason, somehow seemed to have lost his zest for life--the essence of his being showed signs of having drained away during the last hour. His step was still strong and secure, but at the same time, it was hesitant, as though the world that he had always known had changed forever--had become more challenging and, in fact, more unfathomable.

He advanced, with a trancelike stare, his arms hung limply by his side, being swung along by his gait alone; and his entire countenance revealed a foreboding Mark had never before witnessed in him.

Mark tried to change his mood, "Come on, Bert, we've got good news for Allie--you aren't going to have to leave your home! And all of your animals are going to be okay, too."

"Thanks to you guys--not to me," he mumbled.

He was feeling the tug of time--sensing the changing of the guard, hearing the knock on the door of old age; and he reacted by withdrawing from the energy swirling around him. He would continue to be here with the love of his life--and every day of his life, he would be a little less able to protect her.

The Newalls, too, were having to face their future. Being sensitive to Bert's deepening gloom did not bode well for any show of enthusiasm about their newfound freedom. Both Weld and Sam understood that a continued absence from their assigned families in Georgia and California would soon ring alarm bells for whoever was directing their lives. These few golden days here with Mark and the Schmidts could not last--and this paradise loss would only heighten their feelings of being surrounded by prolonged weldschmertz.

* * *

Once the activities of the day had been explained to Allie and the evening meal was over, Weld, Mark, and Sam walked out into the cool evening air, realizing that they had to make some decisions and that whatever they would plan for their tomorrows, it would haunt or excite them for the rest of their lives. The frogs around the pond, down by the pig lot, were beginning their evening serenade, and the call of the Whippoorwill in the distant stand of trees added to the deepening melancholy of the three.

"You think that the VeryFresh people will be back to harass Bert and Allie?" Sam worried.

"If you'd lost 13 planes, a platoon of men, and a 20 story silo, what would you do?" Weld summarized.

"Yeah, true. I think I'd be very angry--but I'd also be really wary. So, I'd probably lie low for a while, try to figure out exactly what had happened!" Sam speculated.

"But, what about us?" Mark asked. He picked up a rock and threw it toward the pond to quiet the evening romances of the frog population. Although he was the optimist of the three, the fact that they seem to be unable to escape the feelings that the puppet master was still directing them--controlling every viable alternative in their lives, caused him to want to lash out—to take action--to get off this treadmill of dead-end decisions.

"We need to do something unexpected--something dramatic!" Mark said, to no one in particular, "We need to get the heck out of Dodge."

"What exactly does that mean?" Weld asked, having heard the quote before, somewhere in his studies of early American history.

Sam struck a pose and, with some drama, said, "Frankly, my dear, I have no idea!"

They all three laughed at this rare glimpse of his, sometimes, unfathomable humor.

In the silence that followed, as they made their way down the long gravel drive toward the main road leading to Wautoma, the increasing sounds of the night continued, affecting their mood.

"I've had it with The United States," Weld shared. "Let's go somewhere far away from here."

"You don't know anything about this country," Sam countered. "We've all been in a cage for the last 15 years of our lives. We know nothing about anything! As a matter of fact, have you ever considered that everything that we've been spoon-fed at the Greenbrier may contain not one shred of truth? Is it possible that this place called America really doesn't exist--that even all of the science and physics we've learned mean nothing?"

"That's depressing!" Mark reacted.

Weld brought them back to their immediate needs: "For the time being, let's assume that our schooling represents the real world: where could we best hide out? Do we need to plan our own deaths again? How do we get out from under the microscope?"

"Are you sure that's where we are?" Sam asked. "Maybe we're just being paranoid. What proof do we have that we're being spied on--that anybody out there gives a hoot about with what we do from here on?"

"Somebody's paying for our upkeep--and you know if money's being laid out for us, it's an investment, not a gift!" Weld suggested.

"Remember, back in the lab, all the times they tried to get us to move that spoon? If they've been watching us today, they know that we can do a little more than that!" Sam declared.

Suddenly, Allie yelled from the front porch, "Boys, better get in here! Those mosquitoes are gonna eat you alive!"

* * *

Sam awoke. His head was throbbing, and he felt a little disoriented. The nights here in Wisconsin were nothing like what he was used to, but he thought that, by now, he was beyond that adjustment. He lay very still, letting his mind reach out for anything unusual in the area, starting in the northeast part of the creaky old farmhouse. He circled the building slowly, and about halfway around, he felt the pain increasing, and realized that it was his brother's pain--it was so pronounced that he concluded it had to be something affecting both brothers. Speaking quietly, "Light," he said. Then, dressing quickly, he left his second-floor bedroom and moved down the hallway. As he opened the door to the deck, which extended out over the top of the kitchen, he recognized two silhouettes standing out against the moonlit sky.

"Mark?" He called out.

"Over here, Sam."

He walked closer, feeling, now, the intensity of the pain.

"You guys sick?" He asked.

"Yes." They said in unison.

As they sat around the picnic table, Sam became the counselor, the mediator, and the Father Confessor. As he listened, he realized several things: though they were brothers, they were not the same. On the outside, their differences were obvious in height, skin color, eyes, hair, gate, gestures, speech, you name it. That part, the physical one, had always been observable. But, the inside was different, as well: Mark was much more sensitive to the thinking and feelings of those around him, in spite of the fact that he was the party boy of the three; Weld was the intellectual, given more to reason than emotion. What Sam was hearing, here on the rooftop tonight, surprised him. The two brothers possessed something in an abundance, which he almost totally lacked: compassion.

Weld and Mark, for the first time in their lives, had killed a human being--in fact, quite a few human beings! And they were now showing signs of remorse, as they reflected on the mercenaries, their children, their wives, and other loved ones. Their anguish was intense because they now felt that they should have tried to find another solution to the problem. Sam realized something about himself, here--he had gone right to sleep--had not even dreamed. And as he thought about how he was so different in his reaction, he searched his mind to try to determine why that might be; for he knew that if he could find the reason, he would be able to help the brothers and reduce their remorse.

One of the salient points of Samuel's many lectures at the lab dealt with the sanctity of life, and it was obvious that he deplored that part of human nature, which caused death to others. He recognized humans were capable of horrible acts, but he could never justify those acts, not even in wartime. Part of every test dealing with the history of war involved his asking the question, "Can you find a solution which does not involve killing? Sometimes Sam could; sometimes not; and reflecting on that fact, Sam, as he tried to deal with his brothers' situation, realized that even when there were solutions, other than war, he could rationalize and justify war!

In the case of the mercenaries, he was able to put their deaths out of his mind and off his conscience by answering the question, What would a reasonable person do in the situation that Bert and the three suddenly found themselves?"

They could have done nothing, and Bert and Allie would have lost their crops, their animals, and very possibly, their own lives.

They could have called the police, but their arrival would have been too late to be affective.

Bert could have signed the document, sold his farm, taken the money and slinked away in shame. But he would not have lived long under those conditions.

Another way Sam was thinking of presenting this case:

"Is it ever okay to kill?"

"Is it ever okay to justify killing?"

"How does one justify killing?"

As Sam continued to listen to Weld and Mark explain themselves, he was able, on a secondary level, to review his options, and at the proper time in these personal struggles, to try his best, without changing their natural reactions to these deaths, to allow them some leeway, provide a door that each could escape through. There had to be away to end their self-flagellation!

Finally, there was a pause in their story and Sam jumped in:

"Give me one word answers to my question.

"Is killing always wrong, no matter what? Yes or no?"

Mark immediately replied, "It all depends... sometimes..."

Sam interrupted, "Stop! Mark, stop! Give me a yes or no. Don't try to rationalize or justify. Yes or no."

There was silence

Finally Mark replied, "No."

Sam continued, "Remember, yes or no: Is killing sometimes wrong?"

Both Mark and Weld answered quickly, "Yes!"

"Good. Now, is killing never wrong?"

Weld answered, "Yes."

Mark tried to correct, "No."

Sam looked at them both, still in pain and still struggling. He was a realist, maybe pessimistic realist would be a better term; and he was sure that, given their situation, in the future there would be even more difficult life or death decisions to be made: he was afraid, that like the old Westerns of an earlier time, there would often be no time for debate--it would come down to *kill or be killed*.

To bring the thinking from the philosophical to the real, Sam looked at each of the brothers in this predawn light:

"We *will* have to kill again, you understand that, don't you?" He said.

"That's what's bothering us," Weld admitted. "What we had to do yesterday was horrible--but Mark and I have agreed that our choices were very limited. But to think about something like that happening again..." His voice drifted off.

"Remember Darwin?" Sam asked. "Survival of the fittest? We have to be willing to do whatever it takes to survive. Are we all in agreement on that?"

They slowly nodded in the affirmative.

"There's something about us," Sam continued, "Something different. That's why the Greenbrier has spent so much time and money on us. Whatever difference that is, we *must* make sure it survives."

Sam could feel that their turmoil was receding--his own pain, too, was lessening, and he felt that, finally, they were ready to return to bed. As the sun rose, the three sons tried to catch a little more sleep.

CHAPTER 10

A week went by and during that time, the three helped Bert move both beef and hogs to the Wautoma stockyards; but at the end of each day, the same problems reappeared: What to do? Where to go? How to exist on their own? These boys did not have passive personalities; but as the summer fled, it was obvious that some outside force would have to intervene in order for change in their lives to occur.

Bert and Allie were ecstatic--life was once again exciting and interesting! And Bert was glowing with pride over the enthusiasm that his 'adopted' children exhibited in their work. The years of neglect of minor things on the farm, such as the painting of all the barns, retrenching the rice fields to prepare for future crops, the repairing of fences...on and on, the little things, which could be neglected for a few years but which, if not addressed eventually, would finally cause a decline in farm production.

The idea of escape, of relocation, of the perfect life began to fade as each youngster enjoyed pitting his growing strength, both physical and mental, against the ordinary and the extreme of farm life!

The contacts from Georgia or California never came, and the feelings of being a rat in a cage gradually disappeared as the sense of hard work and cooperative family life wove its mesmerizing spell. It was not until late fall, after the harvests, that they arrived—an over-sized lab van, an SUV and a cadre of technician-guard types, interrupting the equanimity that had taken hold on the Schmidt farm.

Jonathan Zobek led the entourage up the front walk early on a Saturday morning in September, as the drivers located their vehicles in the Schmidt's side yard. Bert, once again, went for his Imp; but Sam, recognizing the Greenbrier's Crest on the van, asked Allie and him to remain in the house. Mark, Weld, and Sam walked toward the oncoming group. The brothers probed them, wanting to get a read on their purpose for this elaborate show of professionalism.

Zobek was the first to speak, his opening gambit being to suggest that he was here for a final interview, a series of tests to determine how well the former wards of the Greenbrier were adjusting to life 'on the economy' as they called it. Fortunately, being late fall, the boys had on light jackets and did not reveal Allie's handiwork on their arms.

Sam spoke for the three: "Mr. Zobek, we aren't interested in any follow-up--and we aren't going to cooperate with you, ever again. For years you had us under your care. We've undergone every imaginable test, experiment, and observation. If you haven't found what you're looking for by now, all I have to say is, it just doesn't exist! We've always been told that every young person had to undergo the same extensive orientation that we did before entering into the real world: now we know better." Sam gestured toward Zobek's group. "Pack up right now and leave. You are no longer part of our lives!"

Sam was calm and reasonable in everything he said, but he was also very clear that there was no room for negotiation.

"I understand how you feel," Zobek replied, trying to show that he empathized with Sam. "We've come a long way--may we, at least, have a blood sample from each of you? We were hoping for so much more. You must understand that our interest in you has always been of a professional and scientific nature. Won't you agree that all the times that you were with us, you had the best of care, the most thorough education, and a staff who served you well?" Mark stepped forward, able to talk and, at the same time, probe to ascertain the true reason for this visit.

"What you say *is* true, of course. But the one thing we never had, under your care, was the freedom of choice. We've tasted that here with the Schmidts; and you know what, it feels wonderful!" As he spoke he continued to probes Zobek's innermost motivations. They were well hidden, but Mark was unstoppable in his search.

Zobek realized something uncomfortable was happening to him: he took a few steps back from Mark, sensing that somehow this young man was behind his discomfort. He was doing all the right things. It had been rehearsed many times. They were here to extract the three and to put an end to this part of the trillion-dollar experiment: he knew he could not think about what his intentions were for them--his body language or his facial expressions might unavoidably reveal the true reason for this visit. He was determined not to think of the details of how the boys would be killed-- how everything about them would be destroyed, leaving no tangible evidence of malfeasance for future generations to examine and to assign blame. But the innocuous thoughts he was trying so hard to project were no barrier to Mark's incessant probing: he could contain the secrets no longer; and as Mark exhaled sharply, confronted by the realities as they tumbled forth--the real reason for Zobek's visit here to the farm and the logic which lay behind it became evident, as the broken box of secrets spewed forth its contents: the entire history of the program, what it really was, and what the Greenbrier had hoped to learn from the three brothers lay bare before him..

Sam and Weld were following this endeavor and were astonished and repelled, as well.

Sam recovered first. "Mister Zobek, can you give us a few minutes to think about these blood samples?"

Zobek was relieved, thinking to himself that the appearance of a reasonable man certainly has its rewards.

"Of course, take your time. We'll all be waiting right here for your decision."

The boys walked away, distancing themselves from what they now understood would be their death sentence.

"Son of a bitch!" Weld exploded.

"Now we know," Mark whispered. "We finally know. We aren't human--not entirely, anyway. But I didn't get the reason they wanted us dead. Why aren't we still important to them?"

"You should continue the mind search," Sam speculated. "We need to know everything."

"No, I'd better not. He was so close to understanding what I was doing. We can't risk it. But the question is what do we do about all of this?"

The three were so deep in their dilemma that they did not notice two armed men circle around the group and enter the farmhouse; nor did they observe Zobek approaching them, still smiling, still the disarmingly friendly businessman.

"Excuse me, but I've been talking with my laboratory coordinator. He tells me that we *are* going to need at least one of you to undergo the complete exit procedure, including a thorough physical. Which of you would like to be the volunteer? Alpha? Or maybe you, Beta? What about you, Gamma?"

"What about none of us," Sam threw back at him, stepping forward.

"No, I'm sorry. That won't work," Zobek, replied, pointing to the house where the two guards were standing with Allie and Bert. "Beta, spare your new family any embarrassment--just come along with us. It won't take that much time, and then we'll be on our way."

The brothers followed the direction that Zobek was pointing and realized, immediately, that the situation had changed--that the Greenbrier men had outmaneuvered them.

"What the heck," Mark declared, walking towards Zobek. "Sure, why not. Let's get it over with!"

"Excellent! Young man--I knew you'd see it our way. Why make it difficult on any of us? I appreciate what you're doing."

They walked over to the portable lab and stepped inside. Two technicians were preparing for Beta, by adjusting the height of what looked like one of the historic electric chairs used in ancient times for executions. Mark balked, when he saw it.

"Wait a minute!" He exclaimed. "You're not hooking me up to that. No way..."

Zobek was surprised with the reaction, not expecting Beta to view this psycho-physical apparatus as a threat: "Beta, don't you remember, at the Greenbrier lab, we had you sit in one of these--smaller in size of course, but it was fun! And it helped us keep you physically and emotionally in good shape."

Mark did remember--but that was a long time ago; and with the new information gleaned from Zobek's mind, he had no intention of sitting in that questionable contraption.

Zobek saw that the chair idea wasn't going to work, so he directed Beta to a nearby table.

"Let's not start with that. Sit over here across from me. We'll do the Association part of the exit interview first:

Mark sat, hands folded on the table, eyes taking in the entire room, mind alert for any danger. And for some reason, it came to him that Zobek could not leave the trailer alive. As repugnant as the thought was, it was a fact! This was a cold assessment, he realized, but a necessary one. It was essential that he re-enter Zobek's mind--pull out the final bits of missing history on the three of them and find out, among other things, why they were now expendable. When he finally had this pompous little pleasantries pusher stripped of everything useful, the only merciful thing to do would be to end his life. After the earlier encounter with a platoon of mercenaries, Mark felt that this decision was much less barbaric and just as necessary; those men in the platoon were simply ex-soldiers, hired to continue following orders--to perform with no questions asked. But Zobek was different: he was a smooth and dangerous manipulator, a self-aggrandizing toady whose only interests were his own self-interests. Taking him out would not cause Mark to lose sleep; and as those thoughts swept over him, he realized that his childhood was over--that the directionless days of no-fault teen-age dalliance were in the past.

"You understand what you're required to do on this Association test, don't you, Beta? If I say *good* you reply quickly with the first word the comes into your mind."

"Sure, I've done this lots of times at the lab," Mark replied, revealing nothing but innocence to Zobek.

"Okay. Rapidly now: *good.*"

"*Evil.*"

"*Love.*"

"*Hate!*"

"*Money.*"

"*Freedom.*"

"*Water.*"

"*Death.*"

"*Spoon.*"

"*Trick.*"

"*Alien.*"

"*God!*"

"*Earth.*"

"*Conquer!*"

They stopped here. Mark could see the assistants inputting this information rapidly. When they had caught up, Zobek brought out the spoon.

"Remember this, Beta? Today is your last chance to make it move--your last opportunity to prove that all of the training we gave you was worth it."

Mark was only half listening. He had begun the journey into Zobek's memory bank, pulling out treasure and trivia alike--so much clutter, interspersed with revelations! But struggling to be free, also, were the final pieces to this puzzle: the answers as to why he and his siblings were no longer essential. And the last nugget was a bombshell: the existence of a fourth brother: Delta!

Refocusing on the spoon, Mark smiled. "Oh, how I remember that darned thing--it wasn't that I couldn't move it--my problem was trying to figure out why it was so important that I make it move!"

Zobek caught the innuendo immediately: "So are you saying that you *always* had the ability to manipulate it?"

"Of course."

Mark and Jonathan Zobek were in the final stages of the last game that the Greenbrier man would ever play.

"Can you show me?"

"Can you tell me why it was so important to all of you?"

Zobek was trying to be patient, but the revelation that Mark had *always* had the ability but chose not to reveal it was making his head spin. He began considering the ramifications that this information would have for the entire project: Oh, how the Consortium would praise him for being the one to finally show that all their effort and expense had, indeed, been worth it!

"You would be doing something impossible for any other human being to do! For two thousand years or more, scientists--men of learning in every field--have felt that, within each of us, was the hidden capability for greatness--that what we did, at any given time, was but the tip of the iceberg of our potential. The spoon was to be the key to who would help us move our Tomorrows in a new direction."

Mark nodded, in total agreement.

"I can't do this with so many people watching," he said.

The lab assistants looked toward Zobek.

He motioned for them to leave.

They complied.

"Watch the spoon carefully, now—focus on the spoon."

And he did. Zobek's hands shook with excitement and anticipation as he placed it in the middle of the table.

Exerting little effort, Mark raised it slowly and, with a studied motion, turned the handle toward his tormentor across the table from him. Then, unleashing a pent-up vengeance, which he did not know was within him, he drove the spoon through Zobek's left eyeball and, with a final flurry, scrambled his brain.

As Mark sat, quietly waiting for the death tremors to subside, he contacted Weld and Sam, sharing the scene with them.

They could see that Mark has alleviated one problem, but as they looked around they realized they had four others to solve: the two lab assistants and the guards up by the house. Why was it that managing one problem sometimes snowballs, creating more challenges? What were they going to do with these four Greenbrier employees? Could they let them go? Should they kill them as they had the mercenaries? How important was it, at this stage, to maintain the secrecy of their unusual talents? They could simply leave and let the facts speak for themselves. But the problem was that they would be leaving Bert and Allie to clean up their mess, and they knew that, after this, farm life could never be the same for them. Not only the Greenbrier people would be interested in them--they would be vulnerable when the VeryFresh Industry returned with their demands, as well. They needed to huddle a few minutes to talk out their dilemma and to come to some consensus--a solution that they would all be happy with or at least would provide answers, which would insure safety for everyone. Looking toward the house, Sam could see the guards becoming restless. Time was passing and for them, time was not their friend. On the other hand, the two technicians who were leaning against the outside of the lab seemed to have little concern and were simply waiting for instructions from the man within.

Sam and Weld exchanged thoughts quickly, both realizing that this part belonged to Mark, so they contacted him, asking exactly how they should proceed. He replied in short order that he would teleport to the farmhouse and use Bert's Imp to subdue the two guards.

Mark was a man of his word, and a few minutes later, the four Greenbrier employees were lined up against the lab vehicle. Mark had opened the door and allowed each of the four to view Zobek to give them and understanding of the seriousness of the situation and to help them realize what could happen to them if they were not cooperative.

By the look on their faces, there was no doubt that each was a believer. It was obvious that none had seen anything quite like this before and had probably never been exposed to a death scene so strange. The four who lined up in front of the Newalls were simply hired hands, and their deaths would serve no purpose—would, in fact, only cause more sleepless nights for the three.

Taking an extra spoon from the mobile lab, Mark held it by the heavy end, pointing the handle toward the African guard. The guard did not blink.

"I need to know who Zobek works for?"

Sam added, "And the Consortium leader, who is he?" As he spoke, he gently entered the mind of the lab technician directly in front of him: Chairman Blount's name surfaced.

"Where can we find Chairman Blount?" Mark demanded.

The answer was on the cusp of being spoken by each of the four, and that was close enough for the brothers who then advised them to return to the Greenbrier with Zobek and to tell Chairman Blount that Alpha, Beta, and Gamma would soon be paying him a visit.

As the vehicle left the gravel road and turned toward Wautoma, there was a communal sigh of relief.

Mark chuckled: "After 15 years at the Greenbrier--15 years of flatline activity, this has been one hell of a week!"

They slapped each other on the back and headed toward the house and toward Bert and Allie, who were frozen in place, unaccustomed to this continued series of challenges. The boys could only imagine what this old couple was thinking--feeling. No doubt, they were wondering why they ever asked to have a teenager spend the summer on their farm.

"How long you think it'll take them to get back to West Virginia?" Sam asked.

"Took me a day and a half to get *here*!" Mark exclaimed.

"Good. Because we need to get down there ahead of them," Sam continued. "Mark, I was following your thoughts? Did you disable their communicators?"

"Oh, yeah--Greenbrier won't know about any of this until they arrive! Why? What are you thinking?"

"After we make our explanations to Allie and Bert, we need to talk about it," Sam cautioned.

Over a fresh batch of chocolate chip cookies and milk, Mark went over what had happened during their stay at the Greenbrier and why the group had come to the farm. Allie always baked when she was worried--and after the events of the last few days, she was really wanting to bake! All the explanations in the world would not assuage her, would not diminish her concerns for "her boys."

Mark gave her his WristLink connection code and made them both promise to contact him if either the Greenbrier or the VeryFresh people showed up again. Following a series of hugs, they piled into the remaining vehicle and left the farm. They had had the foresight to force the lab foursome to leave via the motorized laboratory.

Mark promised the Schmidts that he would be returning, and he left all of his work clothes and personal items in his room.

As they passed through Wisconsin, Sam, who, uncharacteristically, had taken a backseat in the latest round of activities, asked, "You don't plan to drive all the way to the Greenbrier, do you?"

They had spent the last hour, as they drove, determining their next moves. The plan, as it developed, was to find and to confront Chairman Blount and, somehow, to convince him to cancel the Consortium's decision to kill the three--and they hoped to do it in such a way that they would have to take no further action against the Greenbrier men.

"No," Mark replied. "We'll find a parking caddy where the car won't be noticed for a few days--then we'll jump to the outskirts of the Greenbrier. I think our best way to convince the Chairman to leave us alone is with a face to face and through his family.

"Family?" Weld asked.

"Of course," Sam agreed--buying into the plan even before it was verbally stated. "It's amazing what people will do for those that they love! Let's just hope that he does have a family."

As they passed through the town of Madison, they noticed, near the end of Main Street, a shop that fit their needs: Weld was the first to see it, yelling, "Stop!" And he pointed at the All Hallows' logo, explaining that they should not be seen as teenagers, and that they certainly should not walk into the Greenbrier where there would be a chance that someone might recognize them! This Halloween Store, he knew, could supply them all with new faces!

"I'm not leaving as the Goon from the Lagoon!" Sam laughed.

But they did spend about an hour there: Mark darkened his hair and sported a mustache to match; Weld added a fake set of teeth and a jaunty English cap; and Sam wore small scar on his cheek and an oversized nose. They wanted nothing elaborate or terribly noticeable but enough to make the teen look disappear and reduce the chance of being identified.

Their final act was to walk into the restroom, checking the stalls to be sure they were the only ones there.

"Altogether—and we'll land at the corner of Oak and Main Street!" Sam said.

It was late Saturday evening when they arrived. The gas lamps had been turned on, and there was a cheery glow from the many tourist-baiting stores that lined Main Street. The boys weren't expecting such a gathering. They certainly wouldn't have chosen this spot to reappear had they known. But it seemed, that with the hustle and bustle of the crowd, no one noticed their sudden arrival.

Sam used his wrist communicator to search for Blount, and he learned that he lived in the adjacent town: 704 Sycamore Street. Feeling that they were lucky not to draw any attention to their arrival here, they looked for another restroom. On their way through the KingMac restaurant, they were brought to a halt by the smell of burgers. It'd been a long day: their last food was Allie's chocolate chip cookies.

The Schmidts had given the boys enough money in real currency for them to go a few days. After that, they'd just have to figure out how to deal with life; but here, this evening, the aroma was too tempting--they stopped and ate, dawdling over the food until it was quite dark outside, hoping that nightfall would make their arrival in the next town unnoticed.

CHAPTER 11

From the study of his 10,000 square foot fortress-like house, Blount watched their progress: he was unaware of why they were here and was oblivious regarding the minutia of the earlier events in Wisconsin. Not yet concerned, only curious, but as a precaution, he called his security, asking that they double the guards around the house.

Walking across the room to the bar, he poured himself a Krupnik, his Polish heritage showing up in his choice of drinks. The dark walnut tongue and groove walls suggested money and power: lumber had been a scarce commodity for hundreds of years, but he had no trouble acquiring either; and he was, at this juncture in his life, quite content. He'd never been a greedy man but had always been a scientist, looking to solve the Earth's most pressing problems; and the greatest breakthrough today would be to find a solution to the mystery behind the life and death of the Alien. The Chairman's money and power were inherited--as most during this century were, and he was putting it, in his estimation, to good use.

The fate of Alpha, Beta, and Gamma were of no concern to him, except... except as it impacted his overpowering need to solve this ancient riddle and, thereby, deliver a wealth of new technology to mankind. As with the lab rats, when their usefulness to an experiment was concluded, they were disposed of in the most economical way--and that's how he viewed the three brothers. Hearing a double beep from his monitoring system, his reverie ceased. The three were now in his town! Impossible, he realized. Malfunction? Perhaps. He was tracking them, using their own WristLinks.

It had been a long day for him: an early morning meeting with the Consortium, followed by a conference call with the missing member of the committee, his most trustworthy follower, Jonathan Zobek. According to Jonathan's call, the mobile lab had arrived at the Schmidt's farm in Wisconsin, and the team was preparing to lure the brothers to the lab, subdue them, and return to the Greenbrier where they would dispose of their bodies in the biohazard furnace.

His afternoon was business also, albeit of a different kind: he had met Anton Dressel, the regional manager of VeryFresh, at the local airport to discuss whether the next phase of the Schmidt incursion would be necessary, after all. Chairman Blount was a stockholder in this food chain and was determined and expecting to take over both the Lukazewski's and the Schmidt's farms.

One of the reasons he had sent Mark to the Schmidts was as a way to have Bert Schmidt report the activities of the farm directly to the Consortium and, of course, to use the farm as a way to end Beta's life, should that become necessary.

Blount sat in his oversized Corinthian leather chair, his mind still perseverating on the VeryFresh dilemma; but his eyes were glued to the security screen, as three dots advanced on his house.

"Charlie," he said, alerting his security chief, "I'm expecting trouble tonight--keep a sharp eye--the guys I'm worried about are very dangerous, so shoot first and ask questions later. And if you bag them, use the biohazard furnace at the Greenbrier to clean everything up!"

"Understood, Mr. B."

From across the room, on the couch, Mark commented, "Mr. Chairman, don't you even want to hear our side of the story?"

Blount was stunned but went immediately for the Imp in his shoulder holster.

Sam, who was standing behind the Chairman, grabbed his arm and removed the weapon. "You're not going to need this--not tonight, anyway."

Blount was confused. What was happening couldn't be happening. There was no way these two could have subverted his elaborate electronic and physical security. He looked at his screen. The dots were no longer visible.

Weld remained in the background, monitoring the area, wanting no surprises.

"How did you get in here?" Blount blustered.

"Chairman," Mark said, rising from the couch, "We didn't come all the way from Wisconsin for a friendly chat; we're here to end, for good, your interest in us. We plan to kill you tonight, if it takes that."

Mark stood in front of Blount. "Don't answer me unless you are very sure, because if you lie, we'll know--and if you, at any time, in your entire life, break your word to us, we'll know that and we'll hunt *you* down as well as your entire family. We'll destroy every one of you." He picked up a large family picture. "Who are these people?" he asked.

"My son and his family."

"Do you love them?"

"What kind of a damned question is that?" For a dried up prune of a man, the diminutive Chairman was showing a little spunk! His bushy eyebrows were dancing across his forehead, telegraphing his frustration.

"Do you love them?"

"Of course I do--they're my family!"

Mark returned the picture to the side table. "Remember, the spoon experiment, Chairman?" He said, as he gently raised Blount and his Corinthian leather chair off the floor and allowed it to continue its assent until the headrest banged against the 10-foot high ceiling. Were Blount not such an abbreviated character, it would have been his head and not the chair that cracked the overhead plaster."

Leaving him there, Mark and Sam walked over to the couch and, with a tired sigh, collapsed. It had been a very long and a very interesting day.

After a few minutes of silence, Blount yelled down, "Okay! Okay! You've made your point. What do you want?"

The two boys ignored him. Weld stepped out from the shadows. "May I fix you all a drink?" He asked the pair. "What's your pleasure?"

None of the three had a clue what pleasure it would be--they had never had anything other than vegetable juice, milk, and a soy shake.

"Surprise us." Sam suggested.

Walking over to the Chairman's bar, Mark took the existing pitcher of Krupnik, poured three small glasses and returned with them.

"Prost!" they said in unison.

Looking toward the ceiling, Mark asked, "Can we trust him?"

"Can you trust a snake?" Sam echoed.

"Sure, you can, if he's dead!" Weld laughed.

"What do you want?" Blount yelled down, again. He was an old man, and his muscles were aching from the awkward scrunched position he was forced to assume: he was a scientist turned investor, sometimes a voluptuary, but certainly not a criminal. This was out of his experience. At first, when the two appeared in his study, he was startled--but he was not frightened--but now...

"Are you a man of your word?" Sam asked.

"It all depends--it just depends," Blount replied, honestly, some desperation now appearing in his voice.

"Wrong answer," the three replied, chuckling and clicking their glasses.

"I propose a toast," Sam declared: "Here's to the rise and the fall of a great man!"

They drank. Weld was the first to run for the water spigot at the bar. In short order, the other two were right behind him.

"My God, that tastes like poisoned fire," Weld declared, in a choking voice.

Mark and Sam could not talk. They were scrambling for the spigot as well, trying to put out the fire.

Blount, in another situation, might have been amused by their antics, but he was struggling just to stay on the chair, realizing that a fall from 10 feet, for a man his age, could be fatal.

The plans of the three were unrehearsed but were becoming effective: The Chairman was at the point of confessing to anything, was ready to promise the world, knowing, all the while, that at some tomorrow, he would have his revenge. As he tried to think back on the boys' lives, he could construct no reason for their hatred of him. He had observed them often through the one-way glass, had made suggestions to the lab personnel for ways to make their lives more comfortable—there was never a moment's thought about using torture to get what they so desperately sought--torture was as repugnant to him as it would be for anyone at the Greenbrier. Results were his goal--the goal of all who were part of this StarQuest program. One doesn't mistreat the lab subjects, be they animal or human; but now that the Consortium had been advised by Dr. Farley to end the experiment, to move on, find their solutions by other means, what was one to do? Those were reasonable recommendations to follow, given by a fellow scientist. There was no ill will directed at the subjects of the experiment. As far as the Chairman could see, there was no reason for these three, who were part of this failed endeavor, to react so unreasonable.

Sam walked over to the center of the room and lowered Blount to eye level.

"What do you want?" Blount sniffled.

"We want you to promise to destroy all records relating to our incarceration, disband your tracking system, and to allow us to lead normal lives. Is that so hard to agree to?"

Blount's mind was going a mile a minute. He would agree to that, of course! But the day of reckoning would come to those three lab rats. That day would come!

Mark followed his thinking and was not surprised by this expected subterfuge.

"Mr. Chairman, there is nothing we three cannot do. Nothing we cannot find out. For example, you have been thinking, just now, about trying to figure out how best to lie to us and how, eventually, to get your revenge. We have never revealed who we really are and what we're capable of to anyone--until now. But now that we have, one of two things will happen:

Blount squirmed in his chair, feeling as though he were back in primary school--how could this boy know what he was thinking?

Sam added, "Chairman, we do know. Listen, for a minute! There *is* nothing we don't know, and there's nothing we can't do. Once again, hear me: now that we have revealed ourselves, you understand what we have to do?"

"No, I don't understand," Blount said, in a somewhat pleading tone.

"*You* are the only one in the world who knows about us, so you have to die." Sam walked away, saying "unless..."

Blount was finally ready: "I'll do it. Whatever it is, I'll do it."

The three turned their backs to him and, at the same time, moved him, once again, to the ceiling.

"See that mirror over the bar?"

"Yes! Yes! It's an antique--300 years old--belonged to my great, great, great, great, great grandfather."

"That many greats!" Sam laughed.

The Newalls did an about-face, returning to the center of the room.

"Look at your antique mirror, Chairman Blount."

"I see it--I see it!"

"Are you sure you see it?"

Blount looks again. The antique bar and the mirror had disappeared.

"Repeat after me," Sam commanded.

"There is *nothing* they cannot do."

Blount repeated the words, now truly believing them.

The three rehearsed with Blount what he was required to do in order to stay alive, reinforcing these requirements with an assortment of visual reminders of their powers.

As Mark and Weld left the room, Sam lowered Blount's chair to the floor and, placing a hand on either arm rest, he leaned over to the Chairman's ear: "If you don't do exactly as we have asked, everyone you ever loved will die--and they will not die pleasantly! When your motorized lab returns from Wisconsin, take a look inside. That will show you just how serious we are!"

In the hallway, Mark asked, "Where to?"

The other two replied in a whisper, "To Crazy Horse!"

CHAPTER 12

Some weeks later, Carlton Blount set on the rooftop of his house, in the sheltered area of the Velosoport, waiting for his ride to the airport. It was a beautiful evening, and as the sun dropped below the horizon, he viewed, with some satisfaction and a little angst, the current events in his life.

One of his primary goals, in recent years, had been to acquire a major interest in VeryFresh Industries; and with the sudden deep plunge in its stock prices because of the disaster of Silo 10 in Wisconsin, he was able to purchase a rather large block of its stock: a few more days like that, and I will have achieved that goal, he thought with considerable satisfaction.

He could not say that he had planned the accident to the Silo or had anticipated the drop in the price of its stock; but he certainly reacted swiftly, buying before it recovered.

He called his valet and asked that he bring up a chocolate martini, the perfect dessert, following a wonderful dinner with his wife of a decade. Some called her his trophy wife, but he did not see her that way. Theirs was an attraction like any other couple who were in love: trophy wife, to him, was a negative--he didn't like it; but as his thoughts turned to her, he recalled the last few times they had been invited to dinner with Jeff Slovinski, one of his oldest Polish friends, and the fact that Jeff, at different times, as they would leave his condo, would try to kiss Sherfy on the mouth. It made Carlton realized two things: how much he loved Sherfy and how Jeff's actions had slipped beyond the bounds of friendship.

The martini arrived in short order, and after a very satisfactory drink, he considered his feelings about Jeff's unexpected death: he had fallen from the 10th floor of an unfinished office building which, as the city inspector, he was examining for any code violations before that floor was enclosed. There were no windows installed yet, and the police surmised that he, while leaning out one of them to inspect the façade, had caught a gust of wind. causing him to lose his balance and fall.

The Chairman did not dwell long on past decisions. He was anticipating his upcoming red-eye to Brussels, Belgium and his plan, finally to acquire both the Lukazewski farm and Bert Schmidt's. Unlike his fortuitous purchase of VeryFresh stock, if *this* plan came to fruition, it would be entirely due to the Chairman's long-range plans!

As he continued to reflect on his to-do list, he became a little down, thinking of the three children and how they had placed him in such a powerless position the other evening. The security people and the technical staff who had installed and monitored his electronic protection were never able to determine how the boys had entered the house or how they had exited. This was unacceptable. True, the system was a decade old--nevertheless, not to be able to solve the problem they were being paid handsomely to prevent... Very unacceptable!

They were all fired, and a new firm was directed to install the latest in surveillance, and they assured Blount that break-ins like this would never occur again.

The distasteful reality of the situation was that, in his business, there was no way he could remain locked up like a prisoner in his own house; and yet, this seemed to be the only place where he, now, could be sure of his safety!

Those loudmouth, insolent teen-agers had made him promise never to pursue them--never to try to learn their whereabouts or their plans. Although he'd not brought them into this world, he had been the one who, for decades, saw that they were well taken care of; he was not used to being talked to in such a demeaning way and, certainly, was not happy with having to make such impossible promises: leave them alone? That will never happen, never ever, as long as I'm alive, never ever will that happen! They were still the only hope for rapid technological advances on this Earth, and they were his hope for continued prosperity.

The fear of them and the concern that they would follow through on their promise to destroy both him and his entire family was gradually beginning to fade, as time passed. Blount finished his martini and prepared to meet the incoming craft, his ride to the greater Atlanta airport.

* * *

The three-hour flight from Atlanta, plus the 30-minute ride to downtown Brussels, went by quickly; the Chairman's reason for being here was simply to pick up a vile--the key to the downfall of the Lukazewskis and the Schmidts: no, that was the wrong way to look at it. He reconsidered. I'm not interested in ruining them, he fanaticized; therefore, he revised his thinking: the vile would be the key to his purchase, at a fair price, of their properties. There, that sounded much more civilized! He did love playing with words--this type of exercise would often soothe his, otherwise, overwrought conscience.

When the VeryFresh mercenaries made their appearance at the Schmidts and were followed shortly after by the actors who played the EPA agents, Blount had suggested that if they could, to leave, surreptitiously, a bug in their house--a way for him to eavesdrop on Bert and Allie—to be able to understand and counteract any plans that they might have which would not agree with what he intended for them. That action proved to be the key to this trip to Brussels.

One of the significant points which came from the eavesdropping was that, without the income from the sale of milk and beef, the Schmidts could not make their monthly mortgage and feed payments. That started the Chairman thinking: if he could find a way to cause the Holstein milk cows to disappear, the farm, in short order, surely would be his!

He was a history buff and loved to read--loved to spend hours in another century with their problems and follow their attempts to solve them.

One conundrum that jumped out at him occurred several hundred years ago--a wasting disease, referred to as Mad Cow. It destroyed large sections of the bovine population in the course of two years, and that's what gave him the idea: what if the Schmidt's Holsteins developed this disease? There *was* no cure. The animals would all die in a year or so. Two questions came from this budding plan: how to administer the disease and, especially, how to keep it from escaping the Schmidt's farm and become the scourge that it once was?

Unfortunately, the extreme illegality of the entire plan prevented him from delegating the follow-through to anyone. He would have to dirty his hands on this one! His research suggested that the Brussels' Center for Animal Disease Control (the CADC) was the repository of this infectious agent—not a bacteria or a virus—but a diseased protein.

Fifty thousand Francs had gotten him access to a mid-level research assistant at the CADC and, with some further financial persuasion, she was willing to supply Blount with a modified version of the protein--one which was short-lived and could not reproduce beyond a 24-hour period.

The question became could Schmidt's entire herd be infected in that short a period? And would our own Animal Disease Center in the United States be able to identify this protein and stop the disease prematurely? It was a fine line, but it was essential because he did not want to turn loose this horrible disease on the livestock of the entire United States.

His limo stopped in front of the Hilton-Carlton and, true to her word, Christiana Whitmire was waiting just outside the entrance. The prearranged signal was that Carlton would roll down his window and wave a red handkerchief, which he did. She immediately ran over, and they were soon driving down the rue des Bouchers, no one the wiser as to this secret meeting.

She carried a small valise. Her eyes were large and trusting. Carlton liked her right away. Her long skirt and leather boots covered her entire lower body, but cleavage—oh, yes! And he loved cleavage. Then he looked at her mouth: no lip coloring, no other facial enhancements. Her beauty was totally natural!

"Thank you for meeting me, Christiana," he said, in an almost reverential tone, so taken was he by her appearance.

"I worry." She said with an alluring French accent.

"What do you worry?" He asked, as she gripped the leather valise containing the vial of the deadly protein tightly with both hands.

"I worry you will not know what to do--you must be very careful."

Blount was brought up short by her statement. My God, he thought, is this thing dangerous to humans?

"You must broadcast it carefully. No wind--no rain--very still day."

"Okay. I get that," he said, with some caution and concern seeping into his voice. "Please, Christiana, give me a rundown on what's going to happen—you know, what I..."

"No problem," she interrupted, "it's not like a virus or a bacteria; it's an infectious protein that causes disease in the other proteins--that's how it spreads. Now, I've done some splicing, so that the spread time is limited--but even after an animal gets the disease, it'll take over a year for it to start showing up."

"Okay, what are the signs that it's beginning to take effect?"

"It's neurological, so the animal will stagger, fall, lose weight, act erratically, you know, like that."

The next question was the one that Blount was worried about: "What's the safest way to spread it?"

"Put it in the animals' food or water. Or you can spread it in the grass fields, where they graze. You need to protect yourself, though. Wear biohazard suit and respirator. Positively, don't break your skin— not the least bit. Be very careful about that."

"So I could catch it!" The chairman was beginning to wonder whether this was such a great idea.

"It's not likely, but we're not sure: it *is* connected to some human problems like the Creutzfieldt-Jacob disease and even Alzheimer's. I've combined, in this vial, both the Mad Cow disease properties and the wasting disease--so it certainly should do the job for you!" Christiana smiled as though she had just shared a recipe for her favorite pound cake.

"Anything else I should know?" Carlton asked, hoping not to hear any other troubling facts.

"No," she paused, trying to be sure she'd covered everything. "Oh, also, your fields can't be used for grazing again--the Department of Animal Safety will quarantine the infected area."

"What about for growing crops like soybeans or rice?"

"Not for a long while--even human access to the property should be restricted. Now, since I've linked this protein to a one-life cycle, it should be okay after a few years, but unless the Disease Control Center is aware of its artificially limited lifespan, they will enforce a strict and long-term quarantine."

She handed him the valise containing the infectious protein and reached for his briefcase, which contained the Belgian Francs. (The Euro had long since disappeared from the continent of Europe.)

The limo stopped at her hotel, and she exited, not looking back and not saying goodbye.

Blount returned to the airport, in a deep funk. The whole idea seemed so simple as he first conceived it: spread the poison; let the cows die; wait for the Schmidts to have to sell; arrange for VeryFresh to buy the land and begin converting it to more Silos for food production. He was beginning to see that it wasn't a well-thought-out plan: It is hazardous to broadcast, even in water or food; it would take a year or more to even show up in animals; the land would be quarantined for an interminable time. As he carried the valise to his private plane, it felt more like an albatross than a vile of hope.

* * *

A few weeks later, after reviewing his options, Blount decided he had to follow through on his Mad Cow plan: he was able to hire one of Greenbrier's guards for a little moonlighting. The way the charming Chairman explained it to the guard, it was simply a little detective work: the daily farm schedule of a couple in Wautoma, Wisconsin needed to be documented. Blount always paid well, and generally the locals in this tourist-heavy town were eager for a few extra dollars, especially if it was easy money. The Chairman made it sound almost like a vacation! The two of them would be flying to Madison, Wisconsin, where the pseudo-detective would rent a vehicle and drive to Wautoma where he'd spend a week charting the daily activities of an old couple named Allie and Bert Schmidt. People who were occasionally approached by Blount for one kind of job or another had learned, years ago, not to ask too many questions--just do the job--follow instructions to the letter--and payment in full, plus a generous bonus was the likely outcome of a successful operation. Blount had explained that the only difficult part of their job would be to appear busy at something legitimate, since this farm and its outbuildings were the only sign of civilization for miles around: it would be impossible for one's presence to go unnoticed day after day.

Blount loved to fish, so while his Greenbrier man was spying on the Schmidts, he took the week to hire a guide, fly to one of his favorite isolated fishing areas, and let the traumas from the last few months just fade away.

JC rented a room in Wautoma, as well as a three-quarter ton truck, which he had painted the color and design of the oil pipe inspectors' vehicles. He then found appropriate decals to round out the official look of his truck.

The days went by slowly. Wautoma wasn't the most exciting town in the late evening, and observing the coming and going of the Schmidts was like watching water come to a boil! The only day that they both left the farm was on a Sunday at 10 o'clock in the morning. They went to church and then ate out at a Cracker Crate restaurant.

JC, the Greenbrier man, who was accustomed to the rapid pace of life around the resort was, after ten days of unobtrusive observing, thinking that he was happy to have a full-time job as a guard at the resort and not be here, working for a cow man!

At the end of the week, on a Friday evening, the two met for dinner at The Corner Grill. Blount had almost forgotten his reason for being here, the fishing had been so outstanding.

Listening to JC's report was like hearing the details of a curling tournament.

Over brandy--rather, over a brandy and a bottle or two of Milwaukee's finest beer, they discussed the results of the spying assignment; and that same evening, Blount had his pilot fly JC back to the Greenbrier, satisfied that it was money well spent! He knew when and how to make the poisoning of the Schmidt's Holsteins a reality.

* * *

The Chairman had brought his biohazard suit and respirator with him, along with the vial of diseased protein. His decision, after hearing the report on the Schmidt's daily activities, was that this Sunday morning, after 10 a.m. was the perfect opportunity for him.

Arriving at the farm about 10:30, he drove around to the backside of the barn, an area referred to as the milking parlor. Before exiting the car, he put the respirator on--a perfect disguise if there happened to be surveillance cameras present. Then he suited up in the biohazard outfit: head to toe protection!

The farm seemed too quiet. Maybe it was the respirator that was blocking the background sounds. At any rate, he moved slowly toward the sliding barn door, carrying the valise of poison, along with a five gallon bucket and a hand pump sprayer, his intention being to fill the bucket with water, add the vial's contents, and spray the grain and the hay used to keep the animals occupied and well-fed during the hour of their milking.

Blount had never been inside a dairy barn. He paused to get his bearing. There was a water spigot at the other end of the building, and he noticed that the hay and grain were already piled up at the head of each stanchion, ready for the evening milking. Looks like Bert is a very methodical and efficient dairy man! All the better for my plan, he thought, with a satisfied chuckle.

He was a small man, only 5-feet tall in his boots, and he weighed a flabby 120 pounds. The activities he was now attempting were a strain on this senior citizen, and his breathing soon became labored. "The damned respirator," he swore—"makes it hard to work and breathe at the same time!" He looked around. What had he done with the valise? Oh yeah, at the other end of the barn, of course. He lifted the five 5-gallon can, now filled with water, and began moving slowly in its direction.

He'd heard movement earlier, in one of the side stalls, and figured there was a calf or who knows what in there. As he struggled the length of the barn, he looked again at the stall. There were no windows in it and no lights turned on, but there was definitely something there. Oh, well, he sighed, dismissing that observation, as he assembled the sprayer. The biohazard suit was heavy and cumbersome, and inside the respirator, he was perspiring profusely, salty sweat running into his eyes; but he was hesitant to remove it, fearing that there might be cameras inside the barn.

As his struggle continued, the stall erupted as Bert's mammoth Holstein bull, enraged by the biohazard suit and the strange sounds of the heavy breathing through the respirator, tore through the half door of the stall and charged. Blount barely had time to turn toward the bull when he was struck in the chest by two vicious horns and 2500 pounds of thrust.

He died immediately, but the bull did not know that and continued throwing him back-and-forth in the milking parlor, finally goring the dead body and flipping it into a corner stanchion. Blount's respirator ended up in the loft among the hay bales.

That evening, as Bert went to the barn to open the doors leading to the pasture, so his cows could enter--they were already lined up for the 6 p.m. milking--he noticed that his bull had broken out of the stall and had injured himself--blood being all over his horns and face. He grabbed a pitchfork and herded him into an adjacent stall and locked the door. By this time, the cows were making themselves known, there utters becoming painful, straining from their fullness.

It wasn't until the next day that Bert found the Chairman, a crumpled rag of a man, his biohazard suit looking like a shredded clown outfit, disguising any sign of humanity in the corpse.

By the time the police arrived, Bert had found the briefcase, the 5-gallon bucket, and the pump sprayer. Being unaware of the true intent of the contents of the leather case, the police were hard put to make sense out of the crime scene, were not even sure that it could be called a crime scene. Basically, an old derelict of a man had found his way, maybe just to get out of the cold night air, into Bert's barn and had been gored to death. The stranger had no identification; and it was later discovered that he had used a false name to rent the car found parked in the back of the barn. The respirator was not discovered until the next spring, and no connection was made between it and the death of the intruder.

Eventually this vagabond was buried in a secluded section of the local cemetery, set aside for the John Doe's.

For years, the valise gathered dust in the property room of the Wautoma police.

INTRODUCTION TO BOOK TWO

By the age of 16, the Newalls had watched their handlers and others grow old and eventually disappear with no explanation as to why.

They had no concept of day or night, of the changing of the seasons, or much of anything else having to do with the passage of time. Their entire lives had been spent many levels below ground, in the Greenbrier bunkers. Their isolation and lack of outside stimulation naturally kept them more childlike for a much longer period of time than would have been the case had they been introduced to a normal life sooner; and taking into account the fact that the Consortium had no intention of ever allowing their crowned jewels to experience freedom and independence, there was no reason for their teachers to deal with preparing them for any real-life situations. All of this made their eventual exodus from the compound so much more traumatic.

In the passage of the years in Earth time between their last meeting at the Crazy Horse Monument and when Book Two opens, Earth had undergone a number of additional cycles of famine and pestilence, as well as a devastating global war and a disastrous earthquake in the North West—all of which reduced the arable land by twenty-five per cent and the population by half.

The Cascadia subduction zone had been under stress for many hundreds of years but had been stuck: (the sooner the tectonic plates slide, the smaller the earthquake). This zone had been dormant for so long that when the breakaway finally came, it was catastrophic. Northern California, Oregon, Washington, and parts of British Columbia were destroyed. Past earthquakes of a similar magnitude had created Crater Lake in about 5000 BC and in 1980, caused the Mount Saint Helens' eruptions.

The disruptions in the subduction zone, in the past, often had triggered follow-up destructions associated with the San Andrea's fault. This did not occur in the 2006 San Francisco earthquake but did follow the Cascadia destruction just after the Newalls arrived in Ohio.

When the brothers are reintroduced in Book Two, they are hardly recognizable physically or emotionally: each had eventually fallen in love and married. Each had children who arrived on Earth stillborn, and each watched the love of his life grow old, grow ill, and die. They were naïve enough to try love and marriage again and to do so in the same city. Ultimately, however, word got back to them through gossip and innuendo that they must have a portrait of themselves in the attic--a reference to an ancient text in which the individual does not grow old but the oil painting of him, which is hidden in the attic, ages grotesquely.

Their emergence from the undocumented Middle Years had left them less trusting, in general, and more cynical, in particular, as they viewed man's inhumanity to man. The child-like nature they exhibited in their earlier meetings at The Crazy Horse Monument had been replaced by skepticism and a wariness of those outside their immediate circle; but they had become fully engaged in their purpose in life and skilled in the Alien characteristics inherited from their father.

They moved again and again, reestablishing themselves in distant cities and switching meaningful occupations, paying dearly for newly forged identities.

One of the positives to come from the earthquakes and other conflagrations occurring around them was that, eventually, civilization became so disrupted that customs such as the Biometric Wallet and the Identification Chip went by the wayside.

Then there was a period which scholars looked back on, calling it the second coming of the Dark Ages, a time of about 200 years of cultural and economic decline, during which there were few scientific advancements and very little written enlightenment. The Newalls struggled with these problems, as well as with the previously mentioned earthquake in the Northwest.

Luckily, the three had left the West coast several weeks before that destruction and were headed for Ohio, hoping to establish a new identity and a new business in one of its sleepy little river towns. They were still mourning the loss of their third wives. No living children had come from any of their marriages; and they now looked at Ohio, without any romantic aspirations at all, having decided never to open themselves up to so much pain again. (They had no way of knowing that their first experiences at love, back in the times just after their release from the Greenbrier lab, had also resulted in three pregnancies and three stillborn.)

They moved on again to a new life in a geographically distant area, choosing new names and other personal information; but for the sake of clarity and continuity, the monikers they originally chose for themselves, Sam, Weld, and Mark will continue to be used.

Always, in the back of the mind of each of the brothers were the question and the challenge: how do we incorporate the gifts that our Alien father left us into coherent plans, which will benefit both mankind and us? It was a constant battle which they faced year after year as they tried to maintain a positive and helpful attitude regarding the people and nations around them who seemed to vacillate, going from exhibiting a bellicose nature toward the rest of the world, to being insufferably ingratiating and self-destructive. Frequently, their gaze would drift from the contradictions on Earth and would fixate on the peaceful moonless night sky, as they searched for that one star which represented half of who they were; and they continued to be saddened by the fact that none of the three was able to have children.

The overriding question for them was why they, themselves, were alive? The Alien, their father, *was* able to have offspring, yet they could not. It had crossed their minds more than once over the decades, that the Alien might not have been able to procreate until a certain age: if not at 16, maybe at 20; if not at 20, maybe… But now that they would be approaching another birthday on May 29, they gave up hope.

And then, out of the blue, it happened. Sam's fourth wife conceived, and in spite of all past failures, this pregnancy went full term--12 months: a healthy boy was born, and they named him Richard and from birth called him Rick.

In the same year, Mark's wife had twin girls--but her term was only nine months, rather than twelve. In the days that followed, no one was sure if the length of the pregnancies would make any difference in the long run: there was so much happiness in the families, that this harbinger was completely overlooked.

Weld had decided, after the loss of his wonderful and loving third wife, that he would not put himself through this kind of torture ever again. He would be the doting uncle and resident bachelor.

However, as the children grew and brought such joy and contentment to both Sam and Mark, he began to reconsider, agreeing with them, that it was their particular kind of Alien genes which permitted conception only after the attainment of a certain age. Feeling that this hypothesis was true, he began rethinking his future.

As these three new offspring grew, it became obvious to the brothers, who were observing their children closely, that the youngsters' chronological ages were matching their actual maturity rate. In other words, they were progressing at the same speed as any other child born in The United States. That was both good news and bad news--the bad news was that the children would grow old and die long before their fathers. The good news was that the mothers would be around most of the children's lives.

The Newalls continued to look for other characteristics, which might have passed down to their progeny--characteristics reflecting their alien past; and as Rick, Jody and Kimmy matured and as the adults saw no indication of anything unusual, they hearkened back to the old possibility that nothing would change until puberty.

Once in a great while, when one child or another made a statement which seemed to mirror the unspoken thoughts of Sam, Mark, or Weld, there would be some internal excitement on the adults' parts and a flurry of hope that at least one of the Alien's positive traits had been passed down; but in every case, the feeling that the children might be trailing clouds of glory was proven false.

* * *

As research continues on the details surrounding the missing middle years of the Newalls, all findings will be compiled in book-form and eventually released.

BOOK TWO

MATURITY

CHAPTER 1

Sam Newall wasn't a big man by today's standards, at 6-2 and 200 pounds, but he was solid and was in the best shape of his life. In fact, on his last birthday, he wondered why he showed no further signs of aging. He certainly felt none. He could still press 300 pounds and could still run the mile in five minutes. The same could be of his two brothers—maybe Weld might not be able to press 300, but two easily. The three lived in the same huge warehouse on River Road, in Cincinnati, with their wives and family and conferred daily on a range of national and international topics.

Theirs was an unusual coming together of like minds; and over the last score of years, their interests gradually morphed into a singular topic: The evil that had been accidentally unleashed upon the world long ago—about the time of Rick's birth--had grown exponentially—and, to their dismay, these three most unusual brothers were losing ground in their fight to contain it.

* * *

Day one began innocently enough on the evening of June 7, near the tiny town of Petersburg, Kentucky. For hundreds of years, folks of all ages had explored its cave; anthropologists from The University of Cincinnati and other schools had conducted digs in and around it. The cavern was not deep, and it held nothing of compelling significance; but it was unusual for this part of Kentucky. However, on that June evening, the Richter scale was aroused from its Northern Kentucky slumber, by a 5.5 quake. No significant damage was done in the neighboring towns, nothing out of keeping for that level, except—except for what two love-struck young people discovered as they entered its cool, quiet interior, looking for a hiding place to finalize their feelings for one another.

The back of the cave, which everyone had assumed to be a solid wall of limestone, had given way, revealing a wide access to a domed room about half the size of a basketball court. Lovemaking was forgotten as the two explored the inviting labyrinth. The young man's photo light revealed a raised platform, in the center of the room, on which seemed to rest a sarcophagus-like box approximately four feet by eight and a depth of about three feet. Upon closer examination, they found no writing, no symbols, and no way to open it. Their thinking was that it had to contain some type of treasure—something they could leave with, no one being the wiser. But, finally, realizing that there was nothing to be gained by looking further, they slipped out to the mouth of the cave and notified the sheriff.

Within 24 hours, the media presence at the cave rivaled that of the police and security. In addition, the Boone County Historical Preservation Board arrived and demanded that the site be closed to the public, while the University of Kentucky anthropologists tried to record, catalog, and preserve the find.

After about 36 hours, a decision was made to have a backhoe come in and move the box for transport to a secure location. Orvis Brown, a gravel operator from a nearby pit, had ventured on to the site out of curiosity; and he volunteered to bring his equipment over and make the transfer to a semi. However, after he explored the interior of the cave and inspected the pedestal and the box, he realized he had neither the right equipment nor the expertise for the job. By this time, using imported generators, the cave was as bright as the outdoors. Orvis showed the UK professors the problem they would have to overcome: the box was not placed on top of the platform, but was, somehow, attached firmly to the entire structure.

Plan B became "Let's X-ray the box, see what's in it and, maybe, determine how to open it."

When WCINK heard of that plan, they immediately volunteered to underwrite the effort if they could stream the activities and, especially, if there were a chance that a way could be found to actually broadcast the box's contents. They insisted on an open line to every viewer's mind screen. A deal was struck. UK brought in portable X-ray equipment, established a connection with WCINK, and began trying to penetrate the box. It soon became evident, however, that no images were forming—the X-rays were ineffective. A metallurgist was consulted. She determined that the box and the platform were both made of lead.

Plan C: "Let's drill a one inch hole through the top lid and insert a camera probe."

WCINK again insisted that the results of the probe be broadcast live to any mind screen that was activated.

All agreed.

Sam Newall shook his head, sadly recalling it all: "Stupid, stupid, damn stupid! Why in the hell did they have to drill into that box? Why didn't they ask one simple question: Why was a lead-lined box placed behind a man-made cave? Why? This was one of the damnedest Pandora's boxes ever conceived!"

The third brother, Weld, walked into Sam's office, interrupting his agonizing thoughts.

"Sam, I think we've got another problem."

"Why the hell not," Sam exploded. "It just seems to be one damned thing after another."

Weld was the non-emotional, analytical alternative to Sam. Though they were the same age and had an obvious brotherly resemblance, Weld was certainly no doppelganger. He was a slight man with a high forehead and a white beard, giving his face a more angular look than was actually the case. The blue eyes seemed to have an inner light of their own. He was quick to smile and slow to ruffle.

"Okay, let's have it, Weld. What now?"

"Well, you remember telling me to find Rick—that we were going to need him soon?"

"Yeah."

"Uh, I don't think you're going to believe this—I found one of his hanging paragraphs—I know where he is, but..."

Sam locked his hands behind his head and leaned back in his ergonomically correct chair: "So this is the part where I get the bad news about my son?"

Weld sighed, "Let me put the paragraph on the screen—you decide if it's bad or good."

Hi Dad, Uncles:

You know how you kept telling me when I asked to become part of the Company, that that would happen someday? Well, I began thinking, what if someday never comes—what if my life is spent just hanging around, waiting? You know what I mean? You understand that I can do that only so long—I think the "so long" is here.

I need to be out there testing my skills, broadening my interests and, along the way, seeing if any of the other Newall talents emerge. And I don't plan to dodge any fun that comes toward me on this adventure!

I've just finished a search for the twenty most beautiful women in recorded history and have narrowed my interests to five. I plan to visit each of them in the flesh and, having seen them, decide which one to place at the top of my list. The five are Elizabeth Taylor, Sally Hemings, Bathsheba, Marion Davies, and Lisa del Giocondo.

Foolish, you say. Now wait. Look at the obstacles I have to overcome. What makes Elizabeth easy is that she's a relatively recent American—which means I won't have a language problem; I won't have a wardrobe problem; I won't have a currency problem, and I won't have a chronological problem. I will have access to all of the above before I jump.

Think of the learning curve for Bathsheba: I won't know the exact time frame or location for the jump; I'll have no expertise in the language; I don't know what to wear to make me a friend rather than a foe; and currency? On the other hand, I suppose there would be no tourists if they all shunned countries where they could not speak the language—and, really, who understands the currency of the scores of places that are visited every year? I'm sure I can muddle through.

Quite a lark, don't you think? I don't know how long this will take; but since you have never needed me, I'm not worried about staying in touch.

See you after I've found the most beautiful woman in the history of the world!

PS. In case you're wondering why I didn't include Eve in my list: no where could l find any reference as to her beauty; but equally important, being the only woman in the world at that time, how fair would that be?

And just so you won't worry too much, yes, I am taking a Repeller—and it's the latest model (x14)—it has some new functions I don't yet understand, but I'm sure I'll learn. And, no, I don't plan to use it to screw up History!

Rick

CHAPTER 2

With the gold coins Rick had *borrowed* from the local Heritage Bank, he was able to secure very favorable lodgings, with meals, on the outskirts of Jerusalem. He ate heartily of the bread and thick soup that the innkeeper had provided and was soon in his room, and by the candlelight he unfolded a map, which he had downloaded before jumping. He also had brought along his GPS, which he planned to use to orient himself and to help locate Bathsheba's house.

It's funny how easy it is to become so accustomed to the conveniences of one's own time and country—not even to question the cause and effect of luxuries and necessities alike! It wasn't until he could not get a signal on the GPS that he realized, with an embarrassed grin: "Of course there's no signal, dummy, there's no satellite in the sky to provide one."

And he did not even think to bring a simple compass. Now, that would have really been helpful!

He lay on the floor on a mat, as sleep overtook his chagrin. Just as he began to drift off, worn out from the all-day walk, he felt, deep within his brain, the beginnings of the same emotional high that would flood his body in the final seconds before a jump. It brought him out of his exhaustive stupor. He sat up and placed his hands on his head in a panic. He realized that he had to stop the forward motion of this unforeseen and unplanned teleportation. Focusing his mind on his surroundings, he stood quickly and banged his head against the door's archway. The pain and the concentration caused the cycle to be suspended. It reminded him of the few times he'd been guilty of a premature ejaculation—an action out of his control and not within his overall desires.

Rick stood for a long time, body tense, mind alert for any return of this strange phenomenon. What was happening to him? He'd never before felt that he was not in control of his jump sequence. After some time, he returned to his mat. Gradually, his heart rhythm slowed and his breathing became more regulated, as sleep insinuated itself upon his aching body.

Suddenly there it was again! The sequence reengaged, a jump eminent. He stumbled toward the table, grabbed a pitcher and poured the water within over his head; and at the same time, he slapped himself multiple times with his free hand. Standing there, trembling, he realized that there would be no sleep for him tonight. He paced the floor until dawn, ever vigilant for a return of that pre-jump aura.

Finally, some time after daybreak, hearing the noise of breakfast being prepared, Rick smoothed his rumpled robe, ran his hands through his disheveled hair, scratched the stubble of his emerging beard, and opened the door.

With pantomimed effectiveness, Joash, his host, pointed toward the table, which had been prepared for him, containing a few cuts of mutton, a loaf of bread, and a pitcher of wine. Rick sat and, with some relish, consumed his meal quickly. He then caught Joash's eye and, motioning him to the table, Rick withdrew from his inner pocket his crib sheets: in Aramaic and Hebrew were written a number of questions. He pointed to the first one. Joash held up a finger and left the room, returning shortly with a young boy and directing him to Rick's list, placed his finger on the question "Where is King David's Palace?" Joash said something to the youngster. The boy shook his head. Rick then pointed to the second question, "Where is Jerusalem's old city?"

The boy read the question to Joash, who became animated, pulled Rick to the front door. They walked out into a morning already so bright that Rick's eyes began to water. Should have brought my sunglasses, he thought. Then, reconsidering, he realized that if he were looking for comfort in 1000 BCE, he would be sadly disappointed.

Joash pointed toward the east, then to the sun, and using his fingers, he imitated walking. Rick gathered that it was a day's journey. He was given bread and meat and a skin of water--and something he assumed was a blessing for the road. He waved goodbye to his host and turned toward the rising sun, hoping that his sandals would last one more day.

By evening, he was sweat-soaked, dust-covered and ill-tempered, visibly upset with himself. As he trudged along, he muttered aloud, "Why the Hell" and looking at the distant horizon, he continued, "Why the Hell did I think this was going to be such a great adventure? If I only knew where I was going—if I only knew that I was getting close to the David and Bathsheba encounter. If only...."

As evening approached, another coin bought him a room on the first floor of a flourishing home that accommodated travellers going to or from Jerusalem, as well as a willing lady, if he was so inclined.

Rick watched as Abigail prepared his meal. He pantomimed to her that he needed to wash up. She pointed to the back door, and then led him outside to a shaded area and a well. As she leaned over the well to draw water, Rick became acutely aware of her better qualities. She smiled at him as she poured the water into a large crock, knowing full well what he was thinking. Walking behind him, she gently tugged at his robe and eased it from his shoulders. Removing his tunic, she began washing his face and bare chest. Rick was uncomfortable with this familiarity, but the cold water and her gentle hands felt so soothing that he smiled, shut his eyes, and relaxed.

She smiled also. Bending down to his feet, Abigail picked up his tunic and robe and headed toward the back door of her home; she had disappeared before Rick came out of his reverie and opened his eyes.

Immediately, he noticed that Abigail and his robe were gone. That meant that both his Repeller and his bag of coins were also with her! He started to panic just as she returned, holding a fresh robe and tunic for him. He relaxed, laughed, and held out his arms for her to help him dress, thinking that he could get used to this. She understood the laugh and her reaction was a coy giggle. Once the robe was on, Rick ran his hand along its sides, hoping for the comforting feel of the Repeller and, of course, his money.

The robe held neither.

By this time, Abigail had turned her back and was walking toward her house. She held up the Repeller, with her right hand but did not turn around.

Rick yelled. "Wait a minute."

She reacted by raising her other hand above her head, and in it was the bag of coins. But she did not stop.

In four long strides Rick was behind her. He grabbed her shoulders and swung her around to face him. She looked up with a mischievous smile, just in time to see Rick's eyes roll back in his head, showing only their whites, as his hands involuntarily slammed against his ears.

He grabbed a post, which was holding up one corner of a grape arbor and held on, yelling with extreme pain.

Abigail screamed, dropped the Repeller and coin bag, and ran toward her back door.

The jump sequence had reengaged. Rick felt something form in his stomach—it began working its way toward his chest. Holding on to the post, he resisted the urgency to jump—resisted with all the strength of his youth, the forces in his chest giving him extraordinary power. He could feel the intruder intensifying its hold on him, trying to pull him out of his present and into the jump Corridor. The two vied for power like behemoths struggling to their deaths. He could feel the Corridor coming closer, could smell that pungent odor which every jump Corridor exuded, not unlike that in a men's locker room. His strength and his will continued unabated, as did his formidable opponent's. Finally, feeling the tide of battle turning in his favor, he held tight to the post, which was now loosening from its base, and with a final extraordinary effort, pulled his adversary into the grape arbor. He felt the relief that an expectant mother must feel, when, after a long labor, the child emerges before her eyes.

But it was no child. Weaving groggily and, in obvious pain, Uncle Weld collapsed in Rick's arms. He was bleeding from his eyes and nose, and he was as red as Rick's new robe.

By this time, Abigail was back, bringing her father. Both were speaking rapidly and gesturing excitedly. Rick understood nothing, except the obvious fact that they were very confused regarding what was happening.

Weld roused himself, wiped the blood from his face, coughed for a few seconds, and then reached for Abigail's hand. He spoke to her and she replied, losing the fearful look, which had dominated her features. Nodding, she turned and ran back to the house, as Weld motioned for Rick to help him to his feet.

Malcah, Abigail's father, leaned down and, between the two of them, moved Weld to a nearby bench beneath an olive tree. Abigail returned with a flask of wine, which Weld eagerly accepted. After a few drinks, he looked up at Malcah, and they conversed at some length.

Rick was totally confused by this entire event: Why was his uncle here? How had he been able to speak to and understand these people?

"Uncle Weld! Uncle Weld! What the hell's going on?"

Weld took another long drink of the wine. "Good news and bad news, Rick. You just saved my life."

Rick was in no mood for games. "Well, I hope that saving your life is the good news! It was, wasn't it? And, how were you able to understand those people?"

Weld chuckled. "So you think you're the only one who ever went back in time on a lark! My boy, I spent too damn many months back here when I was only a few years older then you are now. And I really, really never wanted to come back again. This is not a fun place."

Malcah interrupted, speaking to Rick as he returned the coins and the Repeller.

"Honest man," Weld said—"well, only somewhat honest. He wants more money if I'm going to stay for supper and even more, if I spend the night. By the way, I had to explain to him that I was robbed on the road, just before arriving here—had to do something to put his mind at ease over my sudden appearance and the blood. And believe me, robbery is not that unusual around here! Plus, I told him that I'd travelled a far distance from another country to explain my strange clothes! Another one of your coins should make him feel much better."

Abigail brought a wet cloth, said something to Weld, and then began cleaning the blood from his face and hair.

"Uncle Weld, would you ask Malcah who the King is here? I need to figure out exactly where I am in this time period."

Malcah and Weld talked briefly. Rick's uncle then translated: "Looks like you guessed pretty close, my boy. You've jumped back to about a thousand or so BC and come within twenty years of your goal—not bad!"

"How do you know that?" Rick asked.

"Well, from the hanging paragraph you left us, I knew that you wanted to zero in on the David and Bathsheba incident. Saul is king, now, but the interesting thing is that, when I asked Malcah if he'd heard of David, he told me of a battle which took place last year near the Valley of Ellah—a battle in which the King's shield bearer, a young lad named David, killed a giant of a man called Goliath—so I'm thinking we must be in about 1020 BC."

"Damn." Rick exclaimed. "We *are* close. One more jump and we'll arrive about the time of the famous nude bathing scene!"

"Not going to happen, Rick." Weld stood, a very serious look on his face. "This is silliness. You've got to come back with me. We're in serious trouble at home.

Your dad really needs you."

"Uncle Weld, you three have never needed me! I'm staying. I'm going to follow my original plan. Tell Dad I'm doing fine, haven't killed anyone, haven't rearranged history. I know those were his big worries ever since I learned how to jump."

Weld took a step toward Rick and put his hand on his shoulder. "Rick, I can't go back without you."

"Fine, then stay." Rick handed the innkeeper another coin. "Tell Malcah that we'll be here one more night."

"You misunderstand me, Rick. I mean, literally, I can't go back!"

Weld took a deep breath and continued, "Your dad, Mark, and I were so desperate for your help that we tried a Triage extrication--tried to pull you from here back to our present. We had to have your help.

Problem was that you were stronger than all three of us! You pulled me into the Corridor. Once I was there, something or someone grabbed me from behind and tried to drag me deeper into its continuum. That's when you really showed how much you have grown in power. You pulled against Sam, Mark, and me, plus the force that had grabbed me!

"I can't go back because I'd never make it alone. You've heard us talk about this Evil, which began along about the time you were born. We'd been able to keep it at bay up until the last couple years. It's gaining strength, for some reason, and is lying in wait in the Time Corridor. We now have to fight it almost every time we jump—and you know enough about our business to know that we *have* to jump!"

Rick had never seen his uncle so desperate—and, yes, so concerned about his own safety. It brought him up short.

"Uncle Weld, what can I possibly do that would make any difference? Sure, if you're worried about jumping back, I'll go with you—but I'm not staying. I'm coming right back here. You've never needed me. I'm sure you'll do just fine, as you always have. Tell you what, if you'll jump ahead with me to the general time of the bathing scene and, using your language skills, help me get to Bathsheba's house, I'll escort you back home and listen to your reasons why I am now *so* important to everyone. That's the best I'm willing to do."

Uncle Weld held out his hand. "You've got yourself a deal!"

Rick grinned. "Okay, but let's not leave on an empty stomach. Explain to Malcah that we're ready to eat."

CHAPTER 3

They arrived together, without incident, on the road to Jerusalem, and began walking east, looking for someone who would know the whereabouts of King David's palace. According to historians, David looked down from his palace and observed Bathsheba bathing on the rooftop of her nearby house. If they could locate the palace, surely someone would know where she lived.

"Ah!" Weld exclaimed. "We're in luck. See the group coming our way?"

He greeted the three furtive, bearded men. Two carried swords and the third, a spear. Weld knew, from his youthful trip here, that travelers often moved in armed groups due to the frequency of robberies.

As he asked for directions, two of the three men began circling them. This was not lost on Weld, who, without looking at Rick, said, "Now would be a good time to bring out that Repeller."

The traveller with the spear frowned and grabbed his weapon with both hands as he saw Rick reach for something inside his robe; but when Rick withdrew a slender rod, his frown turned to a grin.

He thrust his spear forward and charged. Having no time to look at the Repeller's settings, Rick simply pointed it at the lunging man and pushed one of the three buttons.

At the same time, the other two were rushing Weld, who did not back away. Grabbing one of the swordsmen by the hilt of his weapon,

Weld swung him around just as the third man thrust his sword into his accomplice.

Rick did a double take. *His* opponent had simply disappeared. The spear lay on the sand. The man was gone.

He turned quickly toward Weld, pointed at the remaining attacker, and fired again. Again, the attacker disappeared!

"Damn," Weld exclaimed. "You interrupted what was going to be an interesting few minutes."

"I don't get it," Rick said. "I knew that this x14 was a new concept weapon, but I had no idea what it could do!"

"Let's keep moving, Rick. But don't put that Repeller away! These are worrisome times, my boy."

After walking for a few minutes and still puzzled by the unusual features of the x14, Rick turned to look back toward the dead man. His two accomplices had reappeared and were bending over him. They looked at Rick but were obviously not interested in pursuit.

In the next several hours of walking, the two time jumpers were aware of more and more traffic crowding the road: caravans, oxen pulling carts of spring produce-- sometimes carts loaded with families went by; and occasionally there were groups of soldiers, laden with armor and weapons of war.

After their last experience with travelers, Rick and Weld were hesitant to question anyone. They continued through the heat of the day, stopping, finally, to refresh themselves, at a well, which was surrounded by vendors plying their trade. They rested in a garden area, where food and wine were being served, feeling secure enough to ask their host what the town, that they could see a short distance away, was called.

Weld translated: "Sounds like he's saying Khirbet Quiyafa—never heard of it." His next question to the innkeeper was "How far is it to Jerusalem?" The answer was, "A day's walk from here, further east."

"Hell," Rick grumbled, "I don't want to walk much further in this heat—besides, my sandals are about shot. Maybe we should just take a chance and jump ahead."

"Maybe," Weld replied. "But let me ask a few more questions first."

After a lengthy discussion with the innkeeper, with much arm waving and finger pointing, Weld ordered more wine for them both and returned to the table.

"We may have gotten lucky. King David's palace is *here*—just up that rise you can see in the near distance. The hill is called Mount Moriah. So, Rick, we've found the palace. Now are you ready to go home?"

"Wait a minute! My goal wasn't to find the palace, it was to find Bathsheba's home."

"Okay, okay. You're right, damn it, but we can't spend much more time here. Sam wants you back ASAP—and my job is to take you back." Weld ran his fingers through his thinning hair and looked at his Wristall. "We've *got* to be out of here in a couple hours!"

Rick stood. "Then let's head toward Mount Moriah."

After another hour's walk, they began their assent. Houses bordered the road, now—and the further they walked, the more elaborate and opulent they became.

An old man, dressed in a prosperous manner, was walking slowly in the same direction as they were, holding the hand of a young boy. As Weld and Rick passed them, Weld paused and spoke with him.

"Do you know where Bathsheba lives?"

The man shook his head but asked, "Do you know who her father or husband is?"

Rick listened to the translation, then slapped his hand against his forehead, "Of course!

"You know, we're so accustomed to the equality of men and women—but that's not how it is here. Here women are treated more like slaves—except in the bedroom."

Rick had done his homework before jumping, so he knew that Bathsheba's father was Eliam and her husband was Uriah.

The only words that excited the old man were *Eliam* and *Uriah,* and he exclaimed, "Uriah, the Hittite! Yes, yes! I know him. He's one of the King's generals. He has a wife called Bathshuk. Is that who you're looking for?"

121

"Do you know her? Weld asked. The man replied with some excitement, "Oh, yes, a beautiful lady." He smiled, revealing several missing front teeth and a bit of lechery.

"There, the corner house—that two-story one—that is Uriah's. He's not home, though. Gone to fight against the Ammonites for the King."

"Satisfied?" Weld asked Rick. "You've found the house of a very beautiful lady--has to be Bathsheba. You've got no excuse now--let's go home."

"No, no—you said two hours—I've still got thirty minutes! Let's actually try to see Bathsheba—after all, you'll have to admit, I've come an awfully long way...."

And without waiting for an answer, Rick took off at a fast pace, headed up the hill toward Uriah's house.

A serving girl was clearing one of the tables in the outer courtyard, as Rick approached. He motioned his uncle over. "Ask her if this is Bathsheba's home."

Weld shook his head in disgust: "Rick, this is a fool's errand! You've found the house, let's head for home." But he did ask.

The girl nodded her head and left the courtyard, disappearing in the direction of the portico of the house. Almost immediately, two armed soldiers appeared: "Who are you? What's your business with the House of Uriah?" And, before Weld could answer, the other soldier pointed to his clothes: "Where are you from. You remind me of a Philistine."

"No, no!" Weld replied. "We're from far away—our dress and our customs are different, but we *are* friends of the King."

Rick wasn't getting any of this conversation but, by the sound of the soldiers' voices, he could tell that things were not going well for Uncle Weld.

"Need any help, Uncle?" Rick said, grinning and showing him the Repeller he had pulled from his robe. The older soldier moved closer, touching Weld's belt. "The Philistines are from far away, also; and they, too, dress in a strange way. I'll let my commander decide if you get to see the General's wife."

Weld nodded his agreement to the soldiers; but then looked at Rick and, with resignation in his voice, said, "Zap'em."

And he did.

Weld turned to Rick—"Now, let's get the Hell out of here!"

They walked around the corner of the house and Weld pulled on Rick's arm.

"Look. We need to guard each other on the return jump—don't forget my problems during the last one. Stand here with your back against mine. Now calibrate. We want to land in Sam's office." He took a deep breath. "Let me know when you're ready, then, on my count, we jump."

"I'm ready."

"Okay, on three, then…"

CHAPTER 4

Sam and his brother, Mark, were just finishing their second cup of coffee. It was 9 a.m., Cincinnati time, when Rick and Weld arrived, making no more noise than the sound of a whisper. But that was a sound that the two coffee drinkers were very familiar with. They turned in unison to see the time travelers standing before them, tired, disheveled, dirty, and reeking with stale body odor.

"Wow! This calls for a celebration!" Sam jumped up, excitedly grabbed his son and Weld in an emotional bear hug. But he stepped back, quickly. "Damn, you guys smell awful! Mark, pour them a stiff drink—then off to the showers with you two! Whew!"

As Mark came over with the glasses of sherry, he nudged them with his elbow—"Welcome home, guys! We just didn't know what to think when Weld disappeared."

Mark was built like a linebacker and had blue eyes and reddish hair—but he was the sentimental and emotional one—could tear up quickly—and he was doing that now.

Sam kidded him, "Come on, Mark, this is a celebration. Don't go crying on us."

"That's not it" Mark alibied. "Their smell's making my eyes water. Get the hell out of here, you guys!"

"Ten o'clock in my office—you two have a lot of explaining to do," Sam barked.

After tossing their travel clothes in the garbage, showering, and shaving, they put on their civvies and rejoined the group again at exactly ten o'clock.

An hour later, after a complete debriefing and a few more drinks, the strategizing started.

Sam began: "As everybody knows, Mark is a whiz at the computer—he's been asking it some pertinent questions—and coming up with a puzzling answer. We all know that our time jumping has been greatly curtailed--and when we do go, we have to keep our guard up to prevent being attacked by whatever hangs out in the time Corridor. Sometimes we can jump for weeks and never have any trouble—and then suddenly, on every jump, we feel threatened."

He took another drink of the sherry, along with some almonds, and continued: "This problem is a fairly new one—it's just been in the last few years that the attacks have been troublesome. We're aware, too, of unexplained anomalies throughout the country. We're trying to determine if this malignant force is behind all these activities. Impossible to tell at this point, if the force is human or something else; but we do believe that twenty-five years ago, when those fools drilled into that lead-lined coffin, they freed this evil energy."

Mark interjected, "When I asked the computer about this, it said there was a sixty per-cent probability that this was the case."

Sam continued: "So, for now, we're going to accept the hypothesis that the problem began with the coffin incident—but why, starting two years ago, has it been increasing exponentially? Okay, that's enough from me. Mark, go ahead with your report."

Mark brought out his notes, placed the Memotek on the table and had a look on his face like a kid who'd been caught with his hand in the cookie jar: "I know this is going to sound like a werewolf story but, based on the computer's answers, the only common thread to the increase in the unexplained disasters, train wrecks, atomic plant melt-downs, plane crashes, building implosions, and so on—the only thing the computer has identified is the variation, over time, in the distance from the Earth to the Moon: the closer the Moon is, the more unexplained disturbances there are here. Scientifically, that doesn't make sense. I keep telling the computer to re-compute. It does--but comes back with the same conclusions. At the Moon's closest point, the perigee, it's 225,622 miles from Earth; at its greatest distance, called the apogee, it is 252,088 miles away. The unexplained disasters seem to occur only during the week before and after the perigee, the closest point."

Sam interrupted, "Could the Colony on the Moon have anything to do with this? They've been up there and running full tilt for about four years."

"Good question. We've been monitoring all signals to and from the Moon, and there's nothing unusual that we can determine."

Weld seemed fully recovered from his ordeal and was totally involved with this dilemma. "What about another energy source from the Moon—not just communications, as we understand it?"

"What are you getting at?" Mark asked.

Weld gave a short laugh, "I don't really know, myself. Can we test for other things—other wavelengths, unusual energies—Hell, anything that can't be explained? And, you know, since the Moon rotates on its axis at about the same speed as it takes for it to circle the Earth, we never see its backside. What's going on back there?"

"Specifically, what do you want me to look for?" Mark asked, somewhat puzzled. "If we don't know what we're looking for, how do we know when we've found it? I'm not saying it's a bad idea, I'm just not seeing what good it would do."

Rick spoke up, feeling for the first time included in the *family* business. "In a way, the question makes sense. If the destructive activities here increase when the Moon is closer, there could be a weak power source on the Moon, which becomes dangerous only at that time. We should try to answer the question Uncle Weld poses: 'Is there any other Moon to Earth activity, whether we recognize it as energy-related or not?'"

"It's worth a try," Sam agreed. "Mark, want to investigate that?"

"Sure. I'm on it!"

Sam leaned over the table, elbows splayed on its top. "Now, here's the next problem we need to think about: How can we deal with this thing that's in the Time Corridor? We have to contain it—destroy it.

Jumping is essential to what we do. We can't shut down for two weeks out of every month, during this perigee. Come up with an answer."

Weld spoke up. "I think Rick is the answer. As I explained earlier, he displayed more time-travel power as he pulled against us--plus he was pulling against that thing in the corridor!"

"All right, I'll accept that as fact. Now, how do we use that information to our advantage?"

The group was silent.

Rick finally commented: "I've been aware that there was something in the Corridor from my very first jump—but since it seemed benign, I figured it was just part of the structure. It's only been in the last year that I've felt that it might be a threat—but I'll have to say, it's never bothered me. Dad, what about you—what's your experience with it?"

Sam looked at the group. "You know, the three of us have been jumpers for years, but it wasn't until sometime after the coffin incident that I felt anything in the Corridor; and, like Rick, I never paid much attention to it--interesting." Sam paused. "Humm, I wonder if there's a connection between the lead-lined coffin and the force in the Corridor? Hell, let's expand it: could this entity also be the cause of the unexplained destructiveness that's now part of our everyday lives?"

Sam seemed always to take the lead on these discussions and to pass out assignments, which he hoped would lead to solutions to whatever problems were on the table.

"Mark, make it a priority to find out if there's any unexplained energy of any kind coming here from the Moon. If there is, try to make sense of it. And get an update on any activity on the backside of the Moon.

"Weld, we need to build our own lead-lined coffin. It has to be thicker and stronger than the original—because that evil force which was released when they drilled into the coffin is, itself, much stronger now. And, most important, we need a final solution--a way to re-entomb it—this time, forever.

"And, Rick, how would you like to go to the Moon?"

"Hell, it beats going back to the Middle East!" Rick exclaimed. "But why? What will I be looking for?"

Before Sam could reply, Rick continued, with some excitement in his voice: "I just remembered! My old college roommate, Todd, is there. He's asked me different times to join him for a week or so."

"What's he do?" Sam asked.

"I don't have a clue, but must be important. He said my trip would be paid for by the Guidance Committee which he was in charge of."

"Great" Sam replied. "See if you can get another invitation. We'll talk later about why I want you to go. And, everybody, one last general assignment: let's all try to come up with a plan to rid the Corridor of that presence."

CHAPTER 5

Weld wasted no time with his assignment: he contacted the Oakley Fabricating Plant and negotiated a contract to build a four by eight (I D) lead container, four inches thick on all sides, with a six inch thick top which would be lowered over the box and into a tongue and groove fitting. Molten lead would then be ensconced around the grooved perimeter, sealing it airtight. In one month they would have it ready for transport.

Satisfied with that arrangement, he began thinking about the final resting place for the container. Contacting a friend of their company, Weld asked for a spot in the Government's underground storage facility. He struck out there and again with another contact. "I don't blame you guys—but, damn it, I've got to find a home for our little friend!"

He sat back, reviewing his options. *If I continue telling the truth about our package, no one is going to agree to take it off our hands. I may have to buy a piece of ground and take care of this myself.* Then he had an epiphany! *No, this thing needs to be returned to its original resting place—the small town of Petersburg, where politics is a big player. Where there's politics, there's corruption. And where there's corruption, there are a lot of skeletons. That's my leverage!*

"Where to start—where to start?" He keyed his system and spoke: "Judge Executive, Boone County, Kentucky."

After convincing Judge Poore's secretary of the urgency of his call, she was reluctant, but finally willing to contact his office. The Judge listened to Weld for about thirty seconds before interrupting, "I'm sorry, Mr. Newall, but as you may know, I've just been reelected; and I really don't have time to meet with you—especially since you aren't convincing me of the importance of the meeting. If you can tell me specifically why we need to meet, I'll give you another minute."

Weld tried to appeal to his patriotism, indicating that it was a matter of National Security. "Therefore, Judge, it's not something I can discuss openly," Weld confided.

"National Security, huh." Judge Poore looked at his calendar. He had no spare time: Since the election, he'd been busy repaying his generous followers with jobs or favors of one kind or another. And he had all those election promises to try to follow up on! Furthermore, over the years, he'd had lots of experience dealing with salesmen of one type or another. He was beginning to feel that that was whom he was talking with. National Security, indeed!

"If you have anything else to say, Mr. Newall, make it short. I've got a meeting with the Historical Preservation Board members in about five minutes."

"I appreciate your time Judge, but I guess I'll need to call Governor Burcham. We're old friends. I just thought this problem could be handled locally."

That got the Judge's attention!

As he looked at his calendar again, he asked, "Is there anything you can tell me as to what your agenda would be?"

Weld knew he had him now. "Well, as I'm sure you understand, I can't say much over this connection; but do you remember, about twenty-five years ago, when a coffin was found in a cave in Petersburg?"

The Judge leaned forward toward his desk and rubbed his eyes vigorously. Should have worn my contacts today, he thought. "Sure do. Is that what this is all about?"

"Yes sir, it is. There have been some new developments. I know you'll recall the hundreds of people who died when the coffin was opened. It's that kind of thing we may be facing again. This could be a life or death situation." Weld was pulling out all stops. He had him hooked and was reeling him in!

Judge Poore slumped back in his chair. He wasn't interested in making any earth-shaking decisions; he just wanted to go on with his life--be the respected judge of this county that he loved. But, down deep, he did *not* want this guy going over his head to the Governor. This was his turf.

Looking closely at his calendar, trying to decide whom he could reschedule, he saw it! There it was–the answer he needed. His eyes landed on his four o'clock. The meeting was with one of his biggest supporters, the Mayor of Petersburg. Hell, if this is about that coffin problem in Petersburg, why not let Newall meet the Mayor—good politics, too!

"Mr. Newall, could you meet with me tomorrow at four o'clock— the new court house on Washington Street? Yeah, okay. Good. See you then."

Weld ended the connection. It was pretty obvious that the Judge was going to have to be convinced, bribed, blackmailed—something! If Weld was reading his man right, he wasn't going to agree to have the coffin reburied in Petersburg! Not without some heavy leverage.

He connected with his Subversive Coordinator:

"Helayne, I've got one for you. Gary Poore, Boone County, Kentucky, Judge Executive. I need to convince him, against his better judgment, to do something for us. Can you see what you can dig up on him? Yeah, great—right--real soon. By noon tomorrow. Thanks."

A minute later, he contacted Helayna again, explaining that he also needed a deep probe done on the Mayor of Petersburg, Kentucky. "I don't know who he is, but I'm hoping he's involved in something we can use. Thanks."

Newall Shipping was a legitimate business, involved in moving bulky freight, mostly Appalachian coal, down the Ohio River to the Mississippi, then to the coast and from there, overseas. But hidden within this legitimate business was a covert one. And although Sam was the front man for both, Weld was the contact man—the one who greased the hands of politicians and businessmen alike, garnering information and/or favors needed to stay current in the ever changing world of espionage. And, today, Mark needed to look at the backside of the Moon.

He was good with computers—but this called for a superb hacker—someone to break into government sites that would provide information regarding that half of the Moon hidden from Earth's view. This same person whom he had in mind would also be asked to compromise the "Big Ear" project, an Alien identification attempt, which used acres and acres of dishes in Kansas, pointed at the most likely parts of the sky which might support life. Mark needed just one of those dishes directed toward the Moon to intercept any messages or energy it could detect and try to decode it.

He made one call. That and one hundred thousand dollars assured him that he would soon have what he needed. He was especially anxious to see if, in fact, there were more or different signals coming to Earth during the Moon's perigee phase.

CHAPTER 6

At 3:30 the next day, Weld arrived at the new courthouse in Burlington.

He was there early and needed the name of a local restaurant to kill a little time:

Approaching a deputy just as she exited her squad car, he asked where he could find the best cup of coffee in town:

"That's easy," the deputy said, smiling. She pointed across the street: "*The Little Place*—great coffee—and it should be. They've been open right there for hundreds of years!"

* * *

At exactly four o'clock, Weld approached the Judge's office.

Sheri, his secretary, sized him up and asked, "Are you Mr. Newall?" Weld nodded. "Go right on in. They're waiting for you."

Weld wasn't sure he liked that. "*They're* waiting for you."

"Who the Hell are *they?*" He mumbled, but he did not break his stride.

The two men stood, one extending his hand. "I'm Judge Poore. Welcome to our little town! I'd like you to meet Bill Grote Petersburg's mayor. I thought it best to have him here if we're going to be talking about something that happened in his town."

Bill Grote was a compact middle-aged man, close to Weld's height, had bushy eyebrows, a prominent nose, and thinning red hair. He stepped around the Judge to shake Weld's hand. Smiling easily, he said, "So you're here to talk about my town?"

Weld replied, "Indirectly, yes. It's really more connected to the discovery of the lead casket that was found after the earthquake many years ago." He was glad he'd had the foresight to ask Helayne to research the Mayor—it'll probable come in handy, he thought

Bill nodded. "Yes, terrible thing. I'd just moved to the area that week—to Petersburg, as a matter of fact. I'd gotten a job across the river, and when I came home—that was two or three days after the quake—people started dying. Hundreds of them—local folks--neighbors—anyone who'd had their mind-screens turned on to channel WCINK and were receiving the live streaming. It was a nightmare! But that was a quarter of a century ago. What's your interest in ancient history?"

The Judge muttered, half aloud, "Yes, it was--a real nightmare," then, looking toward his outer office, "Sheri, we'd like some coffee—have Ed start a new pot—also, tell him to bring cream and sugar, just in case."

He turned to Bill, "Told you it was about that problem--but Mr. Newall said that there's something new going on—something involving National Defense or Security—I forget which. That's why I wanted you in on this. So, go ahead, Mr. Newall, we're listening."

Weld had not wanted to attend this meeting without knowing everything there was to know about the Judge. He needed some way to force him to agree to allow the new coffin to be returned to the cave—but he had not anticipated that the Mayor would be here. His mind was racing like a whirligig, trying to think how the Mayor's presence here could be used to his advantage.

Weld was sure Helayne could come up with some dirt on Judge Poore. After all, he was a politician. All politicians were crooks, Weld had always thought that--and with good reason. Hadn't he handed out hundreds of thousands of dollars to them over the years for their cooperation?

The bad news was that the Judge was clean, not even an unpaid or fixed parking ticket; the good news was that Bill Grote was not.

From 1000 AD to about 1650, Petersburg had been home to a group of the Fort Ancient Indians. Through evidence, which came to light during the various excavations by the University of Kentucky, it was proven that there had been an expansive village life over a very long time. This was a historically significant Indian community.

Early in the twenty-first century, when city water came to the area, it was very difficult to excavate for water lines without disturbing the burial sites or the plethora of early Indian artifacts. Finally, through the intervention of the Boone County Historical Preservation Board, spearheaded by Matt Becher, along with the work of Dave Pollack, Director of the Kentucky Archeological Survey, a way was found to provide water for the community.

Weld's Subversive Coordinator, Helyane, had learned that Mayor Grote was involved in illegal nighttime digs on his large farm, which abutted the town's borders; and he was selling the relics and artifacts unearthed. She learned that he had a non interest-bearing checking account in his wife's maiden name, in a Cincinnati branch of Fifth Third Bank, with a balance of two hundred thousand dollars. Not bad for the mayor of a town of one thousand!

The Judge interrupted Weld's reflections, "Please, Mr. Newall, let's hear what you have to say."

"Oh, yes, I'm sorry—just trying to think about how to begin, since this does involve the cave and National Security. We think that it's important to return the coffin to the cave—rebury it, so to speak!"

The Judge interrupted again, "You from around here, Mr. Newall?"

"Sure—just across the river. My brothers and I own Newall Shipping. Ever hear of it? We've been in business on River Road for years. Why do you ask?"

"Well, it's just peculiar—you seem like an educated man—one that appreciates the finer things of life. You enjoy eating out?"

"Love to. But I'm not following you. Why are you interested in my eating habits?"

Judge Poore leaned back, put his hands behind his head. "It just seems strange that you've never heard of *The Cave.*"

"Isn't that what we've been talking about?" Weld said, with a little exasperation revealed in in his voice.

"Well, yes and no. I'm surprised that a gentleman, such as yourself, an epicure by your own admission–that you haven't been to *The Cave*, one of Boone County's best restaurants."

The Judge chuckled, "I know you thought I was getting away from our topic—but really, I wasn't. Just thought I'd have a little fun, before explaining why we are not at all interested in any plan you have for that cave.

"You see, about ten years ago, the farm where that old cave is located was willed to the county. Bill and I, along with a group of investors, decided to go out on a limb—throw some money into it—make a restaurant and marina. We felt that if the state could do that—you know--build all those state parks, we could too! A group from Chicago gave us the best bid on bringing it all together. Took us a couple years, but we've been open now for six years. Business is great. We draw all the fancy river-boating folks to the marina, and people come from everywhere in the tri-state to the restaurant—Indiana, Ohio, Kentucky--Hell, we've had folks from forty of the fifty-two states so far."

"Wow!" Weld exclaimed. "You really did take quite a risk, though. But I don't understand why people would go to the cave, knowing its history?"

Bill jumped into the conversation: "Ah, that's like talking about World War III. It's all ancient history. Life goes on, and memories are short. If we stopped going to every place that held sadness for a few folks, we'd never leave our houses."

The Judge came back, "Hell, this is a big world—shouldn't be hard to find a place to store that old coffin. How'd you get hold of it, anyway?"

Weld was discouraged. He was counting on returning the unleashed Evil to its original grave. "It doesn't, matter," he said, resigned to the fact that he'd have to keep looking.

"Sorry I've taken so much of your time."

He stood, preparing to leave, when Bill brightened: "Hey, why don't you come to the big celebration we're having in Petersburg next week?"

Weld just wanted to get out of there, but his cultured nature caused him to respond: "What's Petersburg celebrating?"

"Damn! Are you sure *you* don't live in a cave, somewhere! Our Moon man is coming home. June 7th is his twenty-fifth birthday! We invited him to come back, and he's taking us up on it. You know who I'm talking about, don't you?"

"No, I'm sorry, I don't. Your Moon man—what does that mean?"

"Todd Eyanni grew up here. Everybody knows him. Great kid. Went off to college and eventually ended up in charge of the Moon Colony. He's coming in on the next cruiser—landing over at our Hebron airport. The whole town is going to meet him there—have a huge parade bringing him home. Then we're throwing a dinner in his honor at *The Cave.* You ought to come!"

Weld rolled the name over in his mind. Could that be the roommate that Rick was talking about? Unusual name, Todd Eyanni. And Sam did tell Rick to get an invitation to visit him on the Moon.

"You know," Weld said, with feigned excitement, "Maybe I will take you up on that invitation. The Moon Colony *is* quite a big deal! Would you mind if I brought a friend?"

* * *

As Weld drove back toward Cincinnati, he contacted Rick—found out that Todd Eyanni *was* his roommate and made plans with Rick to attend the celebration.

Weld did much of his thinking while driving, which, for most of his life, had become a totally mindless pursuit: just punch in or say the coordinates, relax, read a book, or sleep. For a very long time, autos had not required the dangerous intervention of human operators.

Now, his thoughts turned back to the problem of the coffin, which Sam wanted to have built: locating a final secure place to store it for eternity. Damn! With all that lead, it will be one heavy mother. Who could transport it? Where to?"

After a few miles, he smiled. "Sometimes I think I'm the dumbest bastard on the planet! Who transports bulky, heavy items? Newall Shipping does. Where is the most secure place to dump anything? The bottom of the deepest ocean! Who has ships that go there? Newall Shipping!"

He keyed his responder and asked, "Where is the deepest ocean?" And just like that, his problem was solved: The casket would be ready in less than a month, and it could be dropped from one of the Newall cargo ships into the Pacific Ocean, near Guam, at a place called *The Challenger Deep*, at the south end of the Mariana Trench—and when it finally hit the ocean floor, it would have almost seven miles of sea water above it. Perfect!

Sam would have the easy part of this plan: putting the genie back in the bottle.

When Weld's vehicle pulled into their River Road garage, Sam was waiting for him; and as they rode the elevator up to his office, Weld was peppered with questions. He could tell that Sam was on to something. His eyes always took on that blue effervescent-like sheen when he was working his way toward the solution to some problem.

"Rick told me that his roommate, Todd, would be here this weekend—that Todd was coming in for a celebration—for his twenty-fifth birthday—that he was born on June 7. Is that correct?"

"Right. That's what I learned today from the Mayor of Petersburg. But why are the dates so important?"

"Twenty-five years ago, on June 7, the coffin was opened! Todd was born the same day that that Evil Entity escaped its prison. (And by the way, on the night of the Moon's greatest perigee)."

"Yeah, a coincidence. So?"

"So Todd is now living and working on the Moon. Our theory is that all the hell that's been happening here seems to come, at a time, when the Moon is closest to the Earth!"

140

CHAPTER 7

A few days went by. Monday popped up on everyone's calendar; and every Monday, at 9 a.m. Sam was in his office waiting impatiently for his team to arrive. This had been a routine for the three brothers for decades—a routine that involved Sam's passing out everyone's assignments for the week. Although their birthdates were only a few hours apart, those many years ago—there had been, ever since, a pecking order: Weld was the youngest and always complained about getting 'all the crap jobs.' Mark, the middle child, tried to make sure everyone got along. He was very big on fairness. Sam, the first-born, was the natural leader and the one who directed the meetings and determined the importance of the various problems they needed to solve.

His office was the only official one. The other two brothers, of course, had their 'man cave' rooms, their lairs, filled with the curiosities dragged back during a lifetime of traveling.

Sam had a quick sense of humor and could be counted on for a lot of fun but never at 9 a.m. on a Monday morning. This was his time, and it was strictly business.

Today, Rick joined the team, feeling more and more like he belonged. He'd thought about these conflicting feelings for the last week—it was unexpected and undefined. Was it because he had, in fact, saved Weld's life by pulling him through the Corridor and out of the arms of that Thing? Was it because his dad badly wanted him to go to the Moon on some, as yet, undetermined assignment? Was it his upcoming birthday? Did he have to reach a certain chronological age to be on the Newall team?

Whatever it was, it was a good feeling sitting around his dad's conference table, expecting, but not dreading, the probability of his first serious assignment.

"Remember the old Army joke," Sam began. "'I need three volunteers, you, you, and you'? Well, that's where we are this morning. I've been trying to come up with a way to capture this thing, which seems to lurk in the time-travel Corridor. I might add, no solutions have come from you geniuses; so, I'm hoping that, at least, you can react to my ideas. And, by the way, I *am* looking for a volunteer."

Weld laughed, "Well, this is unusual. It's always been like your old joke: 'you, you and you.'"

They all got a chuckle out of that. It was funny and it was true.

Sam jumped right in: "At the perigee, the point where the Moon is at its closest proximity to the Earth, we go into the Corridor and, using our x14 Repellers, we subdue this Evil; we drag it out and cram it into the lead box and dump it in the ocean. End of problem. Any questions?"

"Hell, Sam," Weld said, "That's not a plan–that's a pipe dream." He got up and headed for the coffee pot. "I don't get it. Your ideas are usually damned elaborate, so choreographed, that we have trouble making heads or tails out of them at first."

Sam grinned. "You're absolutely right, but this time you guys are going to fill in the blanks. I've explained what has to be done–okay, now you figure out how we're going to do it."

Mark had just been listening to this repartee, but now he spoke up: "Sam, damn it, you already have the answers. You're just trying to make us feel that we're part of this plan. Why don't you simply lay it out–give us our assignments, and we'll be on our way?"

This meeting was an eye-opener for Rick. He'd followed the comments back and forth, and it reminded him, so far, of some of his old frat house meetings. Not what he had expected. But not being sure of what his place was here with this team that had been working together forever, he decided he would just observe.

"I'm just looking for ideas," Sam countered. He, too, got up and visited the coffee dispenser. His office reflected his personality: no trophies of past glories, no memories to be relived–just a large warm room with furniture and pictures from the Edwardian period, expensive but understated. The company gym was on the basement floor, so there was no need for any strategically placed exercise equipment, no golf bag leaning in one of the corners suggesting a well-rounded personality.

There was no outer office, no administrative assistant within eavesdropping range. Sam had a fetish for security and secrecy--these were two primary ingredients for a company whose major reason for existence was espionage.

Weld began: "Okay. We go in with guns blazing. The Evil is just standing there waiting for us and surrenders. Yeah, Sam. Quite a plan. Remember I've met this thing--almost died in the Corridor! I'd like a few more details."

Mark jumped in, "And what are we volunteering for, anyway?"

Rick began to get it. His dad, as best as he could determine, had had a formal and prolonged education and seemed to know a lot about just about any subject; so it was no surprise to Rick that he recognized Sam's use of the Socratic method! The ancient man of learning could not have done better himself!

Rick thought to himself--this technique is probably necessary to bring these disparate brothers together.

Sam pointed at Mark. "You've hit on one of the two weaknesses of my plan: how do we know the Evil is going to be there and how do we make it reveal itself?"

"What else?" Weld asked.

Sam replied, "Let's just deal with this one first. Give me some ideas."

This was Rick's chance: "We need to give it a reason to show up. The time is right--the Moon's perigee. All we need now is to tempt it–and, Dad, I know what your volunteer comment is all about. One of us needs to go in there alone and unarmed."

"Bingo!" Sam exclaimed.

Rick continued: "What does this thing know about us? I've been in there. I've passed through the Corridor many times. It's never bothered me. Weld encountered it unarmed and alone and, as far as *it* knows, he was strong enough manage his own to escape."

Sam nodded. "Keep going."

"You, Dad, have had the most experience jumping, and you've confronted it and escaped. Mark no longer is a frequent jumper and has no history with this thing. Mark is your volunteer."

Mark pushed back form the table, his blue eyes flashing, "So I'm the tasty unarmed pigeon. Don't I have something to say about this?"

"Now, Mark, sit down. Wait 'til you hear the rest of the plan before you volunteer," Sam said, seeming to enjoy this little scene.

"Let's play it out. Mark is in the Corridor, very tempting and very unarmed. Then what?" Sam was setting the stage here, drawing a picture–waiting for someone to fill in the background. He looked around again, "Then what?"

The brothers looked at one another, but quickly turned to Rick. Weld said, "Your call, Rick, then what?"

Since returning from Jerusalem, Rick had been reading about and playing with the x14. It had many new functions–activated by only three buttons.

"Remember the rodeo we went to a few years ago, the act where the three cowboys went into the arena against a raging bull with nothing but their lassos?"

"They were a bunch of crazy bastards," Mark suggested. "I thought they'd all end up on the horns of that bull!"

"But what happened?" Rick asked.

"Damn! That was exciting!" Mark stood up and pantomimed the struggle. "Each cowboy readied his lasso, and then one of them distracted the bull while the other two threw the ropes around his neck; and, as they yanked on him, the third cowboy threw his rope."

Mark walked around the middle of the room and pulled on the imaginary lasso. "They spread out and tightened those ropes--no matter which way the bull turned, if all three held the ropes taut, he had no where to go."

"That's the plan I like," Rick said, nodding to the group. "But instead of a rope, we'll use our Repellers. We'll all set them on stun and then switch to the Impeller mode—the setting that will pull this thing toward us. With each of us pulling from a different direction, it will have nowhere to go, just like that bull."

"Anyone see a weakness, here, in Rick's plan?" Sam asked.

"Yeah!" Mark growled. "Helluva big one. If I'm in there, alone, baiting this thing, how will you cowboys know when to show up?" And he wasn't grinning when he asked that question.

"That's the other problem," Sam interjected. "How will we know the right moment to jump in with, as Weld said, 'guns blazing'"?

No one answered. So Sam held up a small button, about the size of a quarter: "The special frequency on this communicator will help us. All you have to do, Mark, is push the button. We'll have already calibrated to your jump coordinates. You push the button and, in a Nano second, we'll have you surrounded. All of us, especially you, will be wearing mirror infused suits to reflect the Impeller's rays. It should be like a fly in a spider's web."

"How long will I have to stay in that Corridor? Even if the Evil thing doesn't show up, it's a dark and fetid place to be."

"Good question," Sam said. "Somehow the Evil knows when you arrive. Maybe, like the spider, it comes when the web shakes. In our past encounters, it shows up almost immediately or not at all. I'd say, if nothing happens in five minutes, jump back here. Any other questions? Concerns?"

"When do we go?" Mark asked.

"That's up to you."

Mark grinned, "Then I'd say in about ten years."

That broke the tension. They all had a good laugh. The meeting was coming to an end. One final assignment: "Mark, find out when the next perigee is. That's our ETD." Sam got up, as did everyone else.

"Oh, Rick. I need to see you for a few minutes," Sam said.

Weld and Mark left. Rick returned to his seat.

"Here's what I need for you to do...."

CHAPTER 8

Mark quickly strode into Sam's office without knocking–unusual for him. "It's tomorrow night!"

"What the hell are you talking about?" Sam said, looking up from a map of the backside of the Moon, which Mark had given him earlier.

"The perigee–it's tomorrow night."

"Damn. That doesn't give us much time. I wonder if we should postpone it. Maybe try next month. Let's think about it. Mark, if you're going in there as bait, there's always the chance that it'll envelop you and disappear."

Mark started to protest. Sam held up his hand. "Hold on now–I said only a chance–and a very slim one at that. We're going to be in there as soon as you push that button—but, just in case, we do need a back up plan. You're the tech genius. Give me a way to protect you."

Mark thought hard for a minute. "I've been working on a reverse atomizer."

"Okay. How will that help?"

"You know how a dog can follow a scent–can track a person days after he's left the scene?"

"Keep going."

"Well, I've developed a hand-held device that does the same thing. It's set up so there's a constant airflow through its filters. If I give it a scent, it will remember it. Then later, if I push the button "FIND," it'll give me a visual and audio signal which will guide me to the source of that scent."

"Will it be able to trace the scent through the time Corridor?"

"Sure–anywhere."

"Can you have it operable by tomorrow night?"

"It's ready now."

"Great! Then it's a go. Call Weld and Rick–let's meet and rehearse our strategy. What time tomorrow is the strongest perigee?"

"Ten p.m."

Sam stood up, walked over to Mark, and put his hand on his brother's shoulder: "Now, you know, if you don't want to do this, we'll find another way. I'm never going to put you in an impossible situation. I really think you're on safe grounds here with our back-up plan: the button, the sniffer, and the cowboys."

"Hell," Mark replied. "You've put me in a lot worse situations. It should be a piece of cake. The only thing that bothers me is that I've never gone into a questionable situation like this one without my Repeller. Isn't there some way I can take it?"

"I wish you could, but I think this Evil thing can sense danger. It will know, somehow, whether you're armed or not. Just remember, when you push that button, we'll be there." Something in the back of Sam's mind was flashing yellow: ignore me at your peril, it was saying. There was nothing about the plan, however, which caused him any worry—it seemed fool proof, so he mentally turned off the caution sign.

June 17, 10:00 p.m. came all too soon. Mark had on his mirror-infused suit and, in his hand, was the call button–his lifeline to the remaining three Newalls and their Repellers.

"Remember," Sam cautioned, "You're to stay in the Corridor no more then five minutes. This Entity is either going to be there or it isn't. If you aren't back after five, we're jumping in."

"Got it," Mark replied. "Okay. Here goes." He took a deep breath and disappeared.

One minute went by, then two: they paced the floor of Sam's office, their Repellers already set for *STUN* and *HOLD*.

* * *

Mark hated standing around in the Corridor. It was pitch dark and had a musky smell, and it was damp and devoid of sound. Besides, with his ability to sense the presence and feel the thoughts of others, he was getting strong emotions of raw hatred coming from very close to where he was. The hairs on the back of his neck began warning of impending danger, but he was at the mercy of the darkness.

Suddenly a flash of intense light blinded him. He dropped his call button, grabbed his eyes, and fell to his knees. The pain was excruciating, like a migraine, only worse. Something grabbed him from behind and began moving him down the Corridor. Then he felt the floor give way. They were dropping story after story. Mark was a big man, and he struggled, knowing his life depended on it; but the strength of this entity behind him was so overwhelming that he finally stopped trying to break free. He was lifted like a toy and slammed into a box. There was total silence. Total darkness: Classic sensory deprivation.

The Newall team tensed as the second hand moved toward the five-minute mark. Sam whispered, "Give yourself six feet distance from this thing. Be sure your Repeller is ready. Here we go. 3...2...1..."

They landed in total darkness; but by the light of their lasers, they could see what they did not want to see.

Mark was gone.

"Damn!" Sam exclaimed. "Look around—there should be some sign of a struggle. Mark sure as hell wouldn't go without a fight."

Rick found it. The button lying on the dank floor. And he found one of Mark's shoes.

Sam pulled out the Sniffer. It showed the direction Mark had gone. Not just through the Corridor, but down. Straight down. His heart was beating rapidly, and his mind was trying to make sense out of this unexpected development: he knew that time was his enemy at this point, so Sam made an intuitive decision.

"What the hell?" Weld said.

Sam cursed as only Sam could. "You keep following the scent. I think I know where it's going--where it's taking Mark. I'm going to jump on ahead."

He landed in the Newall Shipping sub-basement--the place where the leftovers of their work-world ended up. Walking to one of the corners, he began throwing items left and right. This was the section of the warehouse where evidence of long forgotten cases was stored. Sam was looking for only one thing: the original coffin from the cave. They had acquired it a few years after the earthquake–a down time for their business, so they had decided to resurrect a few old murder cases–this was one of them.

So much clutter--so many years' worth of ancient history. He ran to the master switch, turned on the lights to the entire storage space and quickly returned and uncovered the coffin. At first glance, it looked as though it had not been disturbed; but then Sam noticed the hole in the top that had been drilled out years ago was now filled back in; and the top which they had sawed off to get a good look at the interior had been replaced at a slight angle—the thousand pound lid had been moved recently!

At that moment, Rick and Weld burst in to the room.

"Sam, how did you know?"

"No time, now. I'm betting Mark's in that coffin. It's been sealed shut again. Airtight. He'll only have a few minutes of oxygen left." Speaking in a staccato-like fashion, "Rick, there's a hardware store down the block. Jump there and bring back a lazer-tipped saw. We've got to get that box open fast."

Rick disappeared immediately and was back in under a minute holding the saw.

"Top or side?" he asked.

"Well, there's going to be molten lead dropping. Let's go through one of the ends."

The saw cut through the lead like it was butter. Rick tried to be very careful because it could go through a head or a toe just as easily.

Weld grabbed a nearby garden hoe, from who remembers what old case, and rammed it into the coffin, hooked it on the cut slab which had fallen inward and yanked it out. Sam shined his light in--there was a pair of feet, one shoe missing.

In unison, Rick and Weld each grabbed a foot and pulled Mark out. His breathing was very shallow and slow, but he *was* still breathing. Sam pounded on his chest and gave him CPR, cursing him at the same time.

"Come on you no good slacker, breathe! Breathe!" Weld took over the CPR and, finally, Mark began wheezing, gradually coming back from near death.

"Weld, get him upstairs. Call an ambulance! Make sure he's okay." Sam was frantic. "C'mon Rick, we're going on the hunt. This thing will be covered with Mark's scent, and we can follow it. Put your Repeller on KILL. We're taking no chances, so when you see it, shoot."

The Sniffer kept beeping–kept pointing the way--Corridor after Corridor, turn after turn, as if the Thing was doing an SDR–a series of evasive maneuvers to throw a person off its trail. But the Sniffer was as good as Mark said it was. Unerringly, it was leading Sam and Rick closer and closer. Every time they turned a corner, Rick fingered the Repeller, expecting to find his target. Finally, as the old saying goes, there was light at the end of the tunnel–and music, and the murmur of a large group of people.

Cautiously, they approached the tunnel's end and stepped into a brightly lit auditorium. They waited a minute to allow their eyes to adjust. A crowd of a few hundred people were seated, all attentive to a speaker who seemed to be in the process of introducing someone: "And to conclude my remarks, and I'll do it quickly because I know you did not come to listen to me give a thank-you speech for my re-election as your Judge Executive; you came here for our Moon man--and here is your Mayor, Bill Grote, to introduce our most famous citizen." He pointed to the edge of the stage, and Mayor Grote walked out with his arm on the shoulders of...

"Well, I'll be damned!" Rick said. "My old roommate, Todd Eyanni."

Sam was not listening. He was distracted by the Sniffer, which suddenly began beeping and showing an arrow pointed directly at the front of the stage.

"Well," he said. "Todd Eyanni–we got you now."

"Dad, that's Todd, my old roommate. Now I won't have to go to the Moon to see him. He's come to us!"

"Yes, he has, son. Yes, he has! Okay, we found out all we need to know; let's jump back home. I'm anxious to see how Mark's doing." And with those comments, Sam disappeared.

Rick did not leave right away. It was great to see Todd again–even at a distance. He was a good friend for four years–great drinking buddy. They had even toured Europe together, following their graduation and before Rick began his graduate studies. He felt a sadness that so many years had passed since their good times. How was it that such closeness could so easily be tossed aside in the name of success—or progress—or what ever excuse one chooses to use!

After listening for a few minutes, to the Mayor's outline of Todd's accomplishments, Rick stepped outside. Having been in the time tunnel for so long and having followed such a circuitous route, he was curious to see just where he had exited. As he walked through the parking lot and headed toward the driveway leading from this complex, he saw the sign, "*Fort Ancient Indian Museum and Meeting Hall.*" That didn't ring a bell. He noticed a group of youngsters gathered around a pick-up truck, so he walked in their direction.

"Get rid of it man, get rid of it!" He heard one of them say. Rick had no interest in breaking up this party, no matter what the refreshments–he was just curious as to where he was.

"Evening guys," Rick said, smiling.

"Yeah, it *was* a great evening," one of them said, under his breath.

"I've gotten kinda turned around. What town are we in?"

"Hey, man, you must be on some kind of happy juice–I'm not exactly in this world myself, right now, but I do know where I am. Greatest little town in Kentucky."

Rick laughed. "Okay. That's a start. At least I know what state I'm in. But I still don't know what town I'm in."

"Didn't you come here to meet the Moon man–he's been in all the news–grew up right here in Petersburg?"

"Petersburg? Isn't that where they had that earthquake a few years ago?" Rick asked, knowing full well that it was.

"Don't know nothing about that, man–why don't you go on in and find out?"

In other words, as Rick paraphrased the speaker, "get lost."

Unlike the old Superman character, Rick had no telephone booth to step into to reinvent himself; but he was able to walk around the corner of the museum, making sure there were no eyes upon him as he vanished. The original GPS system of years ago had a special category called "favorites." Rick, too, had favorites stored in his jump mode; and his dad's office was one; so without having to calculate, he plugged in his favorite and was immediately standing in the dark, by his dad's desk.

He turned on the lights and looked around, hoping to find a note or some information explaining where everyone was.

Then he remembered, Sam had told Weld to call an ambulance-- "He's at the hospital, of course--that's where everyone is." He keyed his system, and his dad answered, immediately.

"How's Mark?" Rick asked.

"He's a Newall—he's going to be fine." Sam laughed. "But he does have three broken ribs and a broken nose from being slammed face down into the coffin. I don't think I'd trade places with him, but you know what, Rick? I'm really on a guilt trip, right now. It was all my plan–I sent Mark into that Corridor knowing the danger. I was so anxious to solve this part of the puzzle, so we could get to the bigger one--the destruction which the Moon was causing every month when it gets closest to the Earth. That focus almost got my brother killed. And I *had* the premonition—you know, that we sometimes get when we should proceed with caution. It was right there—and I ignored it!"

"Dad, you shouldn't blame yourself–that's the kind of stuff you guys have been doing for years. You all know the risks. If Mark had a problem with it, he would've said so."

"I know. I know," Sam replied, in a low, discouraged voice. "Rationally, I understand all that; still, I was willing to send Mark unarmed and alone into a very dangerous situation. I don't like that in myself."

"Is Uncle Weld with you, now?"

"No. He's gone over to tell Mark's family."

After finishing his conversation with his dad, Rick sat alone in the office, at the conference table, in the same chair he had occupied during their 9:00 a.m. meeting. River Road traffic was nonexistent this time of night—most of the west to east cars were using Columbia Parkway, higher up the bluff from the Ohio River. He looked at his dad's chair—could not imagine Sam not being there. Yet, Rick had lived long enough and was sensitive enough to the effects of time to understand the cycles.

He could find no happiness in what he observed. It was a series of endless struggles, of pointless effort--toward what end? At the conclusion of every human struggle, death is always there, waiting--and, in between, a little joy and much suffering. Most of the actors on Earth's stage don't seem to be aware of all of this, Rick felt. They arise each day in sadness and in hope; they perform their rituals of learning, working, loving, and suffering; and the day ends in exhaustion. They are blind to the fact that Tomorrow's job is to provide more of the same.

The effect of sharing the grief his father was feeling and the almost certain suffering of his Uncle Mark pushed Rick further into reflection. He walked to the liquor cabinet, made himself a Manhattan and a cup of black coffee—the perfect combination for his mood.

After a couple drinks, his thoughts turned inward to self-evaluation. Here he was, twenty-five years old, held two college degrees--but had no life—not even a girlfriend. Something was wrong with that picture, he thought. He did like girls, and he smiled at that teasing suggestion that he might be gay. "No, way," he said, "it's just that they take too damn much of my time!"

He realized that he was now a legitimate part of the Newall organization and that frightened him a little. He knew only scattered tid-bits of what his dad and uncles actually did—had no clue as to where their ever-present supply of cash came from. After a final sip of the strong coffee, he said aloud, "Well, I'll know--all in good time."

That lack of knowledge did not bother him; but, as he continued to contemplate, he realized a lack of a significant other did. "Damn!" he muttered. "Significant other–where the hell did that phrase come from? I don't need a significant other, I need a girlfriend!"

His mind wandered back to Jerusalem and to Abigail's smile and her giggle. *I liked her,* Rick thought. *But I guess by now she's a little too old for me.*

Sam laughed, "What are you muttering about over there, Rick?"

Startled, Rick jumped to his feet. So submerged was he in his own misery, that he had missed the whisper that signaled the arrival of Sam in his office.

"Dad! I didn't hear you come in. How's Mark?"

"He's doing great. They're going to release him tomorrow. But he'll have to spend a few weeks at home while those ribs heal; and the doc told him he should see about having his nose re-aligned. But he's in good spirits–I think he feels better than Weld and I do about all this."

They sat quietly for a few minutes. Silence had never been the enemy for either the father or the son. It seemed to bring clarity to the relationship, forming a bond that all of the talking and verbal sharing could never duplicate.

In the early years, Sam was gone a lot, as he developed his niche, his business model; but no matter where in the world he was, Rick could feel his presence and his love; and, now, as they sat in silence, their minds seemed to link up.

Todd Eyanni was my best friend, Rick's mind broadcast. *He still is. I don't believe he's part of the problem.*

Sam's mind reacted. *We traced him to the museum. The Sniffer pointed directly at him there on the stage. We're going to have to act on this information, Rick, and you know what that means. Every day, every night, during the perigee, people are dying. They're dying pointlessly, without reason, because of Todd's agenda–whatever that is. He may not even be human. Todd was born at the same hour and same day the Evil escaped from the coffin.*

Rick interceded. *Please dad, let me look into this. Let me go to the Moon. I know Todd would invite me again. I'd like to find out what I can from the people in the Colony. There has to be another explanation. All you have are a series of coincidences. Nothing more.*

Sam replied strongly, *I put Mark in danger in that Corridor; I'm not going to have you alone and unarmed on the Moon with Todd. I've changed my mind about your going there. Forget it.*

Rick turned to his father and said aloud, "What are you going to do with Todd?"

"He's going into the new coffin and then to the bottom of the sea. I want the Moon to return to what it has always been: an old friend that sheds light on our paths at night and lightens our spirits during troubled times."

CHAPTER 9

Rick took the elevator to the fourth floor of their River Road complex, to Helayne's office; and as he walked into the anteroom, he could hear her booming voice:

"You *will* have that ready by the end of the month. Yeah, yeah—I'm sure you have other customers; but unless you want the world to know about the Cuban deal you were involved with last week … how do I know about that? That's not the question you should be asking. The question should be, what do you need to do to keep that information away from the media? I'll be very quiet if that box is delivered by July 31, okay? Yeah, I thought you would agree. Thank you very much.

"I know you're out there, Rick; just give me a couple minutes."

Rick had gone to Helayne's office many times over the years—never a dull moment. She had gotten a little older, kept her figure, and, as always, was dressed as a fashion model. She was the diva of Newall Shipping but deservedly so. Sam recruited her from G&P, having to promise her a suite on the top floor overlooking the river and a closet the size of his office.

Rumor was that she had so many shoes she had to rent a storage locker for those that were seldom worn.

She strode into the room like she owned the place and grabbed Rick in a bear hug. "Okay, you've got thirty minutes. What's up?"

He followed her back into her office which, quite unlike Sam's, was a decorator's delight: modern furniture, interesting memories collected from around the world, artfully displayed.

Knowing Helayne's penchant for no-nonsense meetings, Rick got right to the point. "There's no question you're the best at what you do as our Subversive Coordinator. Remember being asked last week for a history on Judge Poore and Mayor Grote?"

"Of course. Was there a problem?" She leaned forward, looking Rick directly in the eye, making him feel as he did when he first came to see her a decade ago-- made him feel like a tongue-tied little boy.

Rick had to pump himself up for this meeting–had to say to himself, "I am the owner's son. Someday this will be my business. I'm Helayne's boss; but there was always a doubtful little voice in the back of his head that proffered these short monologues, putting Rick in his place. "Really now, boy. Do you think you're the boss? Really?"

But Rick plowed ahead: "I need more, Helayne–can you go back and broaden your research–give me everything there is to know about these two guys from birth until today? There's something we're missing. Treat them as you would homegrown terrorists. It's that important."

"Your dad was satisfied with my report. What are you looking for? I felt I did a thorough job."

"Yes, you did." Rick did not want to ruffle any feathers here, but he damn well was going to get what he wanted.

"Helayne, the Judge is a politician. Has been most of his life, yet you found nothing we could use. Not one scrape with the law. No secret accounts, no family problems, no money taken under the table, no wayward children. How far back did you go?"

"Twenty years," she said, defiantly.

"Not enough for what I need. I want everything from the moment the two of them were born until this very day. Look at the background of their parents, their siblings. Pull out all the stops on this one."

"That kind of investigation will take a lot of my time. Has Sam approved it?"

"Do you think I need his approval? This *is* company business. I'm following a lead that he hasn't considered. Helayne, you know my dad--once he makes up his mind about something, there's no changing it. I think he's wrong on this one, and the life of a very good friend of mine is in danger."

"Is Sam the danger?"

"Yes."

"Delicate situation. Let me think about this one."

CHAPTER 10

S am's instructions to Rick still reverberated in his ears, as he landed on the Moon—"Don't come back until you can tell me that Todd is an innocent bystander, connected only by coincidence to all the hell on Earth, or that he is the man we're going put in that coffin."

Following the confusion and drama of the landing, Rick was finally guided to his quarters where an evening meal was delivered, along with a schedule of events for the next day. He ate quickly and, without even removing his clothes, lay on his bed, exhausted from the trip. Sleep overtook him quickly, but all too soon, the speaker in his room announced the arrival of his first morning on the Moon. Breakfast would be at 7 a.m., and the members of the Guidance Committee would meet in the main conference room at 9.00.

As he walked down the well-lit corridor, he was met by Carol, the social coordinator, who directed him through the cafeteria to where his old college roommate, Todd Eyanni, was seated. Todd looked up, grinned broadly, and jumped to his feet, meeting Rick a few steps from their table. "Rick! I'm so glad you took me up on my invitation! Sorry about last night. I certainly planned to meet you at the terminal; but things kinda went south. Come on, sit down. Carol, would you mind telling them we're ready for breakfast. Man, we've got a lot of catching up to do! You first, Rick, what have you been up to?"

And so, for an hour, they went back and forth, filling in those missing years and, on occasion, reliving a few of the highlights of past adventures. It was obvious that both were warming to this re-emergence of an old friendship; and the meeting with the Guidance Committee seemed to infringe much too soon on this special time.

* * *

Around a large oak table, six pensive people were seated, drinking coffee, seemingly waiting patiently for the seventh chair to be occupied, as Rick and Todd Eyanni walked in. Those seated rose: three men and three women. Todd walked to the vacant chair, pulled it out and motioned for Rick to sit, then continued to a circular spot, lighted in the floor.

"I see we're all here, so let's jump right in: At our last discussion, we all agreed to have a trusted outsider brought in to hear what we have in mind for our Moon expansion. You voted to have me find that person. I'd like to introduce Rick Newall, a long time friend and associate—a man I would trust with my life—with our lives. I will not waste your time explaining why I chose Rick or what exactly he brings to this table. Suffice it to say, he *is* the man we've been looking for, and he has agreed to hear us out and to react honestly.

"Margaret, would you speak first, outlining, in basic terms, the direction we plan to go and why. Rick, Margaret Jackson."

Clearing her throat, Margaret rose, walked behind her chair, faced the group, and with a hesitant smile, spoke directly to Rick:

"Mr. Newall, as part of our agreement to have an outsider here so that we might share some of our hopes and plans for our immigrant population, it's imperative that that person be brutally honest with us; and at the same time, no matter what that person thinks, no matter what his natural reaction is to what he will hear, he needs to understand that his life is secure only as long as he remains mute regarding what he has heard once he leaves this meeting.

"Mr. Newall, do you understand and so agree?"

Rick glanced at his friend, Todd. "Look, I've already agreed to say nothing about what I learn here today. If that's not good enough, I'm not interested in hearing anything else. Sorry, I don't want to risk my life as a favor to a friend." Rick stood and prepared to leave.

Todd stepped from the lighted floor toward the table—toward what had become known informally as the Guidance Committee: "I think we're getting off on the wrong foot. Rick, all Margaret and the rest of us are asking is that you not divulge anything that we discuss today. You've made that promise to me, but will you now make that same promise to our Committee?"

Rick turned to the Committee. "I've already agreed to that! I will divulge what I hear to no one; but if making that statement somehow puts my life in jeopardy, I intend to leave this meeting now. It's as simple as that. How much more specific must I be?"

"Fair enough. We have no intention of threatening you. Please rejoin the group. Okay, Margaret, cut to the chase on this. We have other speakers, and we have a deadline to meet." With that said, Todd stepped back from the table.

"I'm sorry, Mr. Newall—maybe I was a bit brusque, but I do feel that you now understand the seriousness of our request. After today, nothing must stop our forward progress."

Rick nodded in the affirmative.

"So—where to begin: first of all, as you well know, we are a satellite of Earth and are, therefore, bound by its Charter. That, however, is about to change. No one outside of this room truly understands the implications of our latest technological breakthrough: we have developed a means by which we can move our Moon out of its orbit around the Earth and, using the slingshot effect, begin to orbit the Sun. This move, of course, would be catastrophic to the Earth—millions would die and hundreds of cities and towns near the seas would be destroyed. We, of course, have no immediate plans to do this, but it's a realistic threat, and we feel that the Earth will take it seriously.

"With this mass destruction as part of its future, were we to relocate, the question for Earth becomes, 'will we?'

"The answer depends on the response to two more questions: What do we have to gain if we do—and what do we have to lose if we don't?

"From what Todd has explained to us, you have a thorough knowledge of Earth's history—a history of wars, disease, famine, plagues, pestilence, greed, avarice, persecution, and human decadence, and on and on. We have come to believe that Earth has little to be desired or envied and much to be ashamed of.

"Our Master Plan is to look at all of these evils of the Earth and to be sure we populate our new planet without them. History tells us that having no controls over the peripheries of an incoming pre-selected population to a new land leads, eventually, to its religious, political or economic contamination.

"In the olden days, when the Pilgrims settled parts of north eastern America, they soon aroused the enmity of the native population; this encroachment was followed, over the centuries, by all sorts of factions, extremes of religion, language, philosophies, dogmas, and skin colors--all things that highlight humankind's differences—and Differences, we have concluded, are what lead to conflict.

"Jamal will talk next on how we plan to purify our intended population—a population we, here, can never hope to be a part of due to the nature of our filtering process."

With those final words, Margaret rejoined her seated companions, taking a long and much needed drink from her now tepid coffee.

Jamal was a cocoa-colored bearded man with a middle-eastern demeanor. He rose quickly, speaking, as he positioned himself, so that he was leaning forward, knuckles on the table, his long hair covering his eyes.

Without the customary prelude, he began: "The early arrivals to any parts of the Earth undertook the journey in anticipation of something pleasant or to escape something unpleasant. Each group, in and of itself, would be the nucleus of an acceptable society—one with similar views, dress, ambitions, religion and so on. Sooner or later, however, these groups were infiltrated by new arrivals from surrounding areas, groups with opposing or contradictory beliefs or customs, giving rise to increasing animosity as the established tried to absorb the new: Most problems throughout history did not arise because of sameness, as Margaret has indicated, but because of differences. The job before us is to create Homogeny. And, yes, that means Dichotomy will be discouraged—no not just discouraged—it will be suppressed—eliminated.

"As an example of our desire for Homogeny, we looked at Religion. What would be the best religion for our chosen few? As we all were well aware, there are literally thousands of faiths—and within those, there are innumerable splinter groups—sub-faiths. Which religion would we choose and how would we do it? We reviewed the histories of all the major ones, and we concluded that millions of people have been killed as part of thousands of wars based on religious fervor; but very few people have died either defending or rejecting the concept of 'no religion.' And that's why we have chosen to allow no religion, no faith, among our chosen.

"Take economics as another cause of unhappiness, dissention and war: the haves vs. the have-nots; the rich against the richer; those who have no land against those who do—I could go on and on with examples of how economic disparity leads to conflict.

"Our solution to that problem is simple: the answer is Sameness.

"First, everyone will receive similar pay, no matter what the job assignment is—from us here on the Guidance Committee to those who keep the Moon's machinery humming. Additionally, because of the environmental extremes imposed upon us here, our engineers have gravitated toward creating all homes with a consistent theme—that of safety and simplicity. Everyone's living quarters will be similar, externally. Some leeway will be permitted as far as the interior design, colors and so forth, but still within the guidelines we have established.

"We will encourage vocational happiness and contentment: if you like your job, you may keep it. If you want to try something else, you may apply for one of the training programs, which could lead to the position of your choice.

"Yes, conformity, uniformity, and overall homogeny are the keys to a contented society; but there must be that creative spark in any population for advancements to occur, be they technical, medical—whatever, so we, of course, intend to provide the motivation—the stimulus necessary for innovation and creativity to flourish. But this expenditure of our wealth will not be directed toward the general population, but toward those who are identified, as time often does, as being exceptional. You see, Mr. Newall, although we strive for sameness in our citizens, as a whole, we understand the necessity to identify uniqueness as it arises within our midst, for it is those unique ones who will provide the impedes for future discoveries and growth."

Jamal banged his fist on the table: "I have volunteered to seek out those with this uniqueness. I will find them; I will see that they provide us with the requirements to face tomorrow's challenges."

Looking at each member of the group, he nodded his affirmation, as if that, in itself, would be sufficient to convince them of his resolve; and having done that, he conceded the floor to Gavin Greengarten, explaining that Gavin would deal with the one area on which they were unable to find unanimity.

Gavin rose slowly, looking quizzically at Rick: "Mr. Newall, my question to you is this—just why would you volunteer to be the whipping boy for our group. You know, don't you, that that's what you will be. We can't agree on a number of topics, some small, some huge. We all have our points of view, and we are going to be badgering you to see the logic of our argument–to accept *our* logic. I sure wouldn't want to be in your shoes. Why would you come here knowing what we expect of you?"

Todd stepped forward, once again, guiding his group–keeping them on topic: "Gavin, let's keep to the agenda. Rick's reasons are his own. The only thing that we need to understand is that he *is* qualified, beyond any doubt, to provide guidance to us, and that he has agreed, as Margaret has said, to be 'brutally honesty.' Please, just accept that he is here, in our best interests, and don't try to analyze him, don't try to figure out his motivations." Todd nodded for Gavin to continue.

Gavin grinned. "Just wanted Rick to know where I stood. No offense intended"; and turning to Rick, he began. "Okay, here's the stumbling block we have:

"To ensure *Sameness*, we must have just one race. How do we select the best one for us here on the Moon? We know that race doesn't depend exclusively on skin color—but that's the way many on Earth perceive it. So, to get to the crux of the dilemma, is the *best* race for us Chinese, Indian, Caucasian, African, Middle Eastern or one of the many others that have taken root on planet Earth? And, within that question, which race is the brightest, healthiest, most inventive, most creative—you get the picture. Then again, just because one race does not fit our criteria, does that mean that individuals within that race who are outstanding, should not be considered?

"Looking at Jamal's earlier example of Religion, I think it was easy to follow our progression of thought to the conclusion that the correct choice would be *no religion*. But how can we say that *no race* meets the intended resettlement guidelines?"

Anton Bonovich interrupted: "Okay, Gavin, I think you've made your point—a point which, I might add, is purely academic at this juncture in our planning, anyway. Let's get to the heart of our problem: how to make the Earth capitulate. We have to achieve that before any of today's grandiose schemes make any sense."

"Hell, Anton, there's no point achieving independence if we can't decide on how to populate our Moon!" Gavin leaned forward, in an aggressive stance, Anton having obviously touched on a sore spot. "This quandary is the one reason I voted to have an outsider come to our meeting. Most of the other unsolved problems, I think, sooner or later we'll solve."

Anton stood, pulling on his mustache, "And, my astute friend, of what value are these population strategies if we don't become independent?" He rolled his eyes with exasperation. "This is not the chicken or the egg argument. Logic dictates that we can decide on population criteria after we achieve independence, but we cannot populate until we are free from the constraints of Earth. All I'm saying is let's become free first, then we'll have as much time as necessary to meet the goals of a Homogenous people."

Todd intervened. "Okay, Gavin, is there anything else you need to cover which will help Rick?"

"Well, I'm far from finished, but I'll concede the chair as long as I have a chance later to conclude."

"Thanks, we'll come back to you after our final topic. All right, Anton, let's hear your plan."

The chair scrapped, as Anton scooted back, grabbed his cane and, leaning heavily on it, rose and cast an intimidating stare toward Gavin, the scar in his left cheek flashing red as he began.

"First of all, the meek shall not inherit the Moon! We here at this table are all committed to doing whatever it takes to slip those surly bonds of Earth—to soar beyond the reach of the archaic rules and regulations of a planet which has failed miserable in its eons-long struggle to provide for the peaceful future of mankind.

"Now, with the exciting breakthroughs by our scientists in Repeller technology, we are able both to repel and attract with previously unimagined force—so much so that we will be able to reposition our Moon by pushing forcefully against the Earth. The trajectory of both will change—the Earth's slightly--our Moon's greatly. Since we, at present, have no atmosphere and, more importantly, no seas, we will fare much better. As Margaret has said, millions of people on Earth and hundreds of coastline cities will disappear.

"Yesterday's initial repositioning was very slight, but enough to get the Earth's attention. It has caused a few of their coastal cities to flood. We will present our petition for independence to them tonight. They should accept, considering the consequence of a rejection. However, if they do not, in short order, we will initiate our second stage of repositioning, which will cause considerable damage worldwide. Theirs should then be an easy choice. Granting us planetary status will cost them very little in the short run; refusing us will cause the immediate destruction of seaside cities everywhere.

"I have emphasized the importance of research and discovery to our future. Let me just reinforce that. For the moment, we hold the advantage in Repeller technology, but there is no doubt that the Earth will achieve the same results shortly and will try to force us back into our original subservient Moon orbit; we must accept the fact that we will be engaged in a never-ending technological struggle in order to maintain our independence."

Xiao Fang sat quietly through all these emotional outbursts, remaining patient, waiting for her time. Eventually the fire and brimstone speeches concluded.

Todd pointed to her. She rose, took one last sip of her tea, and nodded deferentially to the group. Placing her hands in front of her in a prayer-like position, she began, speaking softly with the smile that she carried with her at all times:

"I do not wish to disagree with any of my friends here, but I'd like to request what Americans call *a time out.* Mankind has been part of the Earth for tens of thousands of years, and if one were to contemplate the advances of early humanoids toward man's place in today's world, any rational person should be impressed by the ladder of success, which he has climbed. (And when I say *mankind* or use *he* in this talk, I am simply trying to be grammatically correct rather than socially aware.) The adversities mankind has met and overcome have been great and varied. Who is to say that these challenges represented a negative impact: is war always inherently evil and did plagues serve no beneficial purpose in this upward climb? Who is so sure that multiple languages or races have slowed man's march toward his present exalted state in the primate lineage?

"As one looks at history, it is no difficult stretch to argue that subtle and unanticipated advances in various fields of learning come following severe population declines, either due to war or disease. In the grand scheme of life, struggle, adversity and defeat represent the grease for the wheels of progress. Success comes from failure; improvements in life, from death; evil stimulates good. Are we not being too judgmental on the inhabitants of Earth or their progenitors? Are we, in our struggle here, refusing to accept that we are standing on the shoulders of giants?"

Xiao Fang paused to look at the group, assessing how her message was being received. She leaned forward and, with her delicate hand, reached for her teacup. Without drinking, but cradling it in her palms, she continued, coming to the point of this extemporaneous part of her talk: "Can we not achieve what we desire without threatening annihilation? Who are these savages we so vehemently despise? As one of the old sages of Earth said, I'm not sure whether it was Plato or Pogo, 'I have met the enemy, and he is us.'"

She paused here for a moment, took a deep breath and continued:

"And, yet, saying all of this does not decrease my determination to do whatever is necessary to achieve our goals. I am only suggesting that we pause and consider the best course of action."

Todd acknowledged her point but tried to maneuver her toward her assigned topic: "Xiao Fang, we will, of course, take a serious look at what you have said. But would you use the rest of your allotted time to elaborate upon your original scheduled topic of Music, Art and Literature for the new order?"

Anton jumped to his feet, rubbed his scar vigorously and turned toward Todd with noticeable agitation. "Why?" he shouted. "Why are we discussing music? Who cares about literature at this point? Why can't this trivia come up later, once we've achieved our military objective? Let's win the war before we waste our time on peace-time niceties."

Xiao Fang turned toward Anton and, bowing slightly in his direction, said "Oh, Mr. Anton, if we plan well for peace, there may be no need for war."

Anton threw up one of his hands in frustration, grabbed his cane with the other and headed toward the door. "I thought we were finished with this crap. I say we not only speak loudly, but we also carry a big stick."

He shuffled from the room in as dignified a way as a one-legged man can.

Todd quieted the murmuring group and then suggested a thirty-minute break. He beckoned to Singh Leh.

"Singh I'm going to get Anton back in here, and when we reconvene, would you review for everyone the salient points of today's meeting?"

With that, Todd left the room, his long strides leaving no doubt regarding his intention: Catch up with Anton and reunite him with the Guidance Committee.

Rick had listened, mesmerized by the intensity of the various speakers—and was completely taken aback by their plans for the incoming Moon population. Although he was acutely aware of the foibles rampant throughout both the advanced and more primitive parts of the globe, the Moon colonization and its problems was barely a blip on his radar. His life, in recent times, had been so encircled by the rapidly expanding nature of Earth's current problems and the frequent rollout of his own arsenal of talents—the Newall curse or blessing, depending on how one sees it, that he had little background to draw from regarding the intentions of the Moon's guardians.

On the other hand, he had seen most of the world, traveling by every conceivable means, including space and time jumping. He was an accomplished student of history, as well as an ardent fan of the latest technologies; but the planning for the Moon seemed, to him, more driven by sociology than anything else. He had never considered the ramifications of, the difficulty of, or the need for creating an entirely new and different society. Making conscious choices regarding religion, language, race—my God—overwhelming!

He knew that he was going to have to react to all that he had heard and seen this morning. He carried the cup of coffee that Todd had given him earlier, walked over to a distant window, and looked out at the Moonscape.

Lost in thought, he was startled when Todd put his hand on his shoulder and indicated that it was time to resume.

Singh Leh spent about thirty minutes covering the major points of their discussion. Anton had returned and was on his good behavior. Rick was not really listening to the speaker; he was preparing his response, knowing that the entire group was anxious to learn an outsider's reaction to their plans.

And his time came all too soon. He rose, moved to the spotlighted area, and began speaking without notes:

"First of all, as your designated outsider, I'd like to thank you for the confidence you are placing in me. My job, as I see it, is not to take sides, but simply to react. As with most people on Earth, I've been too busy with my own petty pursuits to think much about you here on the

Moon. I've heard of your struggles and sacrifices, and I've been aware of the occasional deaths associated with building a livable community in this extreme environment; but that's about as far as my knowledge and, frankly, my interest, extended.

"From what I've heard and from my own experience with Repeller technology, I'd say that your plans to achieve independence are almost a certainty. Maintaining this independence, as Anton has reminded you, is another story. As far as culling the Earth's humanity for the correct ingredients to populate the Moon—language, religion, intelligence, creativity and so on—these are fairly easy to achieve."

Rick paused here, waiting for the whispering to recede.

"Then we have the race problem. My solution for that may be too long-term and cumbersome. I haven't been given your time line, but if you are in no hurry, it's something to consider: With your language solution, you chose to reject all real ones and to use Esperanto, an artificially created language; do the same thing with race: create your own. Here's how I would suggest you proceed: Choose your best, brightest, and physically superior individuals and mate them, with this one caveat—no two of the same race will mate. The next step is to have these pregnant women settle on the Moon base. The children they birth will be of no single race. Over time, as these children mature, each would be required to mate with an individual unlike his or her racial composition.

"In short order, I'd say about two hundred years (and that is in short order considering the life of a planet) there will be but a single race. The original mothers will be returned to Earth at the maturity of their offspring.

"To further purify the Moon population, all current and future workers at any and every level, will be on a rotating schedule. None will be permitted to settle permanently here. As your indigenous population matures, they will be trained to assume the duties of the immigrants.

"You will have your Utopia. Although it has been tried unsuccessfully many times on Earth, here you will have no interference, no distractions—no competition. How could you fail?

"And, as a final comment, let me say, yes, you should succeed; but I wouldn't want to be a part of this new Moon order, no matter what you paid me or promised me!"

And with that, Rick walked over to Todd, shook his hand and headed toward the exit, much as Anton had done earlier.

CHAPTER 11

Returning to his room, Rick pulled his flight schedule from his jacket pocket—rechecked the departure time: "Not long now--but too damned long," he muttered half aloud. Removing his shoes and jacket, he lay on the bed, reviewing the meeting he had just walked out of: hard to believe, he thought--yeah, hard to believe! What suffocating plans. What a screwed up way to bring life to the Moon. Give me Earth with all its problems, any time!

Todd had promised a tour of the Colony at 2 p.m. so Rick decided on a power nap. The shuttle flight yesterday and the disorienting nature of the activities following his arrival had drained him of his usual morning energy. His eyes grew heavy, and sleep soon overtook his thoughts.

He awoke suddenly, startled by Todd roughly shaking him. "Hey, Rick, wake up, buddy. Come out of it! It's almost time for lunch. We don't want to take the tour on an empty stomach!"

Rick stood, his head groggy--stood with some dizziness. He staggered toward the bathroom and splashed cold water on his face. "Hey, I'm really sorry. What time is it? Damn! I've never slept that deeply!"

"Not a problem. Sorry about the intrusion, but when I knocked several times and got no answer, I was worried. Sometimes our artificial environment really disrupts a newcomer's natural circadian rhythms. You okay?"

"Yeah, sure—just a little groggy."

"Good enough," Todd said, slapping Rick on the back. He seemed honestly relieved. "See you in the cafeteria in about 15 minutes."

As the door closed on Todd, Rick looked at his WristAll. How could I have slept for two hours? Wow! That's never happened before, he thought. This Moon life could take some getting used to.

His flight was in about six hours, so he began piling items back in his shaving kit, packing his travel bag, and thinking about home; so much to do there—and so little incentive for him to stay a few extra days here, as Todd had suggested.

Breaking off his thoughts, he headed toward the cafeteria, a communal structure, built to hold several hundred diners at a time. At this juncture in Moon planning, there were only about seventy workers here, those with the expertise in assembling and using the 3-D Industrial Copiers, the workhorse of building the external features of the Moon's structure.

The din of the conversations sent a hum throughout the cavernous structure. Looking overhead, Rick could see the Earth in the distance, a blue beacon in the darkness; spotting Todd at the far end of the room, he headed in that direction.

"Glad to see that you're looking much better, Rick. We've got a lot to talk about. I thought the meeting went really well. After you left, we were able to nail down some critical decisions." Todd laughed. "Wait, that didn't come out quite right, did it? What I mean is that because of your comments, it became easier to see our way forward. One decision, though, you may not like. But remember, 'The good of the many overrides the good of the few.' Still, you may find it a problem. I hope not. I hope you can just go with the flow—be a good sport about it."

Rick pulled up a chair, but took his time sitting. Finally, he did. Looking across at Todd, he said, "Hell, man, the way you're bouncing that topic around, I'm almost certain I'm not going to like it!"

"Let's not go there yet," Todd said, smiling. "You know, your assessment gave everyone food for thought. It all seemed so natural—so doable-so reasonable. You had them eating out of your hand! Up until the end, that is. The shocker was when you confessed that you were not interested in becoming part of the new order. Sure, we're the first to admit that our ideas are not for everyone—Hell, it damned well *isn't* intended for everyone! But you laid out a way to achieve the perfect society—then rejected it. That was a painful moment for us."

After a short pause, Todd gave Rick a curious look. "Why?" he asked.

Rick laughed. "Well, since you're obviously the force behind this plan for a new world, it would be really hard for me to explain why. I'd do better with an impartial listener. How could you take my line of thought seriously?"

"Sure. Okay. I'm not impartial—but humor me—I really want to know why you're turning your back on us?"

"No, no—you misunderstand me. That's not my intention; I'm merely sharing that the type of society I heard explained today would not meet *my* needs. Really, were you expecting me to join with you?"

Todd looked up at the skylight for a long time. "I guess I had you figured all wrong. Yes, I did expect you to help us. And, yes, in case you're wondering, I have to admit, I got you here under false pretenses. I thought that once you heard us out, this kind of adventure—this real-life puzzle would be right up your alley. I remember all of the way-out things we used to do and figured you'd say, as you often did—'Why the hell not!' I'm guessing I'm one of a very few of your friends—maybe the only one—who's aware of your extraordinary talents. We need you, Rick."

"Not a chance." Rick picked up the menu. "Not a chance."

"Man, I'm really disappointed in you. I was hoping we could do this the easy way."

"What the Hell does that mean," Rick exploded, with obvious tension in his voice.

"I'm sorry. It's the disappointment talking. Forget l said that. Let's go ahead and order," Todd replied, with a finality in his voice, which Rick picked up and filed away for future reference.

The meal became a slow dance for both diners as they tried to maintain some semblance of cordiality, while at the same time being aware of the growing tension regarding the unspoken reality of the elephant in the room: the phrase—'I was hoping we could do it the easy way' ruining both their appetites.

The meal ended abruptly as Todd took an emergency incoming call, rose, and asked Rick to follow him.

Rick caught up with him just as he was leaving the cafeteria.

"What's wrong?"

Todd was almost running now. "It's Dr. Bronson--another stroke!"

Nothing more was said as they rode the elevator up two floors to the infirmary; and as they came to the waiting room, Todd pointed to a chair, "Wait here."

He continued on down the hall and passed through the double doors at the end.

"Dr. Bronson?" Rick said aloud. "Can't be that man--Dr. Ezra Bronson, the inventor of the Repeller? But then he recalled the comments by one of the members of the Guidance Committee regarding their gigantic leap in Repeller technology, but it didn't make much sense-- Bronson was old. No, Bronson was dead! It started coming back to Rick, now: a lab fire three years ago, late at night. Dr. Bronson was working alone. The fire consumed the entire floor. It was a week later that the cleanup squad finally found his body, burned beyond recognition, requiring a closed casket burial

"I'm going to need your help."

Rick looked up. Todd and a White Coat were standing over him. "We don't have much time," White Coat interjected.

"I know, I know. Come with me, Rick." And turning to his companion, "Find me a large ream of paper! Bring it to Bronson's room."

White Coat left; and grabbing Rick by the arm, Todd led him down the hallway, speaking rapidly as he walked: "I hope I can count on you, partner. Dr. Bronson's weakening fast. We need to access his mind--search for the formulas he's just completed on the latest Repeller breakthroughs. These formulas will put us years ahead of where the Earth is in their research."

Entering the hospital room, Rick was surprised to see Dr. Bronson lying on the bed, completely nude, no IVs and no monitors; He was breathing very shallow, mouth slack and eyes tightly closed.

Rick turned toward his old college roommate, "What is it you expect me to do? Looks like the man's dying."

"He *is* dying, dammit!" Todd exclaimed. "We don't have time for these question games. I know what you're capable of--I've seen you do it. We need you to tap into Bronson's mind, find the formulas and copy them down on the sheets that White Coat's bringing."

"What makes you think I even know what you're talking about?" Rick replied, in a whisper. He was not comfortable being forced into this life-and-death situation--was not sure how much Todd knew of his skills or how he even became aware of them.

"Dammit, Rick! Don't play the reluctant suitor with me. I was your roommate for two years--we traveled through Europe together. I've seen your parlor tricks—I've watched you go into casinos in Europe practically broke and come out with a grubstake for another month. A few times, when you were drunker than a skunk, I've seen you do amazing things with your mind! So cut the crap! Help us out here. Just do it--we're running out of time."

White Coat burst in, carrying a sheaf of paper, which Todd took and motioned for the aide to leave the room. Handing the papers to Rick, he said in a very even tone, "Our future depends on getting Bronson's formulas. I'm leaving you here alone, so you'd better damn well get started."

And with that pronouncement, Todd backed out of the room and softly closed the door.

Turning to face the dying man, Rick checked his WristAll. His Earthbound ship would be leaving in a few hours, and, at this point, he felt no assurance that he would be on it. As he looked around the room, he noted the total lack of medical equipment--there seemed to have been no attempt to resuscitate or even provide comfort for Bronson. How long has he been lying here? Rick wondered. When did he have his stroke? Did he even have a stroke? As these suspicions directed his thinking, he scanned the room looking for cameras or observation posts or see-through glass, wondering if, maybe, the people here on the Moon were more interested in him and in learning of his special abilities then accessing Bronson's so-called secret formulas.

At last, satisfied that he was alone and unobserved, he approached the bed. The man was old; that was for sure. Although he still had a full head of hair, his body seemed almost to have been shaved. No pubic hair. Rick lifted one of the man's arms: no hair under the armpits--all signs of advanced age. The body showed no indication of trauma, however. The toes and feet were noticeably blue, contrasting sharply with the extreme paleness of his skin, and there was a slight discoloration in the chest area--possible defibrillation? Rick checked for a pulse: there was none, yet his chest rose and fell. Manipulated? Hard to understand.

Not knowing what to expect, Rick gently entered the man's mind: it was still functioning, but barely. Finding Bronson's mental index, Rick searched, looking for anything suggesting Repeller technology. As he probed more deeply, he leaned closer, until their two heads almost touched. Rick braced himself, placing one hand on the doctor's chest. He could feel the breathing, shallow but steady. And to his surprise, he could now feel a heartbeat, a slight but steady rhythm.

As he found the area reserved for math and science and began separating the detritus from the relevant, the man's hand gripped Rick's wrist; and he thought he heard the one word 'don't.' Reversing his mind search, he slowly exited and looked down on Dr. Bronson, for now there was no doubt that it was he; and he realized that there *was* no hand gripping his wrist. Bronson was, as he had been from the time Rick entered the room, motionless, save for the almost imperceptible chest movement.

Rick checked the time again: he had been probing for over 30 minutes, an arduous task, considering the putrid condition of the outer part of the cortex. There was no smell, of course, but Rick's stomach was beginning to react to the sensation that he was picking up--one of rotting flesh.

Taking a deep breath, Rick returned to the same location in the brain where he had exited moments ago; and suddenly the information began flowing out like water from a broken spigot. He grabbed the sheets of paper and started making notes. He could not write as rapidly as the information was being transferred from Bronson's mind to his own, but he did the best he could. He saw the symbols as they appeared in his mind—he made no sense out of them, but he tried to copy faithfully, realizing that if he failed to get every signal, every squiggle correct that it would change the results of the program. He began sweating—blinking his eyes frequently to keep the stinging sensation from interfering with his task, and he plowed on. His back began to ache; he was having to write in such a cramped position. Finally he flopped on the hospital room floor, thinking that changing his position would confer some relief. Was there no end to the doctor's memory! After about an hour, the images seemed to be speeding up, but Rick noticed that they were also becoming less distinct.

Glancing quickly toward the location where White Coat had piled the ream of paper, he realized that, in short order, there would be nothing to write on. He mind began searching for an answer to that possibility: He could write on the tile or on the wall, if he had to! "Damn it all," he muttered. He hand was now beginning to cramp, his fingers curling up toward his palm. He frantically thought to himself: if I can make a spoon move, surely I can make this damn pen move on its own!

Finally, the cramps became so severe, that he had to drop the pen: he willed his mind to pick it up and continue. Suddenly there was a burst of information, which overpowered him. His eyes rolled back in his head, and he lost consciousness, his body slumping across that of Bronson's. Rick was exhausted. His shirt was sticking to his chest from his own sweat. The headache, a natural byproduct of such intense concentration, began its debilitating takeover. Rick's mind shut down. Bronson's right arm dangled lifelessly over the edge of the bed. There was a stillness about all of this--a finality that suggested an ending and, strangely enough, a beginning.

Rick was so engrossed in those final moments of his struggle that he did not see the one tear hit the pillow near Dr. Bronson's head, nor did he realize, a moment later, that he had stopped breathing.

$$\mathcal{E} = \frac{G}{2c^2} \frac{L - 3(L \cdot \hat{n})\,\hat{n}}{|r|^3}$$

$$Sg = -\frac{c^2}{4\pi G}\, Eg \times 4 Bg$$

$$Bg = \frac{G}{2c^4} \frac{L - 3(L \cdot \hat{n}/n)\,r/n}{n^3}$$

$$L = I\, b_{ALL}^w = \frac{2mn^2}{5} \frac{2\pi}{T}$$

$$\bullet \quad I_{bALL} = \frac{2mn^2}{5} \qquad\qquad \underline{Bg = 2\pi Gm}$$
$$5rc^2\,T$$

$$8\pi\left(T\,bd - T_{ac}\,\eta^{ac}\,\eta\,bd/2\right) = R\,bd$$

$$\cancel{}\ g^{ab} = \eta^{ab} + h^{ab}$$

$$u = \int \frac{P_0}{|X - X'|} d^3 X'$$

$$a_2 < 4 \times 10^{-7}$$

$$6\,\zeta_4 = 3 a_3 + 2\,\zeta_3$$

$$S = \frac{1}{16\pi G}\int (R - 2\Lambda)\sqrt{g}\,d^4x + S_m$$

$$T_{\mu\nu} = \frac{1}{G\pi G}\left(R_{\mu\nu} - \frac{1}{2}g^{\mu\nu} R + g^{\mu\nu}\Lambda\right)$$

CHAPTER 12

An hour later, Todd walked back into Bronson's room and found the disturbing scene: notes scattered all over the hospital room—no way to indicate the order in which they had been transcribed. Ignoring Rick and the doctor, Todd carefully gathered up the many sheets of paper, papers filled with undecipherable symbols and shapes--a trove of secrets which he was hoping his elite Moon team could properly collate, translate, and implement, making the Moon's Repellers far superior to anything mankind has yet seen.

Once he felt that information was secure, he turned his attention to Rick, still unconscious, lying across the corpse of Dr. Bronson. And only seconds after he pushed the red button on his WristAll, two aides appeared: "Remove the doctor and bring a confinement jacket for Mr. Newall."

The important thing, now, Todd knew, was to preserve these sheets of symbols which had been pulled from the dying man's mind, by a surprisingly tractable Rick, and get them to the Moon's analysts--let them decipher Bronson's last and reluctant gift to their Colony and finally, make this satellite a planet! But until they were able to find the connection between his latest breakthrough in technology and the reality of a super Repeller, Rick was staying put.

* * *

Three a.m. here on the Moon was no different than three a.m. on the Earth: the revelers of the night had retired and the morning shift was yet to rise. All was quiet, not even the lonely sound of a barking dog. Of course, there would be no sound like that on the Moon. Here, dogs were deemed to be a waste of food and space--a quaint relationship of millennia ago, which had no relevance in today's world.

And it was at 3 a.m. that Rick awoke: he was disoriented and confused but aware enough to ask himself if he had been drugged; yet, not cognizant enough to immediately realize where he was and what had happened.

Slowly he began to relive those final moments with Dr. Bronson, and he suddenly felt his agonizing migraine and accepted the fact that it was usually the result of a mind intervention. When he tried to raise his hand to his throbbing head, he could not. His entire upper body was immobilized!

"What the hell!" He shouted. "What the hell!" He shouted again.

Immediately, the overhead lights came on, blinding him. He felt a warm hand on his forehead.

"Mr. Newall, are you okay? Are you awake?"

The voice evoked concern and relief.

Squinting his eyes, he looked into the face of the most arresting countenance he had ever seen.

"My name is Kim Su. I'm assigned to you. How do you feel?"

Rick could sense true concern on her part.

"Get me out of this damned restraining harness! Why am I tied up, and where is Todd Eyanni?" And looking around, he asked, "Where's Dr. Bronson?"

Kim answered none of these questions. "We've been so worried about you!" She whispered, leaning close to him to check an instrument protruding from his left nostril.

Rick struggled to free himself from his constraints--but to no avail. He was frustrated and angry--and he had to use the bathroom!

"I have to go!" He said. "Get me out of this bed."

"It's okay, Mr. Newall. Just go. You've been fitted with a catheter. So it's okay--you can go."

"A catheter! My God! What in the Hell are you doing to me?"

"Oh, you're so much better now. I can just tell. The first week, we thought you weren't going to make it."

"First week! That makes no sense. Yesterday, I was with Todd and Dr. Bronson."

"I'll call Mr. Eyanni. He'll explain. But you *have* been under my care for the last two weeks. You were a very sick man, Mr. Newall."

And with that ominous pronouncement, Kim left the room.

Rick was alone again and more frustrated than ever. "Two weeks! Two damned weeks! Bull shit!" He tried to lift his arm to read the time and date.

"Rick! You're awake! Thank heaven." Todd rushed over, grabbing Rick by both shoulders: "By God, I think we're out of the woods with you, finally!"

"What's going on? Why am I tied up? What's this crap about me being here for two weeks?"

"Turn over on your side. Let's get this restraining system off you. You can imagine how worried we've all been. I had no idea how dangerous what I was asking you to do would be." Rick turned on his side and was soon free.

"No, wait, Rick--the catheter!" Kim came running in: both her hands went under the sheets--gentle hands--and soon he was untethered.

While in the bathroom, he looked at himself in the mirror: gaunt, disheveled, eyes bloodshot--could I have been unconscious for two weeks? He looked down at his penis, black and blue and swollen and paining him as he urinated. He looked up to check his WristAll for the time and date, but his wrist was bare.

After splashing water on his face and running his wet hands through his hair, he opened the bathroom door to find himself alone again. Only then did it come to him that he was totally nude, the bruises on his left arm standing out in contrast to the rest of his pale white body. "I've had an IV in my arm," he noted, in surprise.

Escape--he thought--I need to get the hell out of here. "I need to jump," he whispered to himself: he inhaled deeply and started the teleportation sequence; but when he realized that he would be jumping totally nude, he aborted.

Walking over to the closet, he hoped to find his clothes--anybody's clothes! His were there, and he dressed quickly--everything but his shoes. Hell, he thought, I can jump without shoes--but just as he made that decision, Todd returned.

"You're looking better, already. I'll bet you're hungry--two weeks is a long time without food! You've probably noticed the marks on your arm. We engaged a nutrition drip for you. Come on, let's head to the cafeteria, my treat!"

Rick *was* hungry--and he saw no threat to that offer--unless they were planning to poison him! Not likely, he thought. They could have done that while I was unconscious.

* * *

The cafeteria looked especially cavernous at 5 a.m. –empty, except for the two of them. Glancing up towards the skylights, Rick was again surprised at the beauty of the Earth framed in the observation platform window--the Earth, still there, still home.

In the distance, they could hear the kitchen staff as they began preparing for the onslaught of the breakfast crowd. Kim handed Rick his shoes, indicating that she would talk to the cooks about their order. In a few minutes, she returned with two large mugs of coffee.

Rick let the mug warm both his hands as he stared off in space, trying to reconstruct the missing hours--or days--after he collapsed on Dr. Bronson's body.

Todd had been as close to a brother as anyone in his life, and now Rick was beginning to fear him--to mistrust his intentions, no matter what cover story he was concocting. There's no way, in hell, I could have been unconscious for two weeks, he thought. No way--and yet, he wasn't sure. He needed his WristAll to verify the current time and date. From habit, he looked down toward his wrist, and Todd caught this moment and laughed.

"I know you're wondering where your Link is, Rick. The first few days you were thrashing about so badly that you caught the band on a monitor, ripped it right off. Don't worry, we'll have another fitted for you."

"Where are the Earth and Moon clocks that I noticed earlier hanging over the archway?"

"Oh yeah," Todd replied thoughtfully, "We were not expecting *that* problem. When we engaged the Moon's Repellers, in order to change our orbit slightly, they somehow affected the clocks. Neither clock was accurate after that. We're now trying to figure out exactly what happened." Changing the subject smoothly, he segued into breakfast: "Drink your coffee before it gets cold. What would you like to eat? I know it's a little early for breakfast, but it's closer than lunch." Todd laughed and took a sip of his own coffee, giving no sign of any nefarious intent.

Rick had, years ago, made a promise to himself that he would not invade the thoughts of those closest to him--and that included Todd, but now he was sorely tempted. Only the fact that he knew he could jump back to Earth at the first sign of danger kept him from breaking his promise.

"Todd, Dr. Bronson died several years ago in a fire on Earth. How could he be here?" Rick was trying to put the pieces of the puzzle together.

"I know. That worked out pretty well, didn't it! I'm proud of that one! I think our Moon's version of the CIA compares very favorably with that of the old Israeli Mossad network. We'd been negotiating with Bronson for some time to come unite with our cause—join the Colony and help us achieve our independence. But... I guess he was just too Earth bound to see that the future of science and technology and independence lay here. We could have kidnapped him, but that would've revealed our hand--our plan to achieve Repeller superiority and, too, it would be much more difficult to physically transport him here in that manner." Todd looked out at the Earth's menacing closeness, satisfied that the Guidance Committee had planned well. "So, forgive me for paraphrasing Mark Twain, 'Rumors of his death were somewhat premature.'"

"Are you saying that Dr. Bronson did *not* want to be here?" Rick asked.

"That's putting it mildly! But after the fire and a few other not-so-veiled threats, he saw our determination and eventually realized that he had little choice: He came and began providing us with valuable solutions to an earlier Repeller problem, but there never was that breakthrough which would allow us to sail like a galactic cruiser to the orbit of our choice.

"As you know from attending the Guidance Committee's meeting, all of our members think we have achieved this breakthrough--that we can change our orbit with impunity. I'll have to admit that I have slightly misled them, but, at the time, we had to solve the problems, which you addressed at the meeting. The breakthrough, I felt, was right around the corner! Now, I'm in a bind—I sort of painted myself into a corner. That's why I had to get you here--under false pretenses, I know; but you'll have to agree, it was a better choice than we gave Dr. Bronson."

The breakfast order that Kim finally had to place, personally, with the kitchen staff eventually arrived, so they both ate with an intense relish.

Enjoying the last few gulps of his coffee, Rick pushed back his chair: "When's the next cruiser to Earth? I need to be on it. I promised my dad that I'd be home within just a few days."

"I wish I could tell you that that wouldn't be a problem--but you can't leave--none of us can. Earth is playing hardball."

"What do you mean?"

"Well, when we changed our orbit slightly, it caused some problems on Earth--you know--tidal waves, earthquakes. Not that that was an earthshaking surprise for them. We *had* told them what we intended to do! Pardon the pun about earthshaking, but we thought that Earth would negotiate with us--would allow us more independence."

"So what's your next step?"

"We've got to decipher Bronson's information and use it to increase the power of our Repellers. I haven't shared this with you, but..." And here Todd paused, seeming to try to decide in his own mind if, in fact, he did want to share. He leaned toward Rick and took him by the arm: "You're one of us now--you can't return to Earth--you might as well know the entire plan:"

He stood, a strapping man, six feet tall, blonde hair, sporting an anachronistic golden tan. "Walk with me, Rick. We'll go down to the Tactical Room--you need to know more than you do--much more, if you're going to help us."

Ten stories down, the elevator stopped, and they exited into a beehive of activity: lights were flashing; technicians were running to and fro--more a feel of bedlam than organized activity.

Out of nowhere, an orange-suited man with a headset grabbed Todd. "You've got to see this," he screamed, as he yanked Todd forward to a viewing platform at the end of the room. "They've launched!" He exclaimed.

"Trajectory?" Todd asked.

"Can't tell yet, but the launch's from one of their space platforms and it's a big boy--hydrogen--multiple warhead!"

"Can we stop it?" Todd shouted back.

"If it's a solo, we should be okay."

"Very well, sound the alarm. Get everybody down deep. We'll have to wait it out. When do you expect impact?"

"Depends on its speed."

"Ballpark! Dammit, ballpark! Give me a window!" Rick hissed, his face turning bright red.

"Two to three hours."

He thought a minute: "How long before we can engage the Repellers?"

"We can start trying to slow it now, or we can wait and really give it a jolt as it gets closer."

"Recommendation."

"Wait and hit it hard in an hour or so."

"Do it, then."

Rick watched all this with a growing appreciation for his old roommate and a better understanding of the pecking order here on the Moon. College was not so long ago, time wise, but an eternity from the responsibilities that Todd had accepted here.

The room regained its businesslike atmosphere as everyone focused on the job at hand. Having nothing to do in the two hours or so before impact, Rick began thinking back to those earlier years when he and Todd had bonded--became best friends. Those early college years and the time spent bumming their way across Europe--carefree and irresponsible—well, not really irresponsible, just having no responsibilities: so recent and yet so long ago.

Much earlier in his life, Rick had been reminded by his dad that he might experience some physical or emotional changes as he matured--it might happen, he explained--but then again, it might not happen. He was no clearer than that. But he did emphasize that any unusual changes in his life should be treated with controlled responsibility! Controlled responsibility? —That combination of words seemed odd to Rick back then and his reaction had not changed.

About the age of 13, his first wet dream occurred; he figured that's what his dad was alluding to; and at the age of 14 when he fell head over heels in love with his English teacher, he felt that this must also be one of the things his dad was talking about.

But nothing prepared him for May 19, a few days before his 15th birthday: he had been yanked from his high school baseball team for allowing a hitter to take second base on a routine single to right field--his position. This occurred in the first inning before he ever had a chance to bat, and he knew he would be sitting on the second string's bench for the next eight innings, unable to rejoin or to help his team. He was embarrassed by his actions on the field but furious with the coach for not giving him another chance. He sat inning after inning and finally drifted into a daydream: Fillmore's ice cream parlor. He began salivating for a banana split! Suddenly he was there. He was sitting at the corner table where he and his dad often sat. Knowing that this was just a daydream, he blinked a few times; still, the smell of the chocolate syrup covering the Sunday at the next table seemed so real:

he looked over--he *was still* at Fillmore's, and the smell of chocolate was very real! After a minute or two, he realized that this had to be what his dad was actually talking about! It wasn't the wet dream, the puppy love, or the other seemingly dramatic incidents that most kids think of--things that turned out to be of no real consequence in the long run. This was different: Name another kid who could think himself to different location!

Why wouldn't his dad have just come out and explained some of the things that would happen? "Hey, Ricky--you going to order something or you just going to sit there?"

Rick looked up, startled from his reflections: Jody, his cousin, who worked at Fillmore's, was standing there by his table, hands on her hips, just grinning.

"You look kinda goofy, Ricky. You want something or not?"

"Banana split!" He blurted out.

And a few minutes later, as he finished off his favorite Filmore treat, he thought, *Dad, guess what just happened to me?*

And his dad replied, *I know son, I know. Congratulations! I didn't want to worry you about something that might never occur. I had no idea whether you would have the gift or not.* For many years, Rick and his dad had been able to communicate with each other in this way. It seemed so natural, that Rick thought all fathers and sons were able to do it. *There's more to come, Ricky, you're on your way! Don't be surprised and don't hold back--embrace whatever happens!"*

Ten stories down in the Moon's Tactical Room, Rick smiled. His dad was right--there was more--much more in the way of surprises that came his way and were still coming his way!

"Locked on!" Someone shouted.

"Wait... Wait... Not yet--a few more... Abort! Abort! Their rocket's changing course. It's turning away from us."

The chatter stopped, as everyone watched the screen--sure enough, the red dot, which represented the rocket, sporting the latest weaponry, was indeed altering its trajectory.

"The damned things going into orbit! Son of a bitch! It's going to be circling the Moon." The orange suited man exclaimed. "The orbit will be just below our horizon. The Repeller's force field doesn't bend--goes in a straight line, so we can't target it! We've got a rocket with a hydrogen warhead orbiting the Moon, and there's not a damn thing we can do about it!"

"Check and mate," Todd whispered.

"What's all of this mean for us?" Rick asked.

Todd sighed, "Instead of having hours to react to Earth's threat, we'll have minutes." And after a long pause, "It really doesn't make sense: The negotiations were going well--good faith negotiations, I was sure. Why would they react with such aggression?" And after another pause, he stood and began pacing, "Sure, we *were* aggressive with our Repeller usage--moving us ever so slightly away from the Earth--but we told them what we were planning to do. It's as if they knew we would now be helpless--as though someone here told Earth that our technology was not really up to speed."

Orange Suit came over. "Mr. Eyanni, I have an idea."

"Go."

"We could lock our Repellers on to the Earth--let them know that if they target us, we can destroy their coastal cities--maybe more."

"Will they know if we *have* locked on?"

"Absolutely!"

"I don't want to continue making aggressive moves--at some point, one of us will have to pull the trigger--let's do this: lock on, hold the lock for five seconds, then disengage."

Turning to Rick, he said, "We'll be staying here for some time. I expect that you've noticed Kim Su over there in the corner--she'll show you where your quarters are down here. Might as well get some rest."

Rick was overwhelmed by all of this: the suddenness, the seriousness, the...

Kim Su saw Todd leave, and she approached Rick: "You don't look good--you need rest. Come with me."

He looked around the War Room one last time, realizing that there was nothing he could contribute. The life or death of this Colony was out of his hands--out of his control. All of the men and women here who were doing their part to survive and to prosper were not the chosen ones, would not inherit the Moon and all its promise; they were simply caretakers, intent on their jobs of ensuring its survival for those who would come later.

"Come. Come, Mr. Newall, you walk too slow! You need your 10,000 steps. I must help you stay healthy. It's my job, you know."

Rick smiled at this attentive young Asian gal who was so serious about life--about his life, in particular.

"Kim, how did you get the job of babysitting me?"

She entered the elevator, waited for him, and then inserted her thumb into the slot and said 'home.'

They descended another two levels. She paused by the last room at the end of a long corridor and touched her WristAll twice. A door appeared in the wall and began to slide open.

"Your room for a while," she said, extending her hand toward the opening, inviting him to enter.

A sterile 10 x 10 room greeted him: a single bed, open-wall storage, a Visoscreen across from the bed, a door leading to what Rick assumed was the bathroom, and one chair across from the bed. No pictures, no decorations, nothing to soften the room.

Kim opened the bathroom door: "You shower, then sleep." Sounded like a command to Rick, but one he approved of. Once in the 5 x 6 chamber, he stripped, slipped under the shower and turned the water on high, letting it ease the stress out of his body and soul. However, after 60 seconds, it automatically shut off. Of course, he thought--water on the Moon would be at a premium. Seeing a robe on a hook near the towel stand, he grabbed it and returned to his bedroom. Kim was still sitting in the one chair by the bed, and she rose quickly: "I'll take the robe--you go to bed."

Rick hesitated, Kim understood his hesitation and replied, "I see your body while you were sick--no problem--you go to bed."

He did so, but felt even more self-conscious than the time when he was in the Middle East and Abigail made him remove his tunic and washed his body and face.

CHAPTER 13

Time lost its hold on him--he drifted quickly into an exhausted and troubled sleep—re-experiencing his exploration of the mind of Dr. Bronson. Equations tumbled over and over in his dreams, and he began mouthing them louder and louder as they paraded before him.

Kim Su turned the background music off, grabbed a notebook from the lamp stand and, sitting on the edge of Rick's bed, began copying the equation as he vocalized them in his dream. This continued for thirty minutes or so; finally, Rick drifted deeper into the REM phase of sleep. Kim looked over the copious notes she had jotted down, shook her head in a very negative fashion, opened the door, and handed the notebook, along with additional papers, which she hurriedly pulled from her valise, to someone waiting just outside.

With one fluid motion, she removed her smock, stood for a moment at the edge of the bed totally nude, took a purposeful breath, and joined Rick.

Hours later or was it days later--Rick no longer felt that he could judge the lapse of time accurately, he awoke and realized that he was not alone in his bed. Somewhat confused, from his deep sleep, it took a few moments to accept the truth: Kim Su was next to him, fast asleep, one leg on top of the sheet draped across his own legs.

He did not move. His body did not, but his mind was trying desperately to make sense of the situation: did he and Kim Su make love? Why else would she be in bed? Was he being set up some way? Blackmailed? He tried to reconstruct the interval from the time he and Kim walked into the room to the moment that he drifted off to sleep. As far as he could recall, there was absolutely nothing sexual in either his or Kim's words or actions. Moving Kim's leg gently off his own, he quietly headed for the bathroom and closed the door. The light came on automatically, and he observed himself in the mirror above the sink: he still looked gaunt and haggard, and his eyes were red and sunken in. He turned to the toilet and started to pee. The action reignited the burning sensation throughout his penis. He looked down and observed that it was still red and swollen. Not an erection, just puffy and sore. No way I could've made love, Rick decided. He finished, threw some water on his face, and opened the door. Standing sleepily on the other side of the bed was Kim Su, unclothed and unabashed.

"I think I love you." She said in a whisper.

She put her hands around his waist and pulled him to her."

"You will take me with you, yes?" She whispered in his ear.

He did not whisper: "Take you where? What's going on?"

Kim put her finger to his lips, and then pulled him closer, pressing her breasts against his chest. "You must take me," she said, with fear in her voice.

Rick replied and this time he did whisper: "What are you afraid of?"

Kim's forehead was against his chest--he could feel her tears as they slid toward his stomach.

"What are you afraid of?" He again whispered.

"This is an evil place. I want to go home."

"You know we can't," Rick reasoned. "We're stuck here. We're practically at war with the Earth. There's a rocket circling us right now, with a hydrogen warhead--we have nowhere to go."

She pulled him back into the bathroom, shut the door, and still whispering in his ear, shared a secret that would cause her death were her actions to be known: "There's no rocket. There's no standoff with Earth." She paused, "and you haven't been here two weeks!"

"What?"

"It's just a show for you—for your benefit. I don't know why they want you to think we're on the brink of war, or why you need to believe you've been here for weeks--I just know there's evil everywhere, and I want out of this place."

"And was your sleeping with me part of their plan--did they ask you to do that?"

"Yes. I didn't want to--well, I did, but I didn't want to because I knew, somehow, it would end up hurting you."

"How could what we do behind closed doors make any difference to anybody?"

"I don't know--promise me you won't believe anything they say-- don't do anything they ask you to do."

"By they, do you mean Todd?"

"Todd--the Guidance Committee--everyone here--there are some good people, I know there are--but how do you know who? You don't. So don't trust anybody."

"Not even you?"

She looked up into Rick's eyes—"Especially not me."

And with that final revelation, she returned to the bedroom, slipped on her smock, and left.

Left Rick with quite a problem:

He pondered, as he, too, dressed: so I can't believe Todd--or anyone else who tells me I've been here for two weeks. I can't trust anything I saw in the Tactical Room, regarding Earth's belligerent activities, and I can't believe Kim who told me about all these deceptions.

One good thing did come of this night in his 10 x 10 bedroom: he had gotten a restful night's sleep. Though he didn't look the part as evidenced by his own preview of himself moments ago in the bathroom mirror, he did feel much better. His quick mind began spinning out situations related to these several problems--began, also, formulating possible solutions to each of the dilemmas. Based upon what he thought the reality of his predicament was, he saw no advantage to remaining here--could think of no disadvantage to just jumping home--except one: Kim Su.

What to make of her? Who was she, really? Was she assigned to him with some devious plan in mind? But what could that be? Was she supposed to make him fall in love with her, give him a reason for staying, for becoming part of this eccentric community? Was she simply feeding information back to Todd and to the Guidance Committee? And what about the Guidance Committee: were their speakers and the posturing that went on, for his benefit? Was their agenda much more than he understood, as he listened to them? They seemed united on several fronts and yet divided on a few, as well. Did any of their stated plans and goals reflect their true intentions; and why, exactly, was he invited here anyway?

Of course, they could be having the same discussion regarding him. He realized that. After all, he did push for the invitation--did use his and Todd's friendship to wrangle a free ride to the Moon Colony. Maybe they were observing him with a jaundiced eye, as well, trying to ferret out *his* motives; after all, it was obvious that they had secrets that the Earth should not be privy to--and who more likely to smuggle these secrets back and share them with Earth then he.

Then again, maybe he was leaping to conclusions, seeing intrigue and subterfuge where there was nothing.

If he were to jump home, how would Todd and the others interpret his disappearance? As far as Rick knew, Todd was aware of only one of his many unusual talents, that of being able to pick up the thoughts of others--a secret Rick foolishly must have revealed in one of their drunken escapades to Vegas or in Europe. He wasn't a card counter, he simply was able to see through the eyes of the dealer what cards he held--and those winnings had helped him finance their travels around Europe.

But to my immediate plans, Rick thought: I need to go home--but go without revealing my jumping capability. I need to be a rocket-ship passenger, but how to do that?

He was now on lockdown with the others as this real or concocted rocket-orbiting scenario played out. I think I'll do some eyeballing, he said to himself--see where the chinks in their armor are.

As he walked down the long and deserted corridor towards the Tactical Room, Todd burst through the connecting door, obviously surprised to see Rick up and about. It was a dangerous tightrope that Todd was walking with his old friend--needing his help but not willing, at least at this point, to reveal any official long-term goals. Dr. Bronson held the key to the Colony's success, and he had provided them, in the time that he was here, with invaluable Repeller breakthroughs. His stroke and recent death brought any further advances to a standstill. Bronson was a savvy scientist who understood that his value to this lunar undertaking was on solid grounds only as long as he continued to advance the technology that they needed to maintain superiority over Earth. It was essential that the Earth revoke their charter, the one which compelled them to abide by all of its regulations and to continue to share the mutual defense pact--an agreement to be the watchdog of the outer perimeter—be the early warning system, protecting the Earth from distant invaders. The mindset of the leaders on Earth was that if mankind could develop the technology to colonize the moon, beings from other planets of our solar systems, or elsewhere, would no doubt sooner or later discover these advances and attempt to mitigate Earth's astral ambitions.

It did not take Todd long to recognize Bronson's method of operation, which was to announce, on a regular basis, small achievements--limited improvements but no major breakthroughs. Todd suspected that Bronson had already completed the entire advanced Repeller concept and could, at any time, make the most powerful defensive or offensive weapon the Earth had ever seen.

The formulas Rick had pulled from the recalcitrant mind of the good doctor confirmed Todd's suspicion, but… And it was a challenge: the beginning information that Rick had jotted down just before Bronson's death was elementary and sometimes simply garbage; however, the formulas which Kim Su copied at Rick's bedside, as he talked aloud during a troubled sleep, were, with a few early exceptions, extremely to the point and of major importance to the breakthrough they needed. It was, at this time, that Todd realized that in those final moments there by Bronson's bedside, Rick had been able to drain the scientist's mind and had the information, whether he realized it or not. In some compartment of his mind rested the technical information needed to make the Moon's offensive weaponry the deciding factor in this standoff with Earth.

The ruse of the rocket attack was simply to buy time and to try to convert Rick--to help him see the advantage of working with the Colony and cast his lot in a long-term way with them. Kim Su was a beginning, an opening gambit: she was Bronson's right-hand researcher, his muse; he loved her like a daughter, but, more than that, he respected and drew from her as a scientist, younger by far, but just as qualified as he to unlock of the mysteries of the electromagnetic principles on which the Repeller was based. Kim Su's job was, by hook or crook--or love--to learn what Rick was holding.

And at the same time that Kim was trying her approach, Todd was intent on trying his own: greeting Rick warmly, he led him through the vacant hallways to the elevator, explaining their latest discovery: the rocket that was circling the Moon was really not an offensive weapon but a scientific probe, and the Earth was simply using the Moon to slingshot the rocket to a final destination, which was on a need to know basis. He continued, with convincing honesty, to explain that the information which Rick had written down there in Bronson's hospital room did not provide any breakthrough moment, but that he felt that critical information *was* transferred by Bronson during his dying moments.

Rick understood what he was suggesting, but had no memory of anything like that happening, and was fairly sure that this was another ploy of some kind--another attempt to get Rick to do the bidding of the Guidance Committee. Because of Kim's earlier heads-up and due to his natural suspicions, he decided to use Todd's problem to his advantage.

"Todd, if I have the information, its not stored in a way that I can access it; so I don't see the point of your getting your hopes up."

Todd replied, (and he felt that Rick was feeding right into his plans): "Would you be willing to undergo Hypnotic Transitioning? One of our staff has made excellent strides in this area, and it will help us know, once and for all, if there's any undocumented information which Dr. Bronson has given you."

"Sure, I'm willing to help—I know what I told the Guidance Committee, but just because I don't agree with the philosophy of the group doesn't mean that I don't think it's a viable plan for all of you here. And being able to protect yourself from outside forces is a prerogative of any group who wants to be free from the rule of others, benign or otherwise. But I think you can accomplish what you want without this cranial intrusion that you're recommending. That's a pretty powerful and invasive method. I think I can get to your answers, if there are any, in a different way: I'm very good at self-hypnosis; and, in the past, I've been able to bring up information that I didn't realize I possessed."

Rick was thinking, planning, and talking at the same time. He needed leverage--and this opening might get him back to Earth.

"If you trust me, Todd, I think I'll be able to get what you need."

"Absolutely, Rick, we go back a long way--of course, I trust you!"

"Okay, to do this, I have to get back to Earth, to my room, to my comfort zone--to my safety net. I *must* feel completely un-threatened in order to open up my thoughts and to probe as deeply as this will require--and I need Kim Su."

"Damn, Rick, we can make you feel safe here--we can provide you with anything you need, plus Kim's already here."

"Sorry, it's too late for that. Think of everything that's happened since I arrived--being strapped down as soon as the cruiser docked because of the repositioning of the Moon's orbit, the pressure of the Guidance team meeting, your threat of doing it your way or the highway, the sudden announcement that a rocket from Earth was targeting us here—that's really too much to overcome." Rick paused. Todd had taken a step back and crossed his arms--not a good sign.

After a few seconds, he held out his hand: "Okay. One final condition to your request: I have to go with you--be with you, just in case."

Rick grinned, "Just like the old days. And our new team includes Kim Su?"

"All right, dammit, all right--it *will* include Kim Su." They shook hands and walked out on to the Observatory Deck, Todd's arm over Rick's shoulder.

CHAPTER 14

Mark looked in the mirror of the hospital bathroom. Both his eyes were bloodshot and swollen; and the area from his forehead to his frown was a dark blue. The patch over his nose announced more pain. He could not lean forward toward the mirror for a closer look because of the fire in his ribcage.

"I've got the wheel chair for you, Mr. Newall—do you have everything?"

"Everything but my pants," he growled—"and I don't need any wheel chair!"

"Hospital policy," Linda replied. "If you won't agree to the wheel chair, I'm not giving you your pants."

"No wheel chair!"

Nurse Linda continued with her haranguing—"Come on, Mr. Newall, it's time to go.

"Get in the wheel chair--your family's waiting downstairs by your car."

"I can walk!" Rick grumped. "I don't want a wheel chair—don't need a wheel chair! I'm not a damned invalid!"

Mark could feel the cold air against his exposed rear end. "These ass-flashing gowns! Why can't we wear pajamas—this is embarrassing!"

"Hospital policy," Linda said, again.

Except in the bedroom, a man feels very disarmed by such exposure. "Okay, I'll sit in your precious wheelchair—now give me my pants!"

Having made her point and won the case, Linda wheeled Mark, with an authoritative demeanor, to the elevator and down to the waiting area.

Mark's two girls, Jody and Kimmy ran toward him as the elevator opened. Each grabbed an arm and hoisted him from the chair. They then came closer, hoping for a big hug.

"No! Wait! Don't touch me!"

They stepped back, eyes widening in confusion.

"What's wrong, Daddy?" Jody asked.

"I'm sorry, honey, my ribs are killing me. Let me just get to the car on my own."

Mark's wife, Peggy, came running over from the cashier's office: "What's all the yelling about?" She was a tall, slender blonde, who exuded strength and vigor.

They all hovered about Mark, each looking for a way to help him to the car. In obvious pain, he hobbled toward the passenger-side door, which Kimmy was holding open, and grabbing the top of the door, he turned his back to the seat and very slowly eased himself into a quite uncomfortable position.

They all got in, almost afraid to close the doors, fearful of jarring the grouchy patient. Peggy turned to the screen, pushed the HOME button and CONSERVATIVE MODE, her goal being to get the man she loved home with as little pain as possible.

As the kids sat in the back seat giggling over who knows what teenage humor, Peggy put her arm through Mark's, being sure to keep her distance from those ribs. Despite the pain, he smiled, feeling himself being engulfed in a warm cocoon of happiness. Was it the pills Nurse Linda had given him just before leaving his room, or was it an afterglow from his escape from the coffin—or was it simply the presence of his loving family?

It offered a few minutes of silent reflection: How often, over his lifetime, had he dodged death? Was he leading a charmed life or were events building exorable toward that final moment of truth?

I no longer need the money, he thought. Why am I still following the beating of Sam's drum? Why can't I follow my own? I'm not a kid any more--let Rick step into my shoes. Weld can show him the ropes.

But after a moment, he reconsidered, "Ah," he sighed, "That's not fair—maybe just a few more years—what the hell!"

Sam, Weld, and Rick were waiting in Mark and Peggy's condo, as they arrived, and walked over as if to hug him.

"Keep your hands off me!" he warned. "You guys have caused me enough pain already. Can't you see, I'm practically dying!" He moved slowly toward a lounge chair, then thought better of it and settled in a straight-backed kitchen chair. They all gathered around him, Peggy bringing another couple pills and a glass of water.

Sam seemed almost on the verge of crying: "Mark, I don't know what to say—I'm really sorry that I put you in that Corridor."

"What I'd like to hear," Mark grinned through the pain, "is for you to say, 'Your fired!'"

Everyone began to laugh, as did Mark. "Damn!" he suddenly yelled, as pain shot through his rib cage. "No more jokes, please!

"Okay, you guys, I know you've been dodging talking about what happened in the Corridor. The last thing that I remember is having someone try to squeeze the life out of me. Take me through it from there."

And, once the ladies had left the room, they did.

"The most satisfying thing about this whole misadventure," Sam reflected, "is that we did find out who that Entity is."

Sam continued, "The Sniffer you put together led us on a wild chase through an elaborate series of twist and turns—Hell, it seemed that the thing expected that we would try to follow it! And, by god, we did—we followed it all the way to Petersburg, Kentucky! And when we came out in that auditorium, the Sniffer pointed right at Todd Eyanni—no question about that. Now we know who we're dealing with."

"If that's the case, why'd you send Rick to the Moon?" Weld asked.

"Damn it, Weld! You know the answer to that one—you know that Todd and Rick were very close for a long time—through college and several years after that. Rick still looks at Todd as his best friend. We have to convince him that Todd is the one who has to go into that lead coffin—and that we have to drop it into the Marianne Trench! He's resisting like crazy! Thinks it would be murder. We can't continue with our plan unless he's on board--you guys understand that."

"How was the Moon trip supposed to change the way he thinks? Seems to me, it'd just bring them closer together. I don't get your logic. Of course," Weld paused here, "what am I talking about, I rarely get your logic, even in the simplest of cases!"

Sam sat, pulling his chair close to his brother: "He's actually more intuitive than we are—he'll let us know if there's anything suspicious going on up there: he'll feel it—he's better at that than we are. We've talked about that before."

"I know, but he's just a kid."

"No—" Sam reminded Weld. "He hasn't been a kid in a long while."

CHAPTER 15

As they left the Hebron cruiser terminal, Todd wanted to go immediately to Rick's Condo to begin the self-hypnosis--secure the remainder of Dr. Bronson's formulas and return to the Moon where his analysts and translators would transfer the formula from the paper to the practical. He was desperate to have an operational Super Repeller to deal with Earth and its nefarious goals before they become too confident and too demanding.

Rick was, on the other hand, in no hurry. (He was finally convinced that he had not been on the Moon for weeks!) The last 48 hours had been hectic, even for a young man: he was drained and needed to cocoon for at least 24 hours—to shut out reality and retreat to his innermost comfort level--all very necessary, too, before he made any attempt at recovering the alleged formulas still in his head!

Kim Su clung to his arm like it was a life raft, and looking at her, Rick could see the pain and fear that her entire body was projecting.

Todd was expecting to bed down at Rick's condo, staying close to the man who carried the secrets to the Super Repeller; he made that very clear as they hailed a cab and headed across the river to Cincinnati: he was not being unreasonable. After all, that *was* the deal that he and Rick had negotiated.

However, the more Rick thought about it, the less inclined he was to follow through with that particular plan. He needed the feeling of safety and security--and with his old roommate under his roof, he knew that that would not be possible; therefore, on the cab ride to River Road, he explained what he needed in order to find success at the self-hypnosis. He needed Kim Su and space--lots of space!

Kim was necessary to put whatever Rick was able to recall on paper in a legible form and to separate Bronson's garbled dying rants from the essence of his breakthroughs.

In a way, Todd had no solid ground from which to negotiate. He realized that fact all along but was hoping that Rick had not. It was clear, now, that Rick was back within the arms of mother Earth--that he was free to simply walk away. It was a delicate dance, but Todd had danced before; so he agreed to check into a nearby hotel and be available 24/7.

The cab dropped Kim and Rick off and Todd continued on.

As soon as Todd was out of sight, Rick could feel the tension leaving Kim's body. She relaxed her hold on his arm and breathed a visible sigh of relief.

"I'm never going back." She stated flatly.

On the elevator headed up to his Condo, Rick began looking at his situation: it was a two-bedroom layout, so there should be no awkwardness about Kim staying with him; but his mind pulled up the image of her standing by his bed on the Moon, naked and unembarrassed. He had to admit to himself that the thought of her real or imaginary attraction was appealing. Yet, as she had warned him, *Trust no one, including me.*

It was the age-old decision: follow the lofty instincts of reason—or those of lust!

Kim broke his sexual reverie as they entered the Condo: "Where's my bedroom and my bathroom?"

On the one hand, Rick felt relieved that some boundaries were being established, but on the other hand…

The Moon Cruiser had a strict limit on the weight of each traveler's bag, but since Rick came with little and left, headed home, with nothing, Kim Su was able to pack two pieces of luggage--one would have thought she was planning to stay indefinitely. Rick paid no attention to that fact--Todd, however, did, making a mental note to be sure that when he returned, she was with him--willingly, if possible, but with him, whatever it took!

Kim asked Rick if they could order in--could have pizza, a treat not yet a staple in the Moon's cafeteria. While she was showering, he called LaRosa's, which was just down the road, closer to the Reds' stadium, and ordered a sausage and cheese pizza with extra mushrooms.

It must be a busy night for LaRosa's, Rick thought, because Kim was out of the shower and in Rick's extra robe well before it came. He gave her his bank stick and headed for the shower, himself.

Unlike the water conservation of the Moon, Earth still allowed for free access to an unregulated supply. Being on the Ohio River was a plus, of course, and the Cincinnati Waterworks was known nationally for having the purest, best tasting water of any major city.

Over pizza, Kim shared some of her life: born in California of immigrant parents, schooled at the University of California and MIT, going from there to a special graduate program for gifted physicists and finally attaining her PhD at the age of 25. She was immediately offered employment with the Ezra Bronson group and, struck by the fame of Dr. Bronson, she signed on immediately. After he died in that horrible flash fire in his lab, she was offered a position as assistant professor at the Moon's School of Technology at twice what Dr. Bronson's organization was paying her.

Once on the Moon, she was overwhelmed to learn that Dr. Bronson was not dead but was here helping the Guidance Committee develop an offensive military weapon; and she soon realized that she had became a virtual prisoner, along with him. They were treated extremely well, however, and paid as promised. The only down part of her life here was that she could never return to Earth for any reason. Even when her father died in an accident on the Santa Monica Freeway, she was prohibited from attending his funeral.

When Rick arrived and when she realized how critical he was to the Committee, she determined to do whatever was necessary to ingratiate herself with him and, hopefully, to be able to leave for home when he did.

In order to implement this strategy, she made some very unusual plans; and when the dominoes began to fall in her favor, she acted:

Knowing that Rick had been unable to provide anything useful from the information he extracted from Dr. Bronson, she determined to use this void as a way to finagle a ticket home!

She explained to Todd that she would throw herself at Rick in hopes of being close to him just in case he would share additional information that he remembered while exploring Dr. Bronson's mind.

Todd bought into her plan.

Where her deception comes into play is when she spends the night with Rick and ostensibly scribbles down formulas as he talks in his sleep. She then hands them to one of Todd's men who was waiting just outside Rick's bedroom door.

But this ploy convinced both that there were undiscovered Bronson formulas still lurking in Rick's subconscious: it was a far-out plan, but it had gotten their attention; hopefully, it would get her to Earth. She realized, after taking down Rick's sleep-induced mumblings that the reality of a major contribution toward Todd's goal was in doubt.

Compounding these misgivings was the realization that she had no plan B--was not able to think of anything, which would extricate her from this dead-end scheme. As good as Rick might be with his self-hypnosis technique, she knew that he would not be able to provide anything of value. However, the ace up her sleeve was that Todd was correct when he began suspecting that Dr. Bronson was spoon-feeding the Committee information in small doses, when he actually had already solved the Super Repeller problem and had, in his files, a design for the prototype. *And*, Kim Su had brought Bronson's entire file with her!

As she enjoyed her pizza, she began strategizing: If she could again sleep with Rick and could convince him that he talked in his sleep, revealing additional Bronson information, she would have these 'new formulas' on hand-written sheets which he could pass on to Todd. Hopefully Todd would be satisfied with this and want to return to the Moon immediately to work on a prototype.

The part of her plan she was having trouble with was how to convince Todd that she no longer needed to be with him on the Moon. She could, of course, simply refuse to leave with him--but he was a devious man. Bronson had also refused to go, and look what good that did him!

Over Graeter's ice cream, which Rick always kept in his freezer, Kim asked, "When are you going to try your self-hypnosis?"

Rick grinned: "I'm in no hurry, are you?"

She giggled, coyly, beginning her strategy of bedding him as soon as was possible.

"Me either," she replied. "I could stay here with you forever!"

Rick was surprised by that revelation--pleased, but surprised. But then he heard her voice in his head, again: *Don't trust anybody, especially me!*

Women! He thought. Where and when can you ever trust a woman? His mind went back, thinking of various relationships he'd had--not recently, of course. It'd been a very busy, yet very inactive year for him as far as the ladies were concerned. Was it that they were not to be trusted or had he simply run across a few unsavory characters? He wasn't sure. How could he ever be sure? How does one separate the chaff from the wheat?

Sometimes, he felt that he should simply swear off women as Uncle Weld had done; but then, he reconsidered: his uncle had not decided to have no more relationships because they were disastrous. His was the opposite: he did not want to go through the pain again of losing someone he deeply loved. And this thought brought up another for Rick: after his uncles had found and lost the loves of their lives—they were willing to remarry, even knowing the eventual heartache it would cause them when they would outlive their soul mates. What message should that leave him?

Kim broke into his reverie: "We don't have to mess up both of your bedrooms, if you don't want to."

He didn't see that one coming: her initial comments, as she entered the Condo, asking where her bedroom and her bathroom were had convinced Rick that she was distancing herself from him. Now this! Who can figure out women, he thought, followed immediately by his reply, a simple masculine reflex!

"No, I hate making up beds, anyway--one bed will be fine!"

So the next morning over breakfast at *The Day After* restaurant, with Rick and Todd, she handed over a thick bundle of handwritten notes, supposedly, taken while Rick talked in his sleep.

Todd took them with him, after breakfast, back to his hotel, spent an hour reviewing their potential and, surprisingly, asked Rick if he would drive him to the Cruiser section of the Hebron airport.

In his mind, he decided that there was no point in creating a scene, demanding that Kim return with him, knowing that she was really no farther away from the Moon than his decision to have her there.

CHAPTER 16

Helayne wasn't sure what to do—and that was most unusual for her. Having finished her research on Gary Poore and Bill Grote, she sat looking at the results on her computer. Rick had asked her to go back to the birth of each and thoroughly vet them–even take a look at their parents. She had done all that; but being really good at what you do can sometimes come back to bite you.

Gary was still the model citizen–no dirt on him at all–the Teflon man, if there ever was one. On the other hand, there was Bill Grote, the Petersburg native–the well- loved mayor. He was the unraveling enigma. Rick may have been more prescient then he knew!

The problem Helayne had to deal with was not whether Bill was dirty or not, it was how to handle this delicate father-son relationship: Rick had indicated that his father was not to know about this research. And his father was Sam, her boss. And Rick was pressuring her to revisit this original research. Ordinarily, she would follow protocol: the one who assigned her a job would get the results. Problem was that Rick was tied up with Todd Eyanni and the Moon problems now–and this information she had uncovered could possibly be time sensitive. The dilemma: should she tell Sam what Rick had asked her to do and, critically important, was the question--how to share the results and with whom?

From the original research on Bill Grote, she had discovered that he was a grave robber, stealing artifacts from Petersburg's Indian relics and making a small fortune as he went. She had only gone back twenty years. Rick had asked her to go back to their births–and that's where she hit pay dirt.

Bill's personal history was easy to research the twenty years of the original request; but when she continued further back, she ran into a wall. Bill Grote simply did not exist twenty-six years ago. She could find no records. Nothing. Nowhere in the state or federal database did his name appear. She prided herself in being able to find anyone who was ever born–her methods had been honed from a quarter century of sleuthing–and as unaccustomed as she was to failure, she was now looking at it.

But that was only the beginning of the mystery: as she pulled up his driver's license year after year, going back those traceable twenty-five years, she became aware of the fact that he had not aged. His picture from a quarter of a century ago showed essentially the same man as he was today–a balding, droopy eyed, senior citizen. It didn't make sense.

She had no idea what all this meant, but she realized she had to share this information with Sam and share it immediately.

He would not be happy; Rick would not be happy. Yet, if this research helped them solve a bigger problem, maybe they'd both feel that she had done the right thing. All these scenes flashed through her mind as she took the elevator from her office to Sam's command center.

As she entered his conference room, he rose from the table to meet her, positioned a chair for her at the table, which held a cup of steaming mocha coffee and one chocolate chip cookie. She smiled at his thoughtfulness. It had been that way from her first day on the job–almost like Sam was wooing her–enticing her with his charms, as a lover would–yet theirs was not that sort of relationship. It was an affair of the heart for both, but an innocent one with mutually defined boundaries.

"Helayne, we need to do this more often," Sam said, smiling, as he moved to his spot across from her. "How's the family doing?"

Helayne had kept him up to date on the New York wedding of her daughter Ellen, with all its drama and potential pitfalls, as well as the adventures of their younger son, Isaac who was somewhere in the world operating as a recent recruit for Mossad. And, of course, Abe, her beloved husband, who refused to remain retired.

But this was a business meeting, so neither went in the direction of family and friends. "Sam I've got a bucket full of problems—but they're very interesting ones."

"Go." Sam, replied, urging her on.

"Well, first of all…."

* * *

After walking Helayne to the door, Sam returned to his desk, originally a square grand piano from before the war—a piano which would never stay in tune, but which, when converted into a mammoth desk, garnered everyone's attention. He sat for thirty minutes reviewing Helayne's report: for some reason, he was not upset that Rick had gone over his head to request a follow-up on Bill Grote, but he was disturbed by the implications that this request suggested.

He had been certain that Todd Eyanni was the answer to the array of destruction, which had been laying parts of the United States and some other areas to waste.

The fact that Todd was born on the same day that the coffin was breached, releasing the evil on the Earth and the fact that all of the unexplained destruction occurred during the perigee phase of the Moon, drew him to this young man. Also, the fact that Todd worked in some capacity on the Moon cinched the deal, for Sam: Todd was more than a person of interest--all circumstantial, as Rick had argued, sure, but damn convincing—especially after the Sniffer, in the auditorium, pointed directly to the front of the stage where Todd was standing.

But, now, the new information, which Helayne had uncovered, seemed to throw a wrench in his conclusions--in his convincing series of circumstances.

Two other possibilities occurred to Sam: 1. Todd and Bill Grote were working together or 2. The destructive force behind all of their problems was Bill, not Todd.

Plus, upon further thought, the Sniffer was not pointing at Todd, specifically; it was directed at the front of the stage, where both Todd and the mayor were standing. Maybe it was not Todd who needed to be in that coffin.

Sam knew that he had to meet face-to-face with Bill Grote, but under what pretenses? From what Helayne had said, Grote had not changed in a quarter of a century, physically; it was true, he realized, that there are some people who look old at thirty but don't change much for the *next* thirty years.

Weld had met earlier with the Judge Executive, Gary Poore and with Bill—so, the question was, could he play off of that encounter? They would already be familiar with the Newall name.

And then there was Petersburg, the river town--the place where the earthquake occurred and where the coffin was hidden. Too much had happened there over the years not to take a closer look at it--to walk the streets and get a feel for the people.

"Rivertown!" Sam exclaimed, aloud. "That's my entrée—our shipping depends on the Ohio River. Why not a satellite business in Petersburg? That's my reason for talking to the mayor."

Helayne had just returned to her office and was beginning the research on several important topics, which, prior to Rick's requests, were on the front burner; and that's when her communicator sounded. After listing to the caller for a few minutes and taking notes furiously, the conversation ended: "Damn," she said with some exasperation, "I should ask for a raise." It had been Sam, wanting her to give him a thorough history of Petersburg, Kentucky. Why doesn't he just go on Google? She thought.

Sam was able to call and talk with the Mayor of Petersburg, explaining that, as the owner of Newall Shipping, he was interested in opening a satellite location downriver, and that Petersburg was one of the towns of interest. Could they meet to discuss the possibilities?

Sam was expecting excitement and cooperation from the mayor— what he got was backpedaling.

"Oh, I'm sorry, Mr. Newall, a business like you have would spoil our small-town atmosphere—would eventually bring undesirables to our area. I'm sorry, but it would really disrupt our way of life."

Interesting, Sam thought. So there's something about Petersburg, he doesn't want outsiders to see—to experience. No mayor would simply flat out refuse to talk to a man who has indicated an interest in investing ten million dollars in opening a business in his town.

Of the three Newall brothers, Mark was the most empathic—could seek out feelings no matter how well hidden—could enter the most secret parts of the mind to ferret out good or evil. All three had this ability, but in varying degrees; and it had worked well for them over the years. For example, Mark did not excel at jumping—which was Sam's strongest—each had a strength and a weakness.

Sam called an emergency meeting for the next day at 9 a.m. He needed all of their talents for a thorough investigation of Petersburg.

After summarizing the conversation he'd had with Mayor Grote, he laid out the plan: a walking tour by the three through Petersburg—during the middle of the day: talk to as many people as possible—observe and record everything ordinary and everything strange.

Weld, who was a morning person, had just come from his hour-long run down the hiking trail, which ran from the center of Cincinnati itself all the way out to Lunken Airport. He was still on his endorphin high. "Petersburg has only 1000 people—we don't all three need to go there—I can handle it myself. Give me half a day—I'll canvass the entire town in that length of time."

"I'm sure you could," Sam said, chuckling; "but I want overkill. The assignment I gave Helayne to go back twenty years on Poore and Grote seemed more than sufficient to dig up any of their weaknesses—but as Rick taught me, sometimes it's best to pull out all the stops. From now on, overkill is my middle name.

"Besides," Sam continued, "If I were to have just one of us go there, it would be Mark. No offense, Weld."

"None taken—just trying to be efficient."

"Okay, what are we looking for?" Mark asked.

"That just it," Sam replied, with a puzzled frown and a shake of his head. "I don't know. Just keep your mind open to all that you feel. I know that can be overwhelming, especially if we encounter a lot of townspeople and extremes of emotion."

"What's our cover story?" Weld asked. "We're in Petersburg, walking the streets, talking to as many people as we can. Why are we there?"

"Same as I told the mayor—we're scouting out a place for a satellite company—a location with easy access both by highway and by river; and with I 275 within five minutes of Petersburg, this really would make a great location. Maybe this should not be just a cover story. What you think?"

Mark gave a thumbs up, but then cautioned, "Let's cross that bridge after our tour. You've really got me curious about this little town and its people."

Sam indicated that he had done a Google search of the Petersburg streets, and that he'd also found a mom-and-pop restaurant called *Third and Main*. He looked up at his brothers and said, "Let's meet at the *Third and Main* restaurant tomorrow at 9 a.m. Now, we need to go over our strategy." Sam laid a map out on the conference table and started pointing at various streets. "I'll take everything from the river through Third Street. Weld, you take Eighth Street through 12th, and Mark, you cover the heart of the town—Fourth Street through Seventh.

"Next we need a list of similar questions, in case the townspeople start comparing notes. If we really were going to try to open a warehouse here, what do we need to know?" Sam asked.

Weld began, "We'll need a workforce; so what is the unemployment rate, locally? What skills do the potential workers have? Can we gain access to the river for our boats and barges? What is the local tax rate? What city restrictions are there on building? And then we need to know the attitude of the townspeople regarding a new business going in."

Sam grinned, "I can tell that you're the analytical one. Good. Now, Mark, you need to ask questions that will elicit emotions. How would they feel about an Ohio company settling in Petersburg? How do they feel about foreigners—about people of a different race or religion or language? You're good at that sort of thing. We need to know what they worry about, what they cherish, what they fear."

One of the things that made the team so effective was that their talents complemented each other, and Sam played off their strengths and weaknesses as he made assignments. By the next morning, at 9 a.m., they were having breakfast at the *Third and Main* restaurant in the heart of Petersburg. There were about a dozen other customers in various stages of eating; so, as they finished their meal, Sam said, "Let's just sit here a few minutes–see what we can pick up from everyone-- listen to their feelings."

There was an elderly couple at the corner table; and as is so often the case in a lengthy marriage, communications retreat and introspection and silence reign.

Mark hovered on the edges of their awareness, listening, as the man was saying over and over "Our mayor is my friend–our mayor is my friend...."

Mark switch to the old lady with the same results.

Weld zeroed in on the two lovebirds in the center who looked as though they had spent a very rewarding night together. It took some time to get behind their constant jabbering in order to hear what they were really thinking–to feel what they were feeling: "The mayor is my friend–the mayor is my friend..."

Sam broke up the session. "Okay, let's get out of here and beat the pavement. That was a great breakfast! Let's come back here again for lunch before we head home."

There had not been a rain for some weeks, and the Ohio River, here at Petersburg, was well below its bank, running downstream at under 4 miles an hour. Sam looked out across its width toward Lawrenceburg, Indiana, the little town on the opposite shore. This would really be a great place for a second site, he thought.

For the entire length of First Street there was no sign of activity. The homes looked as though they probably were all on the National Historic Register. They were well cared for--their yards were neatly manicured–just no sign of life.

On Second Street, a tall raggedy man was mowing one of the lawns, but when he saw Sam, he hurried inside.

Sam continued walking. As he made the turn on Third Street, he saw, for the first time, the tower of what was obviously a church; but on a closer look, was it really a church? The peak of the steeple was a much narrower protrusion, almost like an antenna reaching skyward.

Walking up the steps of the building, Sam read the large sign by the door: "Petersburg United Church–all are welcome"; and with that greeting, Sam tried the door.

Locked.

After a circle around the building, he continued down Third Street. A middle-aged man was coming toward him, smiling, "Looking for someone?" he asked.

Sam rejoined, "Yes, I'm looking for you!" just as a way to start the conversation. "I was wanting to talk to someone who's been around here for a few years."

"That's me, all right," the gentleman chuckled. "I've been here almost a quarter of a century. How can I help you?"

Sam kept his distance, not intruding on the man's thoughts or feelings–not yet, but there was something familiar about him–it was his voice.

Sam began with a compliment–never hurts. "Beautiful town you have here."

The gentleman smiled and nodded.

"If you have a few minutes, I'd like to ask a question or two."

"Not a problem–I'm headed down to the river–got a park bench there where I have breakfast every morning."

"Sure," Sam replied, matching the man's stride, and turning as he walked, he extended his hand. "I'm Sam Newall, by the way."

"You know, I talked with someone recently–someone with that last name Newall

Construction or Newall Shipping--something like that. I'm Bill Grote."

Sam did a double take. "Damn! You really are the man I'm looking for. I was the one you talked to about a business in your town. But, I'm

222

telling you, now that I've seen Petersburg, I think what I really want is to live here."

As they approached the river, Sam looked across at Lawrenceburg again–and a flood of memories came back: he could see *Hillforest*, built in 1855--an old river captain's house with a widow's walk; it belonged originally to Thomas Gaff and was an Italian Renaissance home, the front porch made to look like the deck of a steamboat. Sam had met his wife, Ann, on a blind date, one of the many he had had after his second wife's death; and he, by this juncture in his dating experience, expected nothing; in fact he was about ready to chuck the dating ritual altogether and remain single.

But Ann had hit him like a Tulsa truck–love at first sight, as they say. It was in that old captain's house across the river that he had proposed to her. Those memories, for a moment, were so profound that he forgot his mission–was unaware that he was probably walking beside Evil itself. It had to be either Todd or the kindly gentleman to his left.

As they approached the mayor's bench, there was a young lady waiting for him. By her side was a four-wheeled cart with two breakfasts laid out.

Sam notice that immediately and turned to the mayor, "Maybe this isn't a good time for our talk–I see you're expecting someone."

"I was expecting you, Mr. Newall. Please join me."

This wasn't going the way Sam wanted it to go. The mayor was controlling this conversation and the meeting–not what Sam was accustomed to at all.

"So, Mr. Newall, I assume you're here to convince me to promote your business--to walk it through the political hazards and the legal steps?"

"Not really, Mayor. I was just so curious about why you would be opposed to my business and, by the way, my money coming to your town. I had to see Petersburg, myself."

"Oh, no doubt about it–this would be a great town for you and your business–it just isn't great for us." The mayor bit into his croissant and, at the same time, reached for his coffee–black, no sugar.

"Not a problem," Sam replied, in his most accepting tone. "Not a problem. After you turned me down, I talked to the folks across the river. Lawrenceburg had no qualms about accommodating my ten million dollars."

"I'm glad to hear that," the mayor slapped his knee with some enthusiasm. "So, I guess your interest in us is over, then?"

"On the contrary," Sam responded. "With our business going to Lawrenceburg, I'm thinking about moving either there or here; and you know, after walking the streets, breathing the fresh air, and looking at Petersburg's wonderful panorama ..." pausing for emphasis, Sam looked at Mayor Grote. "After doing all that, I've decided, I want to settle here. In addition, it's just far away enough from my business across the river, that I'll have a little peace and quiet here, I'm sure."

The mayor grew quite pensive, "I don't think that's a great idea, Mr. Newall. Not at all."

Sam continued, undeterred, "I've not seen any for-sale signs anywhere. Are you aware of any properties I could look at?"

"There aren't any," the mayor said, with a finality that got Sam's attention. "I handle all the property transfers, and I can tell you, nothing is available."

"Oh, I'm very familiar with human nature; and I'm sure if the word got out, here in Petersburg, that I wanted a home—and that money was no object, I would very soon have a dozen offers on my desk."

Grote chuckled, "Well, yes, under those circumstances, that might be true elsewhere—but, take my word for it, even if you offered a million dollars for one of these little places, you'd find no takers. Go ahead, make the offer—I know my town. Spend your money across the river, Mr. Newall."

"Do you mind if I walk around and talk to some of the folks—or is that a problem for you?"

"It's a problem. You see, this is a very interesting town. All the men are gone--out on their jobs; and I'm afraid if you walk up to any one of these houses and ring the doorbell, you'll shortly have a weapon pointed at you by the little lady behind the door. No offense, Mr. Newall, but why don't you go home? We're a strange little town, a throwback to more peaceful times—a time when the men went to work and the women raised the gardens and the kids and were not afraid to defend themselves."

Sam stood up, brushed some croissant crumbs from his pants and said an intentionally pleasant good-bye to the mayor.

CHAPTER 17

The three brothers met again outside *Third and Main* in Petersburg but decided to discuss their impressions of the town at the *Tousey House* restaurant in Burlington, just a few miles away. They wanted no eavesdropping--or remote hidden recording devices. *Tousey House* was a favorite restaurant for many of Boone County's folks and much of the rest of the state. It was named after the original builder and resident, Erastus Tousey, a Burlington businessman in the 1800's. The building was saved from demolition in the 1980's by, then, Judge Executive Bruce Ferguson, one of the distant predecessors of the current Judge Executive, Gary Poore. From that restoration until today, the *Tousey House* had been known for its outstanding fried chicken, biscuits, and gravy—a meal each of the Newalls now eagerly anticipated.

Sam, as usual, began, "I thought we might learn something about Petersburg—now I'm sure of it."

"Mark, you go first—yours is the impression I really want."

"I've never come across anything like what I felt as I walk the streets. It was a palpable fear–I wasn't able to talk to anyone–I saw a few people, but as soon as they realized I was headed in their direction, they literally ran from me."

Mark waved the server down and ordered a second drink. "Sorry," he apologized to his brothers, "but this has really unnerved me—you can't imagine how I felt to be exposed to that much fear—it was so...so real…so personal! I'm sure you felt it, too; except, as you know, with me the effects are really heightened. And the other peculiar thing was that, above the fear present throughout the town, there was a superimposed thought, which was—well, it almost seemed like it was being broadcast to everyone. The thought was 'The mayor is your friend.'"

Sam and Weld both spoke at once. "Exactly, yes. Very distinct—almost like a voice, whispering this message—'The mayor is your friend.' Totally weird."

"Mark, I'd like you to do some research—maybe snooping is a better word. The local church wasn't on your list, but there's something strange there—it holds some secret; I can't figure what it is. I could feel it as I came close to the building. Can you make one of your stealth drones available? I'd like it to spend a week over that church. I want to know, on a daily basis, what the drone sees, hears, concludes. Also, find out where the mayor lives. Make that one of the drone's priorities."

"I can have it flying tomorrow," Mark said, taking a long drink from his bourbon and coke.

"No, not tomorrow," Sam responded. "Let's wait—I'm getting one of my famous hunches—let me think a minute."

The other two brothers looked at each other. "Here we go," Mark laughed. "He's dangerous when he heads for his hunch app."

"The thing that worries me," Weld replied, "Whenever he gets these hunches, we get stuck with some kind of pain-in-the-ass dangerous job."

Sam just grinned, nodding, "Have your fun—these hunches have also saved your skin a few times.

"I think, somehow, this town is connected to the problems that occurred during the Moon's perigee, and after today's encounter with the mayor, I believe *he* may be worth watching more closely.

"I want that drone flying during the week the Moon comes closest to the Earth. And I want it running silent—no communication with it or from it—passive observation only."

* * *

The perigee came and went. There were no unexplained disturbances on the Earth, and no detectable activities around the church. The only thing of interest that it reported on, once it returned to the Newall warehouse, was that the mayor was putting an addition on to his house.

* * *

Rick's major reason for the Moon trip was to be able to vindicate Todd—to prove that his dad's suspicions were simply that and were not grounded in any verifiable truth, but when he returned to Earth, along with his old roommate, and as Sam tried to pin him down regarding the results of his trip, Rick dodged an outright explanation, saying, rather, that he and Todd had some unfinished business, and that he would know more in a little while.

Sam finally relented. "All right, all right—we can't put anyone in the coffin with no real proof, but we have to keep looking; we have to build a case that will stand up to the death sentence. In other words, we stay on high alert, and we keep our guard up."

Todd returned to the Moon a day later, seemingly satisfied with his visit, and Rick said no more about any misgivings regarding his old roommate.

All of the Newalls continued to stay vigilant, day after day, for the next month. But it was futile. And then came an unexpected call.

* * *

"Mr. Newall, I've been thinking about our last meeting and about the good that you might bring to our town. I'd like to meet with you and your team—let's see if we can make both of our dreams come true. Please tell me you haven't committed to Lawrenceburg, Indiana, yet."

Sam was almost speechless, but his mind was already looking for an angle. To say that Sam did not trust Grote, the mayor of Petersburg, would be an understatement. Why *now*, Sam thought. What's really behind this offer? Personal greed would be at the top of my list for this guy—'for the good of the community' would be at the bottom. Play along, play along, he thought.

"No, no, we're taking our time. There are several river towns around you that have shown some interest. May I ask what caused you to reconsider?"

"As I said—the good of the town--that's my main concern. Also, I'll have to admit, when you threw out the line 'money is no object,' I began thinking. I'm not getting any younger; and if you have vetted me as I have you, it's easy to see that I don't have the means to retire. I think you might be able to help both me and my town at the same time, and that's the honest truth."

"I'm with you, so far," Sam replied, noncommittally.

"Good. How about the four of you, Weld, Mark, and Rick coming to my house for a powwow?"

"Sounds like a plan," Sam agreed. "Let me see when I can clear all of their schedules, and I'll give you a call."

"I'll be waiting to hear from you." And with that, the conversation ended; and Sam's various scenarios began. He ran through all the possibilities that could be viable--sifting and sorting the many reasons the mayor might have had for making the call.

The faith he had in his team was very strong, and he exercised that faith now by bouncing this unexpected turn of events off them. They needed to look at all the advantages and disadvantages of such a get-together; and most important, they had to determine what the mayor was really up to. His stated reasons were all very human and all very believable, and yet all too predictable. But if his overt reasons did not reflect his real motive, then they had to divine his actual intent?

And so he admitted that he had done his homework. He knew the team members by name and wanted all of them present. On the surface, that's necessary if he expected to sell his logic to Newall Shipping. On the other hand, to have all of the Newalls under the same roof of their potential enemy—not a wise move on the part of the Newalls....

After an hour of going back and forth with these various uncertainties, Sam decided on safety. He would go alone. The drone would be flying above the mayor's house, riding shotgun, as it were. Weld and Mark and Rick would maintain mind contact— seeing what Sam saw, experiencing what he experienced; and they would be close by, Repellers at the ready. And whether it made any difference or not, Sam would insist on having the meeting at a time his team would calculate–a time when the Moon was at its farthest distance from the Earth.

The meeting was arranged, the time determined, and Sam outlined what he needed from the mayor: a list of sites, price ranges, political and legal pitfalls, as well as other minor items. He was also striving to pick up the emotions of the mayor, especially since he planned to tell him that he would be coming alone.

He would drive. Weld, Mark and Rick would jump to their positions which would, in effect, have them located on the front, back and side of the mayor's house--but discreetly hidden in the woods which surrounded the property.

Rick, remembering his time on the Moon and suspecting that Todd had doctored his food or his beverage, cautioned his dad not to eat or accept any drink.

All carried the new version of the Repellers, and they were set on STUN and on HOLD except for Sam. As much as he wanted to carry, he could not justify it. Since he had sent Mark, unarmed, into the Corridor to face the Evil hiding there, how could he now go to the mayor's house and carry a weapon? Additionally, if the mayor *was*, in fact, the Evil one, he might detect the threat and not reveal himself for who or what he really was.

The new coffin was readied and loaded on a semi-trailer, along with a small crane to lift the top of the coffin up enough to shove the body inside. The semi would remain at the crest of the Route 20 hill, just above Petersburg and, when called, would be at the mayor's house within two minutes.

CHAPTER 18

Sam knocked on the mayor's door, feeling confident, knowing that his team had the house surrounded.

"Sam, come in, come in. I'm so glad you're willing to hear me out." The mayor extended his right hand and with the other gave Sam a good-old-boy pat on the back, as he ushered them into his living room. Mayor Grote seemed at ease, trying to put on his most agreeable face. "You know, Sam, now that were going to work together, you've got to try some of my very rare Kentucky bourbon—it's called Pappy Van Winkle! Let me get a couple glasses."

Sam heard Rick's thoughts: "Don't do it, Dad."

The mayor returned with two glasses and an unopened bottle. "Do you mind opening it? I'll get us some ice."

Sam opened the beautifully labeled container and poured a couple fingers in each glass.

"I hope you were able to free up the others. Are Rick, Mark, and Weld coming together?" The Mayor asked, as he returned with the ice.

"Sorry, I couldn't make it work," Sam replied, "but since the company *is* in my name, only, they aren't really necessary."

"Will they be part of the new company you want to build here?"

"Sure."

"Then it *is* necessary for them to be part of this discussion," Grote said, with a very slight testiness in his voice.

233

Oh, this is really going well, Sam thought to himself.

"I see your point," Sam agreed. "I'll make sure that they're at the next meeting. But at least, now, we can do some preliminary work."

"Well, I suppose so," the mayor concluded. "Come on, let's go back to my office–just built it over the last month. In fact, this will be the first meeting I've had here; some initiation, huh?" He laughed and motioned for Sam to precede him into the room. As Sam did so, he heard the door slam behind him.

What the hell, he thought. You getting all this, Mark?

No answer.

In fact, the silence was so complete, that it reminded him of the room where he'd had his hearing tested recently. Yeah, he reflected, my first sign of ageing—but the only one, he was quick to point out. He *was* having trouble, he had to admit, especially in restaurants, with many conversations going on near him. Understanding the speakers at his own table was becoming more difficult.

Sam looked around for a window or back door. There was neither. He did not want to jump, revealing that part of himself; so he sat at the mayor's desk, in his chair, unafraid, at this point, but definitely puzzled. He tried to put himself in the mayor's shoes. Why would he do this? How was he planning to make this episode part of an overall plan? He was obviously unaware of Sam's abilities—or was he using this a test to see what Sam would or could do?

He sat for an hour, playing out these various situations in his mind. He could not see how locking him in here was, in any way, to the mayor's advantage—it certainly had revealed his hand, but to what end?

Finally, Sam stood, took a deep breath, and calibrated. His jump would take him to the edge of the woods where Mark was waiting.

* * *

The three Newalls watched Sam go into the house and listened to the interesting banter between the mayor and him; and then suddenly, there was silence. They tried separately, then together to contact him. They could not. It didn't make sense, because they had been able to stay in touch mentally despite the distance from one another and from the house. And there was Sam, fifty yards away, and they could not hear him.

At the edge of the woods, across Route 20 from the mayor's house, they gathered to try to solve this problem.

Hearing a noise by the mayor's garage, they turned to see his BMW headed toward them and then turn left on to Route 20, away from Petersburg.

"Did you get a good look inside that car?" Mark asked, speaking to Rick who was out closer to the road.

"Pretty good. The mayor seemed alone, and unless Dad was in the trunk, he's still in the house."

* * *

Sam hit the wall hard, almost knocking himself out. Lying there semi-conscious, he did not yet realize, that although he had tried to jump from the room, he could not; he had been thrown back, head and nose bleeding, onto the mayor's expensive Persian rug.

At about the same time, Rick hit the outside wall and lay sprawled in the hedge at the base of the office addition. Weld and Mark rushed over and brought him to his feet, and although he was not unconscious, he was definitely addled.

"Damn, what's going on?" Mark asked. "What happened to you?" Neither brother could grasp the idea that Rick, of all people, had not been able to jump to the interior of the house.

"Let me lie down for a minute," Rick said, with some hoarseness in his voice. Then, looking at Weld, he asked, "Did you see me jump? What happened?"

"Hell, Rick, you hit the side of the damned house."

"I'll bet Dad's done the same thing, if he's still inside. So now what do we do?"

Weld answered the question even before it was asked by going up to the front door, and with a swift kick, he was inside. The other two followed.

The mayor kept a neat house–immaculate great room, with a massive stone fireplace. There were pictures of him and every politician imaginable hanging on the back wall. After a quick look around, the three began searching for the door to the new addition. There was none. And this meant only one thing: it was somehow concealed by a movable partition. They banged on the walls listening for a hollow sound. Nothing. Finally, Weld took his size 13 foot and began destroying the entire north section of the office. They soon found it–a metal door, hidden behind the wall, which contained the political pictures; but it was no ordinary door. It looked like the door to a bank vault–and the whole wall seemed to be made of metal.

"Damn!" Rick exploded. "The bastard has created his own version of a lead coffin. I remember Dad saying that the meeting was to involve the four of us–now it makes perfect sense. Somehow the mayor has learned something that even we didn't know: we can't jump into or out of a lead-lined room!"

"This is really strange," Weld reflected. "I guess now we've got something in common with the Evil One that we've been trying to corner: none of us can penetrate a lead-lined box. Does that mean we have a similar ancestry–can't be--that's stupid talk."

"Speaking of stupid talk," Rick interjected, "We've done enough talking. How do we get my dad out of that damned house?"

There was silence.

Mark spoke first, "We can't jump in, and he obviously can't jump out. We've got to get some kind of high tech cutting or boring tool and break through that lead wall."

Rick spoke up, "I think I know a way. I'm going to jump differently." And with that, he took a deep breath and disappeared.

Rick and Weld looked at the back wall, expecting Rick to just bounce off of it again.

* * *

Sam was still lying on the Persian rug, bleeding, when Rick found him. Gradually, half carrying, half dragging his dad, they reach the nearest couch; he was able to position Sam on it, and he then went to the mayor's bathroom for a cloth and some water.

By this time, Sam was stirring, but still bleary-eyed. Rick gently wiped his dad's face, removing the dried blood and moving his hair away from his eyes. This was the first time Rick had seen Sam, incapacitated, practically helpless. He didn't like the feeling and tried to push the image from his mind.

In a few minutes, Sam rejoined the real world. "Where are we?" He asked.

"Rick grinned, "Still in the mayor's office. You tried to jump out, but didn't make it."

"Damn! That's never happened before." And after a short pause, he asked, "How did you get in here?"

"The same way were going to get out," Rick explained. "Were going to jump through space and time. We know when this room was built. Remember the stealth drone which sent us records of the Mayor's addition being built? We know it was a month ago, so you and I have to stay within this room but jump to a time one month ago—to a time before this lead barrier was erected; then we jump in time and space to the front yard in real time."

"You know," Sam commented, proudly, "That sounds like one of my convoluted plans. Good thinking! Okay, I'm ready. Let's do it."

And they did.

CHAPTER 19

Because Sam was still a little woozy, they decided they would ride together in his car, with Weld driving. And as they continued up the hill on Route 20, out of Petersburg, they looked for the semi carrying the coffin, planning to tell the driver to follow them back to the warehouse. But the trailer was gone.

Brad Linenger had been with them for years–he was sober and reliable.

"He sure as hell wouldn't have left without telling us," Weld muttered.

"I don't know," Rick rejoined, "We *have* been at the mayor's for over two hours. Our plan was to call him right away--get him down here for his part of the job. What could've happened? Maybe he did leave."

"No, the mayor came this way as he left his house; so, somehow, he's behind the truck's disappearance." Mark held up his hand asking for silence, "Just keep quiet for a minute--just for a minute, let me think– maybe I can sense where Brad is."

They pulled off the road, and Mark cut the engine and began his search. After a few minutes, he realized that Brad was either dead or not in range or perhaps he could be unconscious. "Sometimes I can't tell the difference," he confessed.

Sam spoke up, finally, seeming to have returned from his somnambulistic state, "Contact the drone. It will know what happened to Brad."

Weld flipped a switch, returning the car to manual control, and he increased the speed well beyond its automatic limitations. "Let's get back to the office, so we can download the drone's information. Brad's a good man–we don't want to lose him."

Sam suddenly sat up, "Pull over, Weld. Pull over. I think were going off half-cocked, Let's think this out."

The others were looking at one another as if to say, "What the hell, now?"

"The mayor thinks I'm trapped in his office—he sees it as my coffin. What he obviously doesn't know is that, with Rick's time space jump idea, none of us could be trapped there. What if there was a way to get the mayor to return to his office with us, and a way for us to lock the vault door with all of us inside? He's trapped. We wouldn't be."

"Might just work," Mark said, enthusiastically, but..."

"I hate buts," Sam interrupted. "Go ahead, let's hear why you have a <u>but</u>."

Mark continued, "but we don't know when he's returning–and he expects you to still be in there."

"Right," Sam agreed. "Let me out of here, I'll jump back–I'll be in his office in case he returns. You contact him. Explain that you're worried about me, and that all three of you are headed to Petersburg. I think he'll believe that. He's going to try to get all of us in his office, step out for some reason, and just like that, we're eliminated.

Sam slipped out of the car and disappeared. Weld was able to locate Grote: "Mayor Grote, this is Weld Newall. We haven't heard from Sam. The three of us are on our way to Petersburg to see what's happened."

"Oh, I'm so glad you called," the mayor responded, with real relief in his voice. "Sam is locked in my new office–I haven't been given the key to the door yet; and I'm on my way to the builder to get it. Please wait for me; I should be back in less than an hour. I'm so sorry. The room has no windows and a very heavy door–I had it built to double as a shelter in case of another tornado. You know how frequent they've been showing up the last few years?"

"Please get back as soon as you can," Weld replied. "Let's get Sam out of that locked room—we'll wait for you there."

At the top of the last hill on Route 20, headed down into Petersburg, they spotted him: Brad Linenger, the truck driver. He was standing on the side of the road, blood running down the side of his face, trying to wave them down.

Weld pulled over, and they all piled out. Brad collapsed into Rick's arms, as they muscled him into the car and continued toward the mayor's house.

Brad was able to walk, and once they got to the house, he lay on the couch, as Rick rechecked his head to see how deep the cut was.

"What happened, Brad?"

"Man, I don't know. I was sitting on the tail of my semi, having a G-sig, and I guess someone hit me from behind—I didn't hear anything—didn't see anything. My truck's gone. I'm really sorry, man."

"You can make it up to us," Rick soothed. "When the mayor arrives, we want you to pretend to be passed out on the couch. As soon as we're all in his office, close and lock the door. Can you do that?"

"Hell, yeah, how hard can that be?"

"Well, the door is a really heavy damned thing. We'll have to figure out how it works before the mayor returns."

True to his word, the mayor pulled into his driveway an hour later and, running up the sidewalk, he was surprised to see that his front door had been broken down, and all of the Newalls were inside.

"What happened to my door?" he shouted. "Oh, my God, my wall!" Then he saw Brad lying on the couch, hair still smeared with blood. "Who's he? What's going on here?"

Mark explained about finding Brad on the side of the road, injured—about needing to get into the house in order to stop Brad's bleeding and of his decision to try to break into the office to see if Sam was okay.

Grote looked around, seemed to be disoriented by all this. He glanced at Brad who looked like he was comatose. He sighed. "Well, let's see if we can get the door open. He handed the key to Weld, "Here, I'm too shaky from all this. You see if you can get in."

"Does this wall slide back," Mark asked? "We tried to break through it, because we couldn't find a door anywhere."

"Yes, yes—I'm so sorry. Help me clean away the broken drywall and wood, and I'll get my remote to expose the rest of the door."

The wall slid back, revealing a very large and substantial metal door, much like the one seen in a bank. And, using the key, which the mayor had given to him, Mark unlocked the door and it swung smoothly in.

Sam was playing his part, lying on the floor, over a pool of blood on the carpet. Mark ran to help Sam, and he yelled for the mayor to help, also. He grabbed him by the arm pulling him into the room, and at the same time, throwing the key toward Brad. With the mayor's not-so-willing help, Sam was carried to the couch. Mark yelled "Mayor, get some water—bring a towel." The mayor turned just in time to see the heavy vault door slam shut.

CHAPTER 20

A few weeks later, as the Newalls anticipated the return of the Moon's perigee, they continued reviewing the daily reports sent to them by the stealth drone, which was still monitoring Petersburg, as well as the mayor's house.

Everything was benign, and really, that's what they expected. Also, they were actually looking forward to the perigee, assuming that now, with the mayor caged again, there would be no more unexplained plane crashes, train derailments, car accidents, as well as no building implosions, and other disasters.

They felt that they had solved the long-term problem, albeit, with a short-term solution. People would soon be asking about the mayor's disappearance, and no doubt, at some point, the Sheriff would have to become involved. The Newalls' concern was that the Sheriff would break into the mayor's residence.

The brothers, along with Rick, had bounced the idea around as to how to dispose of the lead-lined room that now contained the mayor's final resting place. They realized that, for the short term, survival was possible since the room had access to water, heat, and air; and as Rick had noticed, it also contained a built-in refrigerator. Because the room was too heavy to airlift to a nice deep ocean and, of course, would not burn, they decided to bury it. Having bulldozers, loaders, and semi trucks of their own, it would be an easy task during the next dark of the Moon to dig a very deep hole behind the mayor's office and, before dawn, come at it from the front, ram through the door of the house and shove the room into the excavation, then cover it over. That procedure would be followed by an intense, accidental fire, which should permanently solve the problem—well, almost permanently. They would eventually have to buy the mayor's property to ensure that there would be no more building on that spot and no more digging.

So involved were they in the logistics of this plan, that the perigee arrived without their awareness; but rather than an uneventful passage around the Earth, the perigee caused catastrophic chaos, the worst destruction seen in a long time, in a swath across the United States and the rest of the world.

There were over one hundred plane crashes, a score of commuter train wrecks, and the atomic plant in Central City went critical, as well as countless auto accidents.

Sam called an emergency meeting. "Could we have misjudged the mayor?" was his first question. "Do we have an innocent man locked up and starving to death in his own house?"

Rick replied, "I hate to say this, but maybe we do need to take another look at Todd Eyanni."

Mark spoke up. "Let's just wait. I've crammed our drone with some new technology which I came up with on my own, and it'll now be able to report on any communication coming from the mayor's house; and as you anticipate, Sam, anything coming from the Petersburg church. So don't break Grote out of jail just yet."

That afternoon Mark pulled up reports from the Petersburg drone and asked the computer to decipher them. In less than an hour, it was finished. He brought the information to the afternoon meeting, arriving early so that he might digest all the facts and implications and be ready to summarize and to anticipate any questions the others may have.

Whenever an afternoon meeting was called, which was rare, pizza was the delivery of choice. And now as they relaxed around the conference table, satisfying their appetites, Mark began his report, hoping also to satisfy some of the curiosity and concerns everyone had.

"Sam, your hunch was on target. That Petersburg church spire is simply a well- disguised broadcast tower. Shortly before all hell broke loose yesterday, the church began sending out a single signal. With the new equipment I had installed in the drone, it was able to pinpoint the target."

"The Moon?" Rick broke in.

"Nope. Any other guesses?"

"If the signal is directed out to space," Rick walked over to the coffee pot. "Anyone ready for a refill? If the signal is directed out to space, it has to be contacting one of the satellites, hopefully one of ours."

"Hold on to your seats," Mark cautioned. "This is going to get kind of weird. The signal went from the church to a deactivated military satellite from the 2050s!"

"A military satellite?" Rick said, trying to figure out the connection. "Do we know the original purpose of this old satellite?"

"Sure do." Mark pulled up a screen of information and looked at it briefly. "You know how it is, at least how it is with the military–what they say they're doing doesn't always explain what they're really doing. According to what we've been able to dig up, it was an experiment on crowd control, using sound waves. Their working theory was that if they bombarded the crowd with infrasound--sounds below the ability of the human ear to detect, it would affect them in a way that would cause them to disperse and would deflate their anger."

"Did it work?" Sam asked, as he finished off the last of the sausage and cheese pizza.

"Yes and no. It depended on the number of cycles per minute. The military eventually worked mostly in the range of 43 to 73 cycles. That seemed to disorient the crowd and caused them to lose muscular coordination, balance, and, surprisingly, even caused them to lose some of their cognitive abilities. At later testing, it was found that their IQ scores were substantially decreased."

"So," Sam theorized, "I'm assuming you're going to tell us that the signal from the church reactivated that military satellite?"

"The mystery deepens," Mark hinted, smiling to himself because of how much stranger the report was going to get. "I was able to access old records on this experiment: the satellite has the same elliptical orbit as the Moon; and when the Moon is closest to the Earth, so is the satellite. Another interesting fact: remember how we were puzzled that the destruction across the globe seemed to be in a straight almost linear fashion, following latitudinal lines? Well, when the satellite was activated, yesterday, it created a swath of the structure directly beneath the path that it uses to circle the globe."

The team was silent, digesting the series of unconnected–now connected–facts. The silence lasted over five minutes. Mark, having worked for years with his brothers, let the silence continue, knowing that from it would come the beginnings of a solution–a plan of attack.

Weld finally broke the spell: "So, the closeness of the Moon has nothing to do with our problem?"

"And" Rick eagerly added, "The Moon and Todd are innocent victims of circumstantial evidence. That's great."

Sam asked, "What is it about these low-frequency waves that cause such chaos?"

"Well, for the planes, it seems that the waves in the range of 70 Hz or below cause people to lose their balance, their spatial acuity, and sometimes causes them to pass out. As far as atomic plants and other high tech facilities, remember what I said about IQ--the very people who operate these facilities, those brilliant scientists and so forth--suddenly they become really dumb. Who can say what they remember or what they forget in an hour or two--or a day or two–who could guess how that would impact their responsibilities?"

Rick walked over to the coffee pot for a refill and returned to his chair, talking as he did. "Since this destruction has been going on so long, why wouldn't our current military recognize what the problem is? How could they not connect this burst of energy from the satellite and the chaos and the Earth?"

"Who says they haven't?" Weld interjected, never comfortable with the military rule. "Can we discount the possibility that they not only were aware of it, but either condoned it or initiated it?"

"No." Sam corrected Weld. "No, were not going to go that route. As far as I can see, they had nothing to gain from such subterfuge. Our enemy is somewhere else. This whole thing is so damned illogical–there is, though, some logic to the reason for this illogic. There has to be. Let's just figure out what it is.

"Give me some illogical reason for these indiscriminate killings–no, wait, maybe they're not indiscriminate. Maybe there is a logical reason for doing something illogical." He paused, "Hell, maybe there is no logical reason for doing something logical."

Everyone laughed. "Sam, you're getting goofier then usual," Weld chided.

"Here's what I think: these problems began in a small way twenty-five years ago. Whoever is behind all of this was just learning his craft. As his methodology improved, the death rate went up. Could it be possible that there is no Evil one, just a highly motivated and very bright but very deranged individual? And as much as we don't want to admit or accept it, could there be someone out there with one or more of our special talents?"

"Not possible," Mark answered. "We'd know it if there were. No, they broke the mold after we were made." He joked. "Okay, one more bit of trivia for you to think about: shortly before the satellite was turned on, there was a message that went from the mayor's house to the church; so I think the mayor may still be plying his trade!"

"And that, my friends, is all we need to know about who that very bright, very screwy guy is." Weld exclaimed. "I say if we bury him, we bury our problems."

Sam stood up, in his business mode now. "Mark, get our dozers, backhoe and so forth down to Petersburg. Get them there tonight. We're going to dig a hole behind that lead-lined room—we're going to dig that hole almost to China; but we don't push the room into it until we do some more checking on Bill Grote. I want each of you to concentrate on this man--use any source, spend any money–well, within reason–I want a thorough biography on the mayor."

"But what about Helayne's…"

"I know what you're going to say, Rick. But she's only human–there's some stone out there that she hasn't turned over. Now, this meeting is over. Go get Mayor Grote."

CHAPTER 21

The next few days went by very quickly, each Newall pursuing his own strategies and theories.

Rick realized that this was his moment to shine--to prove his worth as a team member. He had talked with Weld and Mark and felt he had a good idea how they were planning to conduct their hunt; and he realized that he had to take a different tack, come up with some unorthodox plan. Helyana had done all the right things, searched, by the book, followed all procedures, and struck out, so traveling down that same path would gain nothing.

Some unconventional path had to be taken. To appear to have had no past required the cooperation of a powerful friend or agency. The WPP was the most obvious entity, which could make Grote, or whoever he really was, disappear--or another way to look at it would be that it could make Bill Grote's appearance some 25 years ago valid–a life that would hold up under scrutiny.

After a devastating series of cyber attacks some 50 years ago, the decision was made to have paper back up on everything. A number of caverns formerly used to store oil, back when automobiles and other mechanical devices ran on that fuel, now held the paper trove. Rick had never visited these paper cities, but had read about them–miles and miles of caverns, teaming with library crews, who were skilled in cataloging everything.

That's where he needed to go. Electronic evidence could easily be destroyed. The physical evidence, not so easily. The problem was security. Knowing what fire and/or terrorist attacks could do to this paper contingency plan caused the powers that be to saturate these facilities with cameras, alarms, armed guards, and drones. Down in the depths of this gargantuan paper-hoarding beast, there was no day, no night, and certainly no down time. Rick would have to do his search under the eyes of many cameras and many people.

Without first determining how he was going to be able to ferret out, from the millions of records, the one file he needed without being arrested, Rick decided to Google the storage facilities in New York State, find out the schematics they used as a guide for file placement. He had to be able to retrieve his information in minutes not hours or days.

Almost always, there is an Achilles' heel that is a part of every bloated organization: There it was, as soon as he Googled: the Green Cavern, aisle 324–1050, stored by year. That was easy, Rick thought–now for the real test. How can I sneak in--and out?

He withdrew his Repeller from his side holster and looked at the three buttons. Something in the back of his mind kicked in--something he had read in the instruction booklet that came with the weapon. One of the new features was very special, but what was it? And there was one other small problem: where the hell was that booklet?

He went over the last few weeks in his mind; so much had happened in such a short time span–who can keep track of everything, he alibied.

He took the elevator to the second floor, to his apartment; and whenever he walked in there, a sadness would envelop him. He was the only one of the group who had never been married; and even though he was now ready to share his life with another, he had not found that person. Most guys would appreciate what he had: a solid job, a first rate education, and some quite unusual talents, talents, which he could not reveal to anyone outside his team. As with the brilliant or the rich, life demands more, much more. He recognized the reason for the sadness, and he made a mental note that when this wacky case was over, he would actually look for a lady for life. Sure, everyone had told him that love would come when he least expected it–but it hadn't come in his twenty-five years on this Earth. And he worried that he might grow old surrounded by adventure and mystery but never experience true love or marriage.

He, like his dad, was drawn to the Edwardian period; and it was reflected in his choice of furniture and other accouterments. His desk, a beautiful mahogany piece from the early 1900s was covered with the reflections of his life. None of the desk's beautiful surface showed, only books, papers, zip sticks, and other items trivial and not so trivial. That's where the Repeller booklet had to be, and so he looked and he looked; and a few minutes later, he found it. Turning to the section on Repeller upgrades, he began reading; and there it was--what had been on the tip of his tongue all along: the FREEZE button and its functions. It embraced a new concept of localized time secession. That was the function, which would allow him to jump to the Green Cavern, aisle 334–1050, and, at his leisure, search for the elusive mayor Grote. He wasn't worried about the cameras, for they, too, would be under the influence of the time stoppage.

Now that he had his plan, he wondered if he should share with his team. He really did not want to. His mind played with the idea of just walking into tomorrow's meeting and laying out the complete history of Bill Grote. He would be the shining hero. On the other hand, the team's mantra was that they all needed to know where each member was and what his assignments were at all times.

Rick sat at his desk, fiddling with the Repeller for a few minutes: the picture of him going to the meeting and astounding everyone with his skills overpowered the Newall rule. He set the weapon to FREEZE, made a mental picture, based upon his research, visualized the Green Cavern, and jumped.

CHAPTER 22

Sam took the elevator to his Subversive Coordinator's office, on the fourth floor. He had prepared Helayne by calling and requesting a layout of everything she had on the mayor and asking that she be ready to share every aspect of her search. His goal was to bypass whatever tools and methods she had used. Why repeat a procedure, which no one was better at that Helayne.

"Process of elimination," Sam whispered aloud, as he exited the elevator into her suite. "I'll begin where she stopped in her search."

Helayne was already at her conference table, surrounded by maps, stacks of documents, a computer and her wall-screen pointer.

She looked peeved. Sam noted the look and realized that she must have felt that this rush, rush meeting was, in effect, placing doubt on her research of both Poore and Grote.

But she was ready for Sam—would overwhelm her old employer and friend with her skills and talent. A shadow of doubt crossed her psyche when he had requested this review, wanting to know not just what she found out about these gentlemen, but, also, how she went about her search. He had never invaded her inner sanctum to that degree before; and she reacted almost as if it had been a home invasion. She did not get up from her chair, as she usually did when her boss came to visit. This was Sam's second hint at her unhappiness, plus there was no hug–not even a handshake. Sam knew that he had better explain his motives damned well–share in detail what prompted him to call this unusual meeting.

He did, and it was helpful in de-icing the meeting, although the local weather was still stormy. When she finished her presentation, which took about an hour, Sam leaned back: "Okay, Helayne. I'm satisfied with everything I see. You've covered every base, but we still have a man with no past. How do you explain that? What could have occurred in order to make this possible?"

"So now, you don't want the facts–you want speculation?"

Sam ignored her comment. "Put yourself in Bill Grote's shoes. If you had to disappear–had to reinvent yourself, how would you do it?"

Helayne could see that he was really struggling with the problem, so she decided to cut him some slack. "You know, Sam," she paused, choosing her words carefully: "You're quite aware that I've been, for a quarter of a century, working on espionage—on stealth research, and I'm very good at what I do. You should understand that I've done everything I know how to do. I've researched every avenue; yet, I've struck out. Can you imagine how I feel about this?" She looked him directly in the eye and continued: "Do *you* have any ideas? I'll be happy to go in any direction you point. It's just that I can't conceive of any of the ways he could've pulled it off. One direction I didn't go, and that's because you haven't provided me with it: I could still research the man, based on his fingerprints or his DNA. If he had a life some other time, some other place, we might uncover it. You know, of course, the name Bill Grote isn't going to find him? Give me something else to work with."

Sam interrupted. "Helayne all *that* is in his file—it's part of his drivers' license."

"True. But those prints and DNA scans may or may not be accurate. You know how lax the license bureau is? He could have been wearing a thumb mitten with a fake print and, of course, you know there are ways to misrepresent your DNA. If I were to give you an assignment, Sam, it would be to find his DNA and find his real fingerprints. Bring them to me, and then I can continue my search."

Sam wasn't often given assignments. His job was to pass them out; but he returned to his office thinking maybe that's what he should be doing. Find those two items that Helayne needed. But because of the way the meeting went, he was in a glum mood. He was hoping for some clear path of investigation, maybe--maybe even a eureka moment. He decided it would be worth his while to jump back to the mayor's house. He clearly recalled the whiskey bottle that Grote had handed him and, of course, he could take a look in the mayor's bathroom and find a hairbrush--something with his DNA.

Without wasting time, he jumped, landing at the mayor's front door, which had been replaced, by one of Sam's men, due to Weld's big foot destroying the original one. The new key he had made worked, and he was inside in no time. The back wall had been repaired, as well. He spotted the whiskey bottle immediately and bagged it, and then headed for the bathroom.

"Hello, anybody home?" someone called from the front of the house.

Sam returned to the entranceway. "Hi," he said. "What's going on?"

"My name's Jackson. Where's the mayor? I need to be paid."

Sam always could think well on his feet. "He's on a short vacation. I'm watching over his place. How much does he owe you?"

"Five hundred dollars for painting the addition and two hundred fifty for all the mowing I've done."

Sam decided he'd cover that on his own, and he pulled out the necessary money.

"The mayor never told me he was going anywhere," Jackson said, as he re-counted the cash.

"Business trip–came as a surprise to him; but he did say that if you showed up, I was to give you some vacation money; and that he wouldn't need you for the next month."

"Damn," Jackson said, smiling broadly. "That's real decent of him."

Sam counted out another five hundred, and Jackson left with a jauntiness in his walk which he did not have as he approached the house a few minutes ago.

That should keep him away from here at least long enough for us to bury this damn room, Sam thought, satisfied with his ploy.

He found a hairbrush and that, along with the whiskey bottle, accompanied him back to the office.

CHAPTER 23

Rick landed in the dark, but almost immediately, lights began coming on, down row after row of filing boxes. He looked up toward the ceiling's glare thirty feet above and was surprised that the shelves of boxes reached the top of the cavern. This was the right section, Rick confirmed, as he noted the signs on each room. It was cold, not damp, as he had anticipated--just cold. He had on only a short-sleeved shirt and summer slacks. I sure wasn't expecting this, he thought.

With his Repeller set on FREEZE, ready to be activated, he began his search and after about thirty minutes of getting nowhere, he stopped. He was uneasy. Too quiet. There were over five hundred people that worked in this mountain, a city in itself. Where were they?

Suddenly, a rolling robot turned the corner at aisle 324 and headed his way: "Identify yourself," it said, in a very humanlike voice. Rick switched the Repeller to its original function--that of repelling, and adjusting it to maximum power, he fired. The robot slammed against the back limestone wall and separated into a number of pieces.

Behind his back, he heard another voice, "Identify yourself." Rick turned and fired again.

Looking around, he saw a computer terminal and headed toward it. He punched in the name William Grote and hit the *Go* button. Almost immediately, a message popped up, "Security code required—you have sixty seconds to input before security is notified." Rick cleared the screen, not knowing if that would cancel the sequence or not.

It didn't.

A vehicle about the size of a large golf cart, with lights flashing, was headed his way, still at least 200 yards down the aisle. He could see two men aboard, rifles in the crook of their arms.

Calmly, Rick set the Repeller on STUN and pointed it in their direction. Almost immediately, upon seeing Rick's movement, the guard, who was riding shotgun, brought his weapon to his shoulder; but by that time it was too late. Rick had fired. There was no sound, only results. Both the driver and the guard were thrown against the backseat, the rifles clattering on the stone floor; but the vehicle coming toward him, continued even faster. Quickly he switched to Repeller mode and fired again. The cart stopped its forward motion, throwing the two into the aisle way.

"Enough is enough," Rick muttered. He set the Repeller on FREEZE–MAXIMUM, and turned in a complete circle, theoretically stopping the motion of everything around him.

Returning to the files, he zeroed in on the date twenty-five years ago when the lead- lined casket was first breach: June 7. Each aisle had a computer terminal at its beginning–somehow he was going to have to access one of them. How could he get the code? Who would have it? Would anyone have it? These records had been here for a quarter of a century. His mind reached out, trying to assess his distant surroundings. No human interaction was evident.

He opened the computer and again typed in the words William Grote. And again, the message appeared, "Security code required, you have......"

He cancelled the FREEZE mode and returned the Repeller setting to STUN and waited.

It took longer this time, but eventually another vehicle appeared. No flashing light. A driver about Rick's age was dressed in a well-tailored business suit, and accompanying him was a beautiful young lady wearing a jumpsuit. Neither exhibited any visible threat as they drove toward Rick, so he tried to stand down, lowering his weapon as they approached. She raised her left hand and the vehicle stopped, allowing her to dismount. Smiling, as she approached, she said, "I'm Jacklyn, do you need help?"

This whole scene was confusing to Rick. He was expecting confrontation--some kind of macho-guard or gun--something he would have to react to, and "Do you need help?" was nowhere within his expectations.

"Yes, please. I'm trying to access the file of William Grote—I'm sure that's his a.k.a. I need a code to find his file location."

"Not a problem." Jacklyn confirmed. The code is different for each aisle. Just input the words Green Cavern and the number of the aisle, and that should do it. Need anything else?"

"No. That's been a big help, so thanks."

"No problem. Don't forget to clock out when you leave."

Who the hell does she think I am? Rick mused. His second thought was that, maybe, this is just another ruse, a way to have him relax and let his guard down...

With that, Jacklyn returned to the car, circled her hand overhead, indicating the driver to turn around, and she was gone.

"I need to get out of here," Rick mumbled aloud. "I think things are going to get stupid real fast." Then he looked at the computer and typed in Green Cavern aisle 324, William Grote. What came up was the date and the comment, "For earlier reports, refer to section 17, file 4."

Rick hurried to aisle 4, thumbed through several folders--pulled out a couple earlier reports. "Well, that's a big help," he said, with some disgust—"it's all been redacted!" He kept looking, "Come on, come on—give me something." But there was nothing of value. He closed the file, glancing at its cover briefly before returning it to the box--Mohammed al Pash—and it was at that moment, his sixth sense kicked in: It was a feeling, almost like an insect crawling into his nose. He turned toward the aisle's opening, his Repeller ready. A huge column of vapor was headed his way—thick, like a dense fog. He realized the Repeller would be worthless against this. Afraid to take a deep breath, he waited for the fog's approach, wanting it to mask his escape; and just as it reached him, he pictured his dad's office and calibrated.

Nothing happened. He turned, trying to out run the advancing threat. And as he ran, he inhaled deeply—and the jump sequence engaged.

"Damn. I never knew that," he exclaimed, as he hit the solid floor of Sam's office. "I *have* to inhale as part of my pre-jump preparation. A little late to share that with me, but damn good to know."

He grabbed a pen from Sam's desk and began jotting down on a piece of his father's stationary, *Mohammed L Pash.*

"Let's see what Helayne will do with this guy," Rick said, both with weariness and relief, feeling that they were finally getting close to the end of their search.

* * *

A few days later, Helayne presented her findings to the Newalls. Using the hairbrush and the fingerprints from the mayor's house, along with Rick's Mohammed L Posh contribution, she was able to put together the profile of a real man, as interesting as any that could be imagined. Mohammed was an American citizen born of Egyptian parents in the city of Detroit; he attended the local Detroit schools and went from there to Harvard and eventually received a graduate degree in Celestial Navigation. He left to fight with Egypt against Israel and was captured by the Mossad who turned him. He was a valued asset, very important in their victory over Egypt. He wanted to return to the United States after the war but was on its terrorist watch list, so he stayed in Israel and eventually disappeared. For two years prior to his disappearance, he did all the right things to get his name removed from the terrorist list, even hiring an international attorney; but each time, he was denied permission to enter the country of his birth. He could not seek asylum in Egypt because they were aware of his traitorous activities; and, in fact, they had put together a hit squad to take care of him. The Mossad finally became re-involved with Mohammed, and a few weeks later, he disappeared.

The DNA and fingerprints, provided by Sam, matched those in the terrorist file: Mohammed and the mayor were the same man.

* * *

In the wee hours of the next morning, well before dawn's light, the Newalls were in the mayor's side yard, as two dozers rammed through the front of the house and shoved the lead-lined addition over the lip of the fifty-foot deep hole that had been excavated earlier. They watched until the dozers had refilled the cavity and disposed of the extra soil; then, with varying degrees of relief, they headed east on Route 20 to the top of the Petersburg hill, where they pulled off the road and watched, as the remainder of the mayor's house went up in flames, illuminating the faces of the Newall family members: "Well, at the next perigee, we'll know for sure," Sam reflected.

The fire died down just as the sun came up behind them, casting its long shadow across the town of Petersburg and, unknown to the Newalls, across the gravesite of their fourth brother, Delta.

THE END

FROM THE AUTHOR

Sometimes I look at myself as the Grandma Moses of literature: I didn't begin writing until I was in my mid-70's; but to my delight, I've found that one of the most satisfying parts of being published is talking to book clubs, libraries, classrooms of students, and others. Students, more than anyone else, occasionally, bring me up short with their brutally honest questions--one in particular, I remember:

"Why would an old guy like you want to write a novel?"

It wasn't the first time I'd been asked this question (not quite in the same way, however!) and by then, I had a few stock answers--answers which were true, but which did not delve into the depths of the why.

I had been a speech and drama teacher, an English teacher, and a school counselor. Once I retired, my immediate goal was to take an old barn on a farm I'd owned for a quarter of a century and converted it into a house. I'd seen that done on *This Old House*, years ago. My entire life, I had envied people who could do things with their hands--the tradesmen who kept all our lives more civilized. My constant chagrin was the thought of my being marooned on a Gilligan's Island type place, because I would ask myself the question "What could I really do?" My background gave me no skills, which could be used in such a situation.

The barn undertaking was an attempt to become qualified for this deserted island possibility! My goal was to learn how to drive a nail, lay tile, and do electrical and plumbing work. Drywall was also on this list, and it was really a challenge.

To make the story a little shorter, I did build that house within a barn--and I emerged five years later feeling pretty good about what I had learned.

Then I looked around and said, "Okay, what next?"

I was retired, had no major debts, and at least a fixed income, along with, up to this point, a fairly patient wife.

But what to do next weighed heavily on me, causing me to loose sleep. I was still strong and very active but becoming more restless day by day.

I began cruising the web, trying to find an answer to my dilemma of what to do with the rest of my life, and I ran across an interesting article which suggested that every person needs to have at least these three things in his background: he needs to have planted a tree, had a child, and written a book. That intrigued me. I had been given the Kentucky Forester award some years ago for planting 10,000 trees, so one was down: all I needed to do was the other two.

I told my wife, Barbara, about my three requirements. "So are you telling me you now want to have a child?" She asked.

"What do you think?"

"I think you're about 50 years too late for that! For God's sake, quit moping around and find something that really interests you!"

"It was the barn project and I've done it." I replied.

She thought a minute and then asked, "Isn't there some mystery in life you'd like to research--some answer you need to find? Isn't there something in your past 75 years that demands another look on your part?"

In the middle of the night about a week later, it came to me! When I was a youngster, there was a horrible multiple murder in my town, followed by a trial and a jury's decision which was unpopular with everyone. The accused was found not guilty and, shortly after, disappeared, never to be heard of again. My mother had gone to the trial every day and would come home with lurid stories of what the prosecutor was presenting as evidence of the murder, trying to prove to the jury that the beautiful bright, energetic teenage daughter, Joan, had tried to kill her entire family. My mother was among the very few who was convinced that the girl was innocent.

When I was in high school, I spent two summers working for a man who formerly was the deputy sheriff and had investigated this murder. He was certain that the girl planned the killings and carried them out in a cold-blooded fashion.

Who was right? I decided to conduct my own investigations, and although it was almost 70 years after the fact, I would try to solve this old enigma!

After a year of research and personal interviews with those still alive who were a part of the investigation or who had direct knowledge of the events surrounding the murder, followed by a year of actual writing about what happened that fateful night in the summer of 1943 at the Kiger's summer home, Rosegate, I published *A Dream Within A Dream.*

In the year following the writing of this novel, so many folks would stop me on the street, email, or phone me with one complaint: "I bought your book so that after almost 70 years, I would finally know who killed the Kiger's; but I'm still not sure who did it. You needed to make it a lot clearer."

The readers' unhappiness over my not identifying the killer to their satisfaction was one of three reasons for considering doing some kind of follow-up about the Kiger murders. The second one was that this story stirred up a lot of old memories in people who had attended the trial, who were involved with the Kiger family, whose parents were on the jury, and the reasons go on and on; but these people came to me, in one way or another, *after* they had read my book, saying that they wanted me to know about what they saw or heard before they died, feeling that their *new* information might just affect the outcome of my research and, therefore, my conclusion as to what really happened that horrible, hot summer night.

So with all this recent information on people, events, plots, and motives, I felt there *was* more to this old tale than I had previously covered. Furthermore, as I would talk to my friends about the additional scenarios being uncovered, they began pressuring me to do a sequel—and maybe even decide on a different ending, based on the recent facts and conjectures, which were coming to light.

I eventually confessed to my wife, that I really didn't want to write another Kiger novel, even if it *would* allow for a new slant on the plot and characters. After giving it some thought, she suggested that the two of us try our hand at a play, instead of a novel.

That was the third reason, and it appealed to me on several fronts:

It opened up a larger challenge to my writing, and I jumped at it, thinking that I could expand my write goals to include something in each of the major forms of literature. *A Dream within a Dream, the Joan Kiger Story*, was historical fiction; the play would represent another form of writing; and looking down the road, I could see myself doing a straight fiction, followed by one of my earliest loves, Science Fiction!

I was excited, too, because of the opportunity to write with Barbara. She was much more successful and prolific than I, having ten books under her belt and having appeared on many of the national talk shows, including Oprah; and as we began brainstorming, her reason for wanting to be involved with this project became clear: as a psychologist, she had a keen interest in mother-daughter relationships. (Her best-selling book was *My Mother was Right*). She now wanted to explore the interconnected dynamics between Joan, who was accused of trying to kill her entire family, and Jennie Kiger, her mother.

Years went by, and I kept researching and writing; and one by one, I was able to check off the various types of literature:

A Dream Within a Dream--historical fiction

Farewell to Rosegate--a two-act play, which, by the way, was picked up immediately by the Union Community Theater and produced.

Braving the Shadows--fiction/adventure

Fear the Moonlight – science fiction

The Life and Times of Dexter—a children's story

I'm not ready to think about an autobiography, maybe because I've always felt that that was something a person did just before dying; and I'm not ready for that great adventure just yet.

I think poetry might be next. That form will be the most difficult to accomplish, for me: I suppose I could do free verse, but that's not much different than writing a novel or short story--there's no rhyme, no set rhythm--no rules: writing should have rules!

Another reason for this plan to write different forms of literature was that I simply did not know what I was particularly good at, if anything.

How does one find out where one's talent lies? What if Shakespeare had tried only poetry, or Hemingway, only plays, or Shaw, only novels? They would have missed their calling and the world would have been worse off because of it!

In conclusion, looking back upon my attempts, I find that I'm probably adequate in each of the literary genres but not particularly good at any one: as I approach the end of my writing career, I have learned that I am average. Is that so bad? Isn't that preferable to never having tried at all?

BIOGRAPHY-- HAL MCFARLAND

Hal McFarland is a Burlington, Kentucky, native and a graduate of Georgetown and Xavier Universities. He also attended Butler University and, in Germany, the Goethe Institute.

He is a retired school counselor, as well as a former speech and drama teacher, and has been named Kentucky Forester of the Year. He has written a local best-selling historical fiction novel called A Dream within a Dream, *a story of the 1943 Boone County Kiger murders. For this novel, in 2009, he was awarded The Anne W. Fitzgerald Research Award by the Historic Preservation Review Board.*

Hal has been invited to discuss his books with such diverse groups as The Rotary Club, Kiwanis Club, Boone County Library, Campbell County Library, the Gallatin County HS Forensic Science Classes, and numerous private book clubs throughout Northern Kentucky and Cincinnati.

He is a member of the Boone County Historical Society as well as a former member of The Boone County Historic Preservation Board.

This is his fourth journey into the realm of fiction, the others being the co-authoring of The Life and Time of Dexter *and, in addition to the novel mentioned above, his recent international intrigue,* Braving the Shadows.

In 2010, he co-authored a two-act play called Farewell To Rosegate, *which was produced by The Union Community Theater and performed at Ryle Theater in Union, Kentucky.*

Hal, with his wife, Barbara, (also an author and playwright) lives on a Western Boone County, Kentucky farm, in a 19th century barn which he, over the course of a decade, converted into their home.

SUMMARY OF *FEAR THE MOONLIGHT*

Three children imprisoned for years because of their ancestry, their final release into a world as foreign to them as it would be if they were on another planet; their struggles, failures, and triumphs as they yearn for and finally achieve adulthood, trying to manage the gifts left to them by their progenitors: all of this combines to produce a fast-paced novel encompassing scenes which would be familiar to aficionados of *The Time Traveler's Wife,* as well as to those who lean toward *Star Trek*.